My Sunshine Away

M. O. Walsh

WHEELER PUBLISHING

A part of Gale, Cengage Learning

GALE
CENGAGE Learning·

Farmington Hills, Mich • San Francisco • New York • Waterville, Maine
Meriden, Conn • Mason, Ohio • Chicago

GALE
CENGAGE Learning®

Wheeler Publishing Large Print Hardcover.
The text of this Large Print edition is unabridged.
Other aspects of the book may vary from the original edition.
Set in 16 pt. Plantin.

LIBRARY OF CONGRESS CATALOGING-IN-PUBLICATION DATA

Walsh, M. O. (Milton O'Neal)
  My sunshine away / by M. O. Walsh. — Large print edition.
    pages cm. — (Wheeler Publishing large print hardcover)
    ISBN 978-1-4104-7823-8 (hardcover) — ISBN 1-4104-7823-8 (hardcover)
    1. Family life—Fiction. 2. Dysfunctional families—Fiction. 3. First loves—Fiction. 4. Large type books. 5. Domestic fiction. I. Title.
  PS3623.A4464M9 2015
  813'.6—dc23   2014049373

Published in 2015 by arrangement with G. P. Putnam's Sons, a member of Penguin Group (USA) LLC, a Penguin Random House Company

Printed in the United States of America
1 2 3 4 5 6 7 19 18 17 16 15

For Kathy, who called me Bird

You are my sunshine
My only sunshine.
You make me happy
When skies are gray.
You'll never know, dear,
How much I love you.
Please don't take my sunshine away.
— *Jimmie Davis, Governor of Louisiana
(1944–1948 and 1960–1964)*

1.

There were four suspects in the rape of Lindy Simpson, a crime that occurred directly on top of the sidewalk of Piney Creek Road, the same sidewalk our parents had once hopefully carved their initials into, years before, as residents of the first street in the Woodland Hills subdivision to have houses on each lot. It was a crime impossible during the daylight, when we neighborhood kids would have been tearing around in go-karts, coloring chalk figures on our driveways, or chasing snakes down into storm gutters. But, at night, the streets of Woodland Hills sat empty and quiet, except for the pleasure of frogs greeting the mosquitoes that rose in squadrons from the swamps behind our properties.

On this particular evening, however, in the dark turn beneath the first busted streetlight in the history of Piney Creek Road, a man, or perhaps a boy, stood holding a long piece of rope. He tied one end of this rope to the broken light pole next to the street and wrapped the other around his own hand. Thinking himself unseen, he then crawled into the azalea bushes beside Old Man Casemore's house, the rope lagging in shadow behind him like a tail, where he perhaps practiced, once or twice, pulling the rope taut and high across the sidewalk. And then this man, or this boy, knowing the routine of the Simpson girl, waited to hear the rattle of her banana-seated Schwinn coming around the curve.

You should know:

Baton Rouge, Louisiana, is a hot place.

Even the fall of night offers no comfort. There are no breezes sweeping off the dark servitudes and marshes, no cooling rains. Instead, the rain that falls here survives only to boil on the pavement, to steam up your glasses, to burden you. So this man, or this boy, was undoubtedly sweating as he crouched in the bushes, undoubtedly eaten alive by insects. They gnash you here. They cover you. And so it is not a mistake to wonder if he might have been dissuaded from this violence had he lived in a more merciful place. It is important, I believe, when you think back about a man or a boy in the bushes, to wonder if maybe one soothing breeze would have calmed him, would have softened his mood, would have changed his mind.

But it did not.

So the act took place in darkness, in near silence, in heat, and Lindy Simpson remembered little other than the sudden appearance of a rope in front of her bicycle, the sharp pull of its braid across her chest. Months later, and after much therapy, she would also recall how the bicycle rode on without her after she fell. She would remember how she never even saw it tip over before a sock was stuffed into her mouth and her face was pushed into the lawn. The crush of weight on her back. The scrape of asphalt against her knees. She would remember these, too. Then a voice in her ear that she did not recognize. Then a blow to the back of her head.

She was fifteen years old.

This was the summer of 1989 and no arrests were made. Don't believe what you see on the crime shows today. No single hairs were tweezed out of Old Man Casemore's lawn. No length of rope was sent off to a lab. No DNA was salvaged off the pebbles of our concrete. And although the people of Woodland Hills answered earnestly every question the police initially

11

asked of them, although they tried their best to be helpful, there was no immediate evidence to speak of.

All four of these primary suspects therefore remained unofficial and uncharged, as the rape had occurred so quickly and without apparent witness that the crime scene itself began to fade the moment Lindy Simpson regained consciousness and pushed her bicycle back home that night, a place only four doors away, to lay it down in its usual spot. It faded even further as she walked through the back door of her house and climbed upstairs to her bathroom, where she showered in water of an unknown temperature.

There are times in my life when I imagine this water scalding. Other times, frozen.

Regardless, Lindy never came down for dinner.

She was likely thought by her parents to be yapping with friends on the telephone, twirling the cord around her young fingers, until her mother, a woman named Peggy, made her evening rounds with the laundry basket. It was then she saw a pair of underpants in the bathroom, dotted with bright red blood, lying next to a single running shoe. The other shoe, a blue Reebok, was missing.

By this time, her daughter Lindy was curled in her bed and concussed.

A bed that just that morning had been a child's.

I should tell you now that I was one of the suspects.

Hear me out.

Let me explain.

2.

One and a half miles from the Woodland Hills subdivision sat the Perkins School, grades 4–12. It was a private and well-funded place. Great white columns stood in front of the main school building, and the rolling lawn was shaded by oaks. Brick walkways scrolled throughout the open quadrangle, each embedded with copper plaques to memorialize past accolades. It was a prideful place, and deservedly. Behind the main campus, adjacent to the parking lot, was the football field and track that Lindy Simpson traveled to at precisely five o'clock every summer evening, where she would train with friends as the sun went down — stretching, jogging, sprinting, laughing — until returning home for supper in the growing darkness of half past eight.

So, at roughly four fifty-five each summer afternoon of the late 1980s, I'd lie on my stomach in the family room of my home

14

and watch from beneath the blinds of our floor-to-ceiling windows as Lindy's piano lesson ended and mine got set to begin. Across the street and two doors down from me, the dowdy figure of Mrs. Morrison would appear first from the Simpson house. She was a teacher at the Perkins School, my school, who taught private lessons during the summer, a lady so polite it is hard to imagine her even having a cameo in a story that begins this way. She wore bright floral blouses with shoulder pads. She carried folders crammed with photocopied scales and sheet music. She often wore hats. She is the innocent stuff in the background of time. Pin her up in the sky of this place. And though I often complained to my neighborhood friends that I hated these lessons, that I hated her, this was a lie.

Before Mrs. Morrison could reach the sidewalk at four fifty-nine, Lindy Simpson would hustle up the driveway with the bike at her hip. Children, and we were all children then, never wore helmets in those days. So, Lindy would stop at the edge of the lawn to pull back her hair. She would knot a loose ponytail, tuck a few wayward strands behind her ears, and be off.

Due to the bend in our street, and the fact that my house sat right on the corner, right in the crook of the elbow, I could watch Lindy Simpson pedal toward me beneath the blinds. And then, after coming up with a host of scenarios in which she might dismount from her bike and trek more permanently into my life, I'd watch her pedal away. Each day at five. This ritual was my pleasure.

She wore tank tops and thin cotton shorts, and she was a track star.

In one of many such memories about Lindy, I can recall a race at my school conjured up by your typical eighth-grade boys during lunch hour. We all wore uniforms at Perkins, white oxford shirts and blue slacks, and the boys who wanted to race were often those who pulled up the collars on their shirts, rolled their pants legs in a fashionable way. These were boys who already had girlfriends, boys who played in summer sports leagues and had straight blond hair. Our school was small and, for this reason alone, I often found myself among them, pencil-thin and curly-headed.

The goal on this day was to get to the central oak tree, standing some fifty yards away in the common area. The unspoken prize was a half hour of glory, maybe the bud of some reputation, and this was everything. Kids tightened up their laces and stretched out their hamstrings. I remember taking a pair of pens out of my pocket and setting them in the grass while, behind us, Lindy Simpson stepped out of the red-brick library. She was fifteen, like I've said, one year older than me, and therefore in high school. This was in the school year before it all happened, before we all knew, so I was undoubtedly not alone in wondering about every inch of her. She wore the same plaid jumper that all the high school girls wore, baring their golden collarbones and slender calves, but Lindy wore it with her blue Reebok running shoes while the other girls donned sandals and Keds. Yet she was no goddess. There were other girls whose names were more hotly bandied, other more beautiful girls my friends and I evoked in the dark. But as Lindy was a female, and as she was older, and as the small of her hairless ankles peeked above her white cotton socks, she held dominion over us all on the playground.

"I want in," she told us, and so I picked up my pens off the grass.

I would never race Lindy. I had seen her run my entire life, outpacing even the older boys in my neighborhood, and this was a privilege not shared by the other dolts on the lawn. I watched them take off toward

17

the tree, the lot of them, and the sight of Lindy's jumper flitting around her legs as she ran, the flash of the pink boxer shorts she wore beneath it, the flex of her thighs, it still comes to me in dreams, the youthful vision of it, in surprise moments alone in my car.

And although Lindy was never a tomboy, not thick-waisted or dusty like they often are, she used to romp through the woods with us behind our neighborhood. She played football with us in the street. She was fast. She was nimble. We didn't know if she was tough because she never got caught. So when she beat my schoolmates to the tree that day and placed her ringless fingers on top of her head to tease them, I looked around the playground for someone to say, "I told you so" to, to prove that Lindy and I were connected in some small way, but I was the only one who hadn't run after her. I then watched Lindy wave at me from the tree, as if we were back on Piney Creek Road, and jog toward the high school building. I don't remember waving back. I only remember staring at the building she entered, the high school building, and feeling one year away from some brand of paradise.

I tell you all this because I was not there yet, not in high school, when I used to lie on the living room floor and watch her pedal. I was young, just a boy, and yet I didn't mind Mrs. Morrison waddling up my driveway at five o'clock each summer afternoon. I was ready to play scales if she wanted me to, to smell the coffee on her breath, to feel her cold hands on top of mine. I was prepared to follow instruction for hours if need be. What did it matter? When Lindy rode by, my thoughts scuttled after her. I was mindless to all else in my crush.

With Mrs. Morrison, I was only fingers.

So it is true that I thought of possessing Lindy Simpson as furiously and as constantly as any fourteen-year-old boy could that hot summer of 1989. The summer of her rape. It is true that I cast us no separate futures.

I opened the door for Mrs. Morrison.

"Look at you," she said. "Every day. The front of your shirt is so wrinkled."

3.

At the beginning of that same summer, in 1989, all of our crepe myrtles shed.

This is not uncommon. Gluttons for the heat, these trees line all the major roads and boulevards of East Baton Rouge Parish. You can cut them down to nothing each year if you like. They are unbothered. This is their home, and our Junes are filled with pink, red, and purple flowers because of it. During this time, however, when they are in full bloom, long shards of bark peel off their trunks. They lie in circles upon the roots like skins.

As a kid, it was my job to pick these skins up when I did yard work. Where I'm from, this is how children help out.

So, once a week, I'd rake the spiky gumballs that fell from the sweetgum trees. I'd pull up the centipede grass that crept over our sidewalks like tentacles. And, more often than not, other boys would be in their own yards doing the same. A few doors down, for example, were the Kern boys, Bo and Duke. These were guys who worked on old cars, guys with useful knowledge I had no clue how to gather. Bo Kern, nineteen years old at the time, had a harelip and a fierce crew cut. He was cruel to his younger brother, Duke, who was seventeen and the type of guy who did well with girls.

As either the result of or reason for this success, Duke Kern was rarely seen with his shirt on. His body was hairless and trim, muscled and lean, and he was vain. Looking back now, I realize that I idolized him. Whenever I glanced over to watch him laboring shirtless on the lawn and pictured myself at his age, our bodies were indistinguishable. Yet it never turned out that way. He and his brother worked with heavy equipment, weed eaters and push mowers, and I raked. They cleaned out carburetors and replaced sparkplugs. They stopped often to argue and have fistfights.

I didn't have any brothers to fight with, but rather two sisters, ten and eleven years older than me, who'd already moved out of the house. At fourteen, I was too young to drive. I'd no idea what a carburetor even looked like and I had never in my life been punched. So, we lived in the same neighbor-

21

hood, sure, the Kern boys and me, we saw each other often, but we inhabited different worlds.

The same could be said about our neighbor Mr. Landry, a man who needs much mentioning later, who I would often see on these days of chores riding his lawn mower through the large acreage behind his lot. An enormous person, some six-foot-five and three hundred pounds, he wore dark glasses and high cotton sweat socks and would sometimes stop the mower for no apparent reason and walk into the woods. I'd then see him, often hours later, return. He and his wife had an adopted son named Jason, a troubling character who is also on our docket.

But most important to me was that across the street and two doors down, Lindy Simpson also worked in her yard. She plucked weeds from the flower beds and swept off the sidewalk. She bent over, stretched out her muscles, and gave me ample reason to sit beneath the blossoming crepe myrtle trees and cool off. Her parents, still a beautiful couple at the time, would place cold pitchers of water and red Kool-Aid on the railing of their porch. They would then stand on the lawn with their hands on their hips and watch carefully, like I did, as Lindy climbed the ladder to pick leaves out of the storm gutters. They would laugh over some family joke that I could not hear and they had no idea what was coming. Lindy wore homecoming T-shirts, sports bras, and pink running shorts. She had a green friendship bracelet tied around her ankle, sent to her by a Christian pen pal in Jamaica.

She was a sight.

On one particular day, in the weeks before the crime, I fiddled with the shedding bark of the crepe myrtle trees as I sat in the grass watching Lindy. I saw a golden shade of brown in this one piece of bark that resembled the color of her hair, so I shredded it into fine strands. I saw a piece as lean and small as the curve of her nose in another, so I laid it on the lawn before me, as well. I then found a knotted shard, a likeness of her eyes, and put it in place. A curly wooden ribbon, her chin.

I searched the surrounding area to find shavings to match her breasts, a soft *W* shape, as well as her proud body and raised arms, a capital *Y*. I found an upside-down *V* to signify her legs and put it to my nose, inhaling what I thought would be the scent of her knee (a Band-Aid), her inner thighs (a vanilla candle), and finally the part of her anatomy that seemed to me the greatest

23

mystery. I was mortified to see my mother standing behind me.

She looked down at what I'd done.

I felt discovered. I felt exposed. I felt ashamed.

"Oh, honey," my mother said. "Is that me?"

It wasn't her fault.

She simply underestimated the distance already between us.

4.

Summers before this, when I was eleven and Lindy twelve, a group of us kids spent the day gathering moss. We were back in the unkempt part of our properties, where we often played soccer and shot garden snakes with our BB guns. There were five of us: Randy Stiller, my next-door neighbor and best friend, a girl we used to call Artsy Julie (because this is how our parents referred to her when she did things like draw dragon-flies on her arms in permanent marker or conduct elaborate wedding ceremonies for her cats in the front yard), Duke Kern, Lindy Simpson, and me. None of us were in high school then, and so tribes like this weren't unusual. The idea on this day was to make the biggest pile of moss we could, and we did this by taking running leaps at the long beards hanging off the trees. We pulled down handfuls at a time.

I later found out that these lots of land

were eventually developed for residential use, that there is now a Woodland Hills East, and I wonder about those trees. These were oaks that likely stood when Jean Lafitte was around, exploring territory along the Mississippi River. These were oaks that hid dark-skinned Coushatta Indians, stalking meals of rabbit and deer.

For us they were a jungle gym.

Duke Kern, always tall, could climb any of them he pleased by grabbing the lowest branch and swinging his legs over his head like a gymnast. He had access to moss that we didn't, so he sent down scores of the stuff. Randy and I collected it all in a pile as Lindy handled and shaped it. Meanwhile, Artsy Julie sat in the grass and made necklaces out of clovers, as if we weren't even there.

When the gang of us had stripped every tree in sight, we had a pile about six feet long, maybe five inches deep. We stood around it, confused and breathing heavily, not having considered what to do once it was made. After a moment, Lindy suggested we jump over it.

Randy agreed.

"Whatever part of your body touches it," he said, "gets eaten by alligators." He tapped the moss with his toe and then limped around in pained circles. "So, you have to walk around like this."

Artsy Julie laughed. We all did.

Duke Kern said that he thought it looked like a bed.

This idea struck me as so unimaginative, so uninteresting, that I was disappointed to see him and Lindy lie in it. The story now was that this was the Royal Bed, fit only for the king and queen of the yard. There had been no election to this effect, no discussion among the rest of us, but there was also no argument. If we were to couple up at this age, this would be the only thing to make sense. We understood that. And so Randy, always a trusty sidekick, took up his station as an imperial guard.

"Be careful, Your Highness," he said. "If you step out of bed you'll get eaten by sharks."

Artsy Julie soon fell into the scene as well, tossing clovers at the feet of the royal couple and strumming an invisible harp. Duke and Lindy smiled. They pretended to drink from jeweled goblets, orchestrate the world with their scepters, and feed each other grapes.

Duke said, "Lindy, we must have an heir."

Then Randy stood at attention. He said, "Intruder alert!" and cast an imaginary sword toward the edge of the woods.

27

I looked over to see Mr. Landry lumbering toward us. He wore a green T-shirt and blue shorts, both drenched in sweat, and had a long walking stick in his hand. I was terrified of this man. We all were. We had our reasons.

One of mine was that on rare occasions, back when my father still lived with us, or later, when my sisters would come home from college to visit, my family would sit on our back patio longer than originally intended. Night would fall and there might be a piece of meat on the charcoal grill, a solo light glowing from the deep end of our swimming pool, all made comfortable by the lilt of my mother's laugh in family conversation. It was like paradise.

Rarer still, but too often, these moments were disenchanted by the booming and indecipherable fights of Mr. Landry and his wife, Louise, two doors down. And though kids don't know, I could tell by the concern on my family's up-lit faces that adult business was going on over there, and I was lucky to have no part of it. I remember once the sound of a bottle breaking in the Landrys' driveway, another time a car engine being revved without purpose. I remember the force in his voice. And it was here I first heard a phrase I'd never heard before, that

I didn't understand the literal meaning of, uttered by my mom, I believe, when she said, "I shudder to think."

So, I was glad Mr. Landry kept his distance.

He called to us out on the lawn.

"Have you kids seen a dog running around here?"

"No, sir."

He looked as if he didn't believe us.

"If you see it," he said, "don't go near it. If you see it, come and tell me."

"Yes, sir."

I watched Mr. Landry walk back into the woods and cross a small creek. He stabbed at the water with his stick. He had a mop of black hair and was, by profession, a psychiatrist.

When I turned back to my friends, Lindy and Duke were again lying on the bed of moss, the conversation with Mr. Landry already forgotten. They giggled and whispered to each other and I watched Lindy rest her hand on Duke's stomach, where she fiddled, playfully, with his belly button.

A few days after this, our telephone rang. My mother pulled me into the bathroom and riffled through my hair with her fingers, a small flashlight between her teeth. Wiry and gray, she told me, Spanish moss is a living thing, and among the many creatures that reside in its wig are lice. So, by lying in a bed of it, Lindy and Duke were infested. My mother explained to me how they had them all over, nearly microscopic, and feasting on every inch of their bodies. I replayed the scene in my head, the way they had eventually helped each other up off the bed, as if some new allegiance had been formed between them, and tried to recall swarms of tiny bugs on their skin.

"I didn't see anything," I told her.

"That's why you have me to look for you," she said.

But the whole story, I suppose, is the shared history that this event established between Duke and Lindy. From there out they often stood to the side at times when the rest of us played. Duke, with his head shaven the next day, took to calling her Queenie. Lindy, who would not have allowed anyone to shave her head in those years, wore Duke's baseball cap to cover the overwhelming smell of vinegar that her mother had used to delouse her hair. She drank from his Gatorade bottle, he ate from her Twizzlers, and it became the assumption that Duke would pick Lindy for his side in tackle football every single time, as if there she could never be hurt.

A couple years later, after the crime, when Lindy and I stayed up late to talk on the phone, she confessed to me that she often snuck out of her parents' house in the weeks that followed the bed of moss and met Duke Kern in his driveway. She told me they kissed on the hood of his father's '57 Chevy and that she let him put his hands beneath her shirt. Oddly, I was neither jealous nor angry.

They were young. They were both beautiful.

Duke Kern was never a suspect.

5.

Bo Kern, on the other hand, was a suspect.

He had graduated from the Perkins School, but just barely, the year before the crime. He was well known around town and, with his unsettling harelip and crew cut, immediately recognizable. Teenagers and school friends knew him as the guy always willing to go one step beyond what any of them dared to do and, as such, he was the wild card of every social event. House parties screeched to a halt when Bo Kern knocked over some antique table in a fit of dancing. Young hostesses cried when he dented a parent's car hood while wrestling and drunk. He was the guy who would publicly accept any challenge volleyed forth, trying desperately to impress girls the world knew had no interest in him.

The football coaches at the Perkins School knew Bo Kern as the slow-witted boy who had ballooned into a formidable blocking back in the summer before his senior year. This was the only position he could play, fullback, or blocking back, as it requires zero agility. The sole purpose of this position is for the athlete to turn himself into a missile, a battering ram, and destroy whatever obstacle steps in his way. His sacrifice makes room for the more skilled running back to show his stuff and light up the scoreboard. It is a position of little reward, fullback, yet Bo Kern had so distinguished himself in the first few games of his senior year that he drew the attention of scouts from Millsaps and Belhaven College, a pair of Division III rivals in Mississippi. This was big news. Banners that read *Bo Knows Blocking* and *Geaux Bo* were written by pep squads and taped up around the chain-link fencing of the football field for the game the scouts were attending. It was October and still warm.

Before this game was finished, Bo Kern had committed two illegal procedure penalties, three personal fouls, and had been ejected for fighting with a player from our opponent, Dutchtown Catholic. Parents and fans alike looked over to explain to the well-dressed scouts that this was surely the product of nerves, some unfortunate anomaly, but they had seen enough. So, kids my age thought about Bo Kern whenever we flirted with failure. The notion was that if *he* could graduate, there was hope for us all, and he was a legend in this capacity. He was therefore a guy that many people pretended to know all about, as people do, if only to nod gravely at his name.

As far as the neighborhood was concerned, when it came to Lindy's rape, he was also a person of interest.

The fact that physical abnormalities were so rare at the Perkins School, so rare in Woodland Hills, didn't help. There were no disabled children that I remember. There were no wheelchairs or deformities. We were all middle- to upper-class white kids, all the products of our parents' success, and when we played with one another at school we played in the mirror.

In this environment, Bo Kern's harelip rattled you.

He was a stocky guy, impossibly so that senior year, and the jagged turn of his lip bared constantly the gums above his front teeth. He rarely smiled, and even when he did you couldn't be sure. So, I have to wonder about people like him, about children perhaps doomed from birth by circumstances beyond their control. What chance did he have among us? How early is the future defined?

I can think of others like him as well, such as a boy named Chester McCready.

Thin and pale and a classmate of mine, Chester did not shave the dark hairs that appeared on his upper lip in high school. He wore shirts with stains on them, sneakers that stank up the classroom, and had the look of some apprenticing con man, a boy who would rather be left alone in the dark. During our sophomore year, a girl named Missy Boyce claimed that Chester tried to feel her up at the concession stand during a football game that previous Friday. Desperate to be desired as well, other girls soon pretended the same, and the name Chester the Molester followed.

When we originally asked him about this Missy incident, Chester told us, "Some guy pushed me into her. It's not my fault Super Bitch was there."

He was emphatic about this and, I believe, honest.

Regardless, many of us who knew him began to pretend that we didn't, and he was known only as Chester the Molester throughout the rest of high school, a time that must seem to him like an excruciating string of years. Even at our ten-year reunion, his name was still on our tongues, as he had recently been accused of sexual harassment at a local sandwich shop where he worked. This didn't strike me as irony, as it did some of the other people at the reunion, but rather as the inevitable end we had sent him to in our youth. Even as children, you understand, we set our paper boats on a stream. We watch them go.

After hearing about this, I went to the public library to look up the newspaper article about this event. I stared at Chester's picture when I saw it, pasted among the other criminals' photos in the Metro section, and I barely recognized him. He had a goatee now, sharp and trimmed, and his hair was thin and brushed forward. His mouth was small. The article said the girl was sixteen at the time of the incident, and it struck me that this was likely Missy's age when this whole thing began, as if his troubles had never matured. I felt an accomplice to the words as I read them that day and a surprising pity for the man he'd become.

Still, it was hard to feel sorry for Bo Kern despite the hand he was dealt.

Unapologetic and mean, Bo took his anger out into the streets beyond Woodland Hills, even in high school, and had a reputation for violence. One time, Bo was brought home by the police for assaulting a boy at Highland Road Park with a stop sign he had pulled from the ground. He was let off with a warning. Another time I saw him put his fist through the window of a car in the school parking lot for no discernible reason.

After gym class one day, all the talk at school was about a brawl that had taken place in the Taco Bell parking lot the night before, where Bo Kern had beaten a boy from across town so badly that he had to be hospitalized. My friend Randy told me that after this fight, he heard that Bo had tried putting the unconscious boy in the back of a friend's pickup truck before the cops showed up and he fled. This was only a rumor, he admitted, but it stuck with us.

"Where was he taking him?" Randy asked me. "Where the hell was he taking him?"

We shuddered to think.

Yet in the year after he graduated from Perkins, Bo grew even wilder.

He had not been accepted to any colleges, had no athletic scholarship offers, and instead worked nights as a bouncer at Sportz, a local eighteen-and-up club near the LSU campus. He still lived at home in these months and would drunkenly return down Piney Creek Road at three and four a.m., squealing around the curve in his father's '57 Chevy. After only two months of employment at this place, Bo had a restraining order issued against him by a college girl, an English major, who was a regular at the bar. She won the case and he was fired.

In the court document, a public record, she described Bo Kern as "a menacing figure" and complained of having nightmares about his face.

She summed it up for all of us.

The evidence mounted.

In the months immediately before the rape, Bo Kern totaled his father's '57 Chevy in broad daylight. He broke the finger of a boy in the next neighborhood who pointed at him and accused him of cheating at basketball. He gave his own brother a black eye on the front lawn. He told us stories about breaking into cars at LSU football games and stealing credit cards. When anyone else in the neighborhood spoke, Bo Kern asked them, "What the fuck are you looking at?"

Where were the consequences? Where was it all leading?

I imagine this must have been the worry of our parents, as well, when the news spread about Lindy's rape. So, recently, when I began revisiting all of this, I asked my mother if she had originally suspected Bo.

She told me that after the police had gone door to door asking people in the neighborhood if they had seen any suspicious activity, Lindy's parents had themselves gone from house to house. She said they were teary-eyed and supportive of one another. She said they looked tired and old. The story went that Dan Simpson, Lindy's father, was particularly suspicious of Bo, despite the fact that he had an alibi and witness to say he wasn't home that night, and when the Simpsons finally visited the Kern house, Betty Kern, Bo's mother, sat down with them in the kitchen. Then, before Mr. Simpson could even mention that he wanted the police to question Bo again, Betty Kern burst into tears.

She was inconsolable.

"I'm so sorry," she cried. "I know what you're thinking. It kills me. He was the first person I thought of, too."

So, "Yes," my mother told me. "We all did."

6.

It is important when I learned the word "rape."

In the school year before the crime, Randy and I were sitting on his kitchen floor. It was a wide and open space with yellow linoleum tiles. We sat with our backs to the refrigerator and faced the wall some twenty feet away. We had caches of action figures in those days, primarily G.I. Joes and Star Wars characters, and I lugged mine around in large plastic tackle boxes my father had left at our house, while Randy kept his in see-through Tupperware containers. On that day, we'd spread the characters out on the floor before us; Boba Fett, Cobra Commander, and the like.

We were thirteen years old, and the only people who knew we still played with these toys were each other.

We shared many secrets like this.

For example, Randy's parents, sweet-hearted people, never got the courage to tell him about Santa Claus, and so his fantasy lasted well past the norm. When my oldest sister, Hannah, told me, I was around nine, and I rushed over to Randy's house to commiserate. It was the week before Christmas and, when I got there, Randy was lounging on a swing outside, chewing the end of a pencil and working on his list. The document was three pages long, complete with simple sketches of the most coveted items, and I couldn't bring myself to tell him. So I spent years like this, changing the subject every time he brought it up. It was no easy task. Randy eventually gathered the facts on his own, of course, and one day in high school, when we had become very different people yet found ourselves together at a classmate's house party, he drunkenly asked me why I'd let him carry on like that.

"I don't know," I told him. "I guess I just didn't want to spoil it."

Randy shook his head and smiled. He put his arm around my shoulders.

"There's just one thing I don't get," he said. "All those letters I sent to the North Pole. Where the hell did they go?"

"That's a great question," I said. "I have no idea."

But Randy also had the goods on me.

The night my father left us, I snuck over to his house and cried like a baby. We were both ten years old then, up in the middle of the night during a school week and, I thought, the only two people awake in the world. I can't recall what I blubbered to him. I only remember lying facedown on his bed, my head sopping up the pillow, and hearing a short knock on the door. I scrambled around to hide, thinking we'd been caught, and crawled underneath his bed. Randy opened the door and rubbed his eyes, pretending to have been asleep. On the floor outside his room was a plate of warm cookies. Two cups of milk. We heard footsteps going back down the stairs.

We were friends.

We had decided enough was enough with our toys, however, and so that day in the kitchen we made a game out of slinging them violently across the floor to crash against the opposite wall. Points were scored if you broke a head or a limb off the figure, and we kept tally by drawing in erasable pen on the fridge. The toys made red and blue marks along the baseboards, I remember, and his dog, Ruby, swallowed the decapitated heads.

After several rounds of this, Randy's older sister, Alexi, came in.

In college but living at home, Alexi was thin, blond, and followed constantly by boys. One particular boy I remember was named Robert, and he slunk around Randy's house for a year. He looked perpetually wrinkled, as if he had slept in his clothes, and wore baseball caps even at night. He worked as a short-order cook in a restaurant near campus, where he and Alexi had met, and always smelled to us like fried onion rings.

When Alexi saw the mess we'd made she said, "What are you two idiots doing?" but didn't wait around for an answer. She told Robert to make her a glass of lemonade, so he did. Then she walked directly to the telephone, attached to a wall near the den, and dialed a number. "Jenn," Alexi said into the phone, "what's this bullshit I hear about you not coming to Robert's party?"

Robert stood over us and grabbed ice cubes out of the freezer.

He asked Randy, "Did you know your sister's insane?"

"You don't have to tell me," Randy said.

We liked Robert, as he described nearly everything he saw as "insane" and made us wonder what type of revelations awaited us in college. We followed him outside to the patio while Alexi talked on the phone. We watched him smoke cigarettes and ash into a Dr Pepper bottle. Their dog, Ruby, then came outside through the dog door and trotted onto the lawn, where she vomited up the brightly colored heads of our action figures. Robert said, "That dog is insane."

We laughed and slapped at the mosquitoes biting our ankles.

Robert then asked Randy a number of questions about his sister, like what type of flowers she liked, what her favorite place to eat was, and if she had ever dated any fraternity guys. Randy, of course, had no idea. After a few minutes, Alexi stepped outside, holding the telephone at her neck, still attached by its cord.

"Robert," she said. "Jenn wants to know what the score was."

The subject was LSU football, as it often is in Baton Rouge, and this was a time of depression. "It was forty-four to three," Robert told her. "We got *raped.*"

So there it was, burning for me.

There have been other words like this in my lifetime, words so mysterious that I had to possess them, even if I didn't understand their meaning. Diaphragm. Prophylactic. Swoon. I remember a day in the sixth grade when a boy named Chuck Beard, a red-headed kid, called me a dildo at recess. We had been playing Four Square along the brick walkways of Perkins and I'd sent him out of the competition with a lob that careened off the boundary line. He was furious. After school that day, my mother picked me up in the parking lot. She asked me how I had done on a project I had turned in to my teacher, Mrs. Williams, a woman who wore massive amounts of blue eye shadow. "I got a B," I told her. "I think Mrs. Williams might be a dildo."

My mother pulled to the side of the road.

"What did you say?" she asked me. "Do you even know what that means?"

She was beautiful and still young, my mother. She had a new haircut since the divorce.

"Of course I do," I told her. "That lady is a pain in my butt."

Cars passed as she composed herself.

The situation was more serious, however, when my mother called me out from my room in the days following the crime. I saw Mr. and Mrs. Simpson standing beside her in the den, and it looked as though my mother had been crying. The three of them directed me to a chair that had been pulled out from the table and stood in a semicircle around me.

"Honey," my mother told me, "I don't

know how to tell you this. I can't believe I'm even telling you this, but Lindy Simpson was raped."

"If you know anything," Mrs. Simpson said.

"We're not accusing you," Mr. Simpson said. "Your mother's already told us y'all were inside, finishing supper. But, please, if you know anything."

I sat there looking up at them, unsure of what to say, and then I heard a soft clinking noise in the kitchen. It sounded like someone was milling around in there, perhaps using a spoon to stir a cup of coffee or tea. I knew that my sisters weren't home and, by this point, my father was long gone.

"Mom," I asked. "Who's in the kitchen?"

"Sweetheart," she said, and before she could tell me anything else, a police officer in full dress turned the corner from our kitchen to our living room and leaned casually against the door frame, still stirring his hot cup of coffee. He was tall and well built and looked indestructible in his uniform. The shining badge on his chest, the thick utility belt and pistol he wore around his waist, it all sent a panic through me. I wondered how much information he could draw out of me if he tried. Not just about the crime, necessarily, but about my rela-

46

tionship with Lindy in general. About the way I thought of her so often that she had become a figure not only alive for me in my waking hours but active in my dreams as well. I sat up straight as the officer looked me over.

"Don't mind me," he said, and nodded toward the Simpsons. "Just answer their question. Do you know anything about this?"

I looked at my mother, who in turn smiled at me so gently that I knew I could say anything, in those years, and she would believe me.

"Honey," she said.

"Lindy was raped?" I asked her.

"Yes," she told me.

"That's terrible," I said.

"Yes," she said. "It is."

I thought about this for a long time.

"But I don't understand," I said. "Who was she playing?"

This comment seemed to confuse the adults in that room to such a degree that they began shifting the weight around on their feet and picking at the lint on their clothing as if they were the guilty ones now, because they had said a thing to a child that the child was not ready to hear. The police officer shook his head, sipped from his cof-

47

fee, and walked back into the kitchen. My mother then walked over and kissed me on the forehead.

"Thank you, God," I heard her say. "Thank you, Jesus."

The police officer left a card on our refrigerator door and asked us to call him if we thought of anything. He then thanked my mother for the coffee and patted me kindly on the shoulder as he and the Simpsons, like unfortunate salesmen, walked back into the heat of that brutal summer. My mother and I returned to the kitchen, where she took the policeman's card from the fridge and studied it before slipping it into a drawer by the phone. She then took out a carton of eggs, some sugar, flour, and a mixing bowl, and began to make cookies.

Later that week I walked into my room to find a pamphlet about sex on my bed. There was no note attached to it, and when I opened it up a loose roll of condoms fell out. We have never spoken to each other about this, my mother and I, but I can remember her lavishing praise on me in this time. She made macaroni and cheese with every meal. She brought oranges to all of my soccer games. Things were remarkably good between us for a while, until she found a real reason to suspect me. It was hard for her, I suppose, to realize that committing the act does not depend on knowing the word.

7.

The day I fell in love with Lindy Simpson was January 28, 1986.

This was also the day the Space Shuttle *Challenger* exploded, and seven courageous astronauts died. I was eleven years old and in the fifth grade.

Along with nearly every other school in America, the Perkins School had structured its entire science curriculum around this mission. We focused on stars and galaxies and made crude Styrofoam mobiles of the Milky Way that we hung with fishing line from the ceilings of our classrooms. In preparation for the *Challenger*'s liftoff, to be broadcast live on CNN, similar grades had been lumped together, fourth through sixth, seventh and eighth, et cetera, and ushered into rooms with televisions. This was exotic to us then, watching cable at school, and the TVs stood on carts that had been pushed in front of the blackboards.

They had plastic knobs and buttons beneath the screens. To make additional space in the classrooms, our wooden desks had been stacked and moved out into the hallways and we were seated in long rows along the carpeted floor, organized by homeroom.

As a class project, the sixth grade, Lindy's grade, had written a letter to Christa McAuliffe. She was the elementary school teacher chosen from more than twenty thousand applicants to accompany the astronauts into space, and she was a national hero. Their letter to her was simple, written in pencil on lined paper, and it thanked her for her bravery. In the weeks before takeoff, Mrs. McAuliffe had returned to the sixth-grade class an American flag and signed publicity photo of the entire crew, both of which were now hanging on a large bulletin board lined in red, white, and blue crepe paper. Our teachers gathered in front of it and chatted energetically. The whole place had the buzz of a holiday.

We drank fruit punch and ate cookies shaped like stars. We wore flag pins and sang the national anthem. We felt good, all of us did, and I had no way of knowing that the image of Mrs. Knight, my homeroom teacher, singing along in front of that flag would never leave me. She was a young woman with a bob haircut, although all teachers looked immensely old to me then, and she was a brunette. This was her first year teaching at the Perkins School, at any school, and it would be her last.

I remember that it was cold and dry that morning, oddly enough, as even January offers no promise of winter in Louisiana. I've spent Christmases in T-shirts, Thanksgivings in shorts and sneakers. On this day, however, we all wore pants and long-sleeved button-downs, and two rows across from me, sitting Indian-style on the carpet, Lindy Simpson wore a navy blue sweatshirt over her jumper.

I paid her no mind. I wanted to see the rocket.

When it came time for the countdown, our teachers turned up the volume on the television and asked us to pay attention. We stared like tourists at the shuttle in its launch position, filmed at long distance by a handheld camera. I remember the Kennedy Space Center looking completely deserted but for the craft: a white shuttle perched atop three cylindrical rocket boosters, the middle one some fifteen stories high and blood red. This was a good time in America. We were dreamers, teachers and students alike, all aboard that mission by patriotic proxy.

So, as the countdown began, we joined along. Our chorus swelled at T minus eight as smoke released from beneath the rocket in purposeful plumes. We then bellowed out the final "one" and watched the *Challenger* take off, heavy and miraculous, breaking away from the launch pad and burning everything beneath it. Our teachers applauded. The announcer said "Liftoff! We have liftoff!" and told us we were witnessing history.

We believed him, and watched the shuttle rise atop a column of fire.

Seventy-three seconds later, it ended.

Due to a massive amount of wind shear, along with the failure of the right rocket booster's O-rings, a flare breached the external fuel tank of the *Challenger* and destroyed the integrity of the ship. From the ground, all systems looked normal. We could hear the joyous cheers of people standing behind the camera, the excitement in the announcer's polished voice. We had no clue. Even Mission Control was unaware of the problem until the very end, as was evidenced by the last transmission made by NASA to the crew. It came ten seconds before the explosion and said, "Roger, *Challenger*, go at throttle up," which means *Ev-*

erything's okay, you guys. Give it all you've got.

After a federal investigation into the event, and public disclosure of every detail, we learned that there was a bit more to this story. The disaster was not a complete surprise to everyone. It turned out that an additional transmission had been made, one second before the explosion, from the crew of the *Challenger* back to the ground, when Pilot Michael J. Smith, while either reading something on the gauges or feeling something in his heart, said, "Uh-oh."

Often, in times of tragedy, there is a delay period, a moment of collective disbelief.

Not this time.

I immediately heard shouts from the halls.

Our teachers reacted first, clutching their chests and screaming as the shuttle burst into flames, and so chaos had us before the first piece of debris splashed into the Atlantic. Mrs. Knight scrambled to turn off the television and Mrs. McElroy, a parental volunteer, tripped over a boy curled up on the floor and fell against the snack table. When the punch bowl broke and spilled red juice all over the carpet, we hit maximum hysteria. I heard people running up and down the hallways. I heard the worried voices of eighth graders in the adjacent classroom. I heard the squealing of pigtailed girls. I didn't know what to do.

So, I sat on the carpet and watched this. I tried not to get stepped on.

Across from me, Lindy Simpson sat on the carpet as well.

When a space cleared between us, I saw that her sweatshirt was covered in vomit.

Lindy looked over at me and pressed her lips together, not out of any form of embarrassment, I don't believe, but rather as if she were merely glad to see someone she knew. She did not smile, necessarily, and she did not cry. Instead she had a look on her face that still haunts me. It was as if Lindy had unplugged herself completely from the event.

This was a look of hers I would see later in life.

Mrs. Knight eventually noticed her, too, and rushed over. In one expert move, she pulled the soiled sweatshirt over Lindy's head and balled it up so that no one would see. Then Lindy, coming to, began to cry. Mrs. Knight helped her off the floor and ushered her out of the room, stroking her hair. As they passed in front of me, I heard Mrs. Knight say, "I know, honey. I know."

I'm not sure why this ignited my heart. I suppose it was the fact that I, myself, was not crying, that I hadn't even had time to react. Or perhaps it was the sight of Lindy's bright pink vomit that did it, strangely enough, so full of candy and sweet punch. Was she so sensitive that this was always inside of her? When I saw her running carefree through our neighborhood, or eating a sno-cone on the curb of Piney Creek Road, was it possible she was this tender and vulnerable? How deeply did she feel what she saw? How intensely can one experience life? Were all girls like this? The idea broke over me. These were separate creatures altogether, I realized, these girls. If not, then how could Lindy have felt so immediately the panic in the classroom, the concern over the death of our heroes? How could it make her sick before I even got off the floor?

So say what you will about men, our massive failures on Earth, but some understanding flickered inside me at that moment, something hardwired came alive. I was just a boy, not even a man, and yet I suddenly felt it my warrant to defend this particular girl from there on out, against any vague threat that might arise. In the days that followed this event, I got into arguments with other kids my age, boys who said they, too, had seen Lindy throw up, and tried to gain an audience to laugh at her expense. I threw fits. I denied it vehemently. I raged against an unchangeable history, something that would later become a habit of mine.

In a curious turn of events, many years after this, I ran into Mrs. Knight at a local restaurant. I was in college then, and she still looked young and lovely. She now worked as an assistant at a contracting firm, she told me, and had given up teaching completely. But she remembered me well, she said, from the day the *Challenger* exploded. She introduced me to her husband and explained to him the nightmare it was, having charge of all those shell-shocked children, and how she still revisits the day in her head. Then she told me a story I didn't remember.

After Mrs. Knight had taken Lindy to the restroom and rinsed out her sweatshirt in the sink, she led her back into the hall. Apparently, I was standing there waiting for them, she said, and had taken off my long-sleeved shirt to give it to Lindy. Embarrassed and upset, Lindy ran off in the crowd without acknowledging me. Mrs. Knight said that she still remembers the lump in her throat at that moment, how ill-prepared she was for pandemonium, and what I told her as Lindy ran away.

"Do you remember what you said?" she asked me.

I didn't.

"You came up and took my hand," she said. "You told me, 'I guess it's true what they say, Mrs. Knight. When it rains, it pours.' "

I smiled at this small memory, as did she.

"I never forgot that," she said. "You seemed so mature. I don't know. You were like an old wise man in a little kid's body. It stuck with me. I always wondered how you'd grown up."

"Well," I said. "Here I am."

"And the Simpson girl," she said. "I felt so sorry for her, too. Are you still in touch with her?"

"No," I told her. "Not anymore."

So on the day I fell for Lindy, school was canceled by noon.

There was a line of traffic in the carpool lane, and even our parents were distraught about the shuttle, thankful to have been let out of work to come get us. Randy and I rode the short distance home in my mother's car, and he kept making crashing noises with his mouth. My mother begged him to stop. We saw Lindy walking home alone on the sidewalk with her sweatshirt in her hand. She looked cold and sad, and my mother pulled to the side of the road. I hopped out of the car and let Lindy sit in the front. She didn't say a word to me. I was crushed.

Later that night, my mother called me into the living room to watch Ronald Reagan on TV. "Honey," she said. "It's the president."

I remember it clearly.

Reagan sat in the Oval Office, his face placid and genuine. He wore a dark blue suit and fiddled with a paper clip in his hand. The credenza behind him, barely visible, was covered in family photos. And instead of delivering the State of the Union Address, which he was scheduled to do, President Reagan mourned our nation's tragedy and mentioned each of the fallen astronauts by name. My mother broke out in quiet tears as he spoke of them, something she did with regularity in these years. She then put her arm around me and pulled me close to her on the couch. We sat in the darkness and listened.

The president said, "And I now want to say something to the schoolchildren of America who were watching the live coverage of the shuttle's takeoff."

My mother looked down at me. She ran her fingers through my hair.

"I know it's hard to understand," he told

59

us, "but sometimes painful things like this happen. It's all part of the process of exploration and discovery. It's all part of taking a chance and expanding man's horizons. The future doesn't belong to the fainthearted," he reminded us. "It belongs to the brave."

I looked up at my mother. She was already broken, I realize now, and had yet to even face the greatest tragedies of her life. She dabbed a soft handkerchief at my eyes and held my head in her hands.

"Were you listening, honey?" she asked me. "Do you understand what he's saying?"

This was my first day in love. I didn't understand anything.

I put my head on her shoulder.

She covered my eyes with her hand.

8.

Back then, I was not the only one in this Lindy fix.

In middle school, a boy named Brett Barrett fell so hard for Lindy that he mowed lawns for two summers just to buy her a ring. It was thin and gold-plated, with some blue stone in its center. Legend goes that she had bested him in a round of kiss-chase years before, a game we played in our youth, and planted one on his cheek. Then, as if this peck were a promise, or the culmination of some ancient courtship ritual, Brett Barrett assumed that he and Lindy were meant for each other, and he got immediately to work. He saved every penny. He thought of little else. Finally, in the eighth grade, he presented her with the ring underneath a live oak near the center of campus.

"Why would I want this?" Lindy said.

She wasn't being mean.

The thing was, during his years of steadfast pursuit, Brett Barrett had forgotten to speak to her.

A boy named Kyle Wims also fell for Lindy when she stood up for him during a pickup basketball game at lunch hour. Chubby and pale, Kyle didn't run much, and hovered instead near the three-point line, waving his arms. He fancied himself a three-point specialist, I imagine, and to be honest I remember him being decent. Still, he rarely got the ball as the more athletic kids drove the lane and made improbable layups. Lindy sat near the court in a row of girls who would later turn out to be the type to play volleyball, softball, and soccer, and together they watched the game. In the middle of their conversation, Lindy got so flustered that she called out to the boys, "Hey, dipwads! Why don't you pass it to Kyle? He's wide flipping open!" and Kyle lost his mind.

He dropped thirty-two pounds in the coming year, either through puberty or devotion, and asked Lindy to the back-to-school dance. She said yes to him out of pure kindness, which made it all worse. Lindy was beautiful and athletic, and at this time, she was still popular. There was never a chance between them. So when she posed for pictures with him in the gymnasium and asked him to hold her shoes while she danced with her friends, Kyle ate it up. The rest of us laughed. I believe it was Tommy Gale who eventually told him to open his eyes and get real, and so Kyle just stood in the corner for the rest of the night. Lindy rushed up to grab him for the last dance, however, and pulled him into the crowd. She put her soft hands on his shoulders, and Kyle flipped us the bird behind her back. That next week he taped their pictures up on the inside of his locker, but we never heard him speak her name again.

A boy from across town was also affected. He had seen Lindy compete in a cross-country meet when they were both in the eighth grade, and he fell in love with her, too. She had won her heat easily, as he had his, and so he assumed it would be a natural fit. In his defense, at this time of her life, Lindy was easy to imagine yourself with. She seemed to walk that perfect line between a person you suspect you might not deserve and the prize life would be if everything turned out just right. She was playful but not silly, pretty but not exotic, and close but just out of reach. So, after the race, this boy took to frequenting the malls and movie theaters, looking for her. If he saw us wearing our school uniforms around town, he approached us as well.

"Do y'all know Lindy Simpson?" he'd ask us. "Tell her the guy that won the mile is looking for her."

He gave us little slips of paper with his parents' phone number on them and so we prank-called his house for years. We figured he deserved it, like some trespasser caught fishing our pond, and made sure nothing ever came of his love.

But not all of her suitors were so virtuous.

Clay Tompkins, an awkward boy with dandruff, was known to spend all his free time scribbling in a green composition notebook. He had few friends at school and didn't seem to want them, although I know now that this couldn't have been true. The last semester of our eighth-grade year, Clay made the mistake of leaving his notebook underneath his desk when he went to the bathroom, and since it was a burning mystery to all of us, we riffled through it. The first page contained a list about twenty names long, all girls at our school. The page was titled GIRLS I'D LIKE TO BANG, and was apparently a scientific ranking. I saw Lindy's name at number 7.

A crowd gathered around the book as one of the boys flipped the pages. Each page had a detailed sketch devoted to one of the aforementioned girls in some pose that they had surely never assumed. Anna Jenks, for example, was drawn swinging from a vine with her breasts hanging out, a pair of skimpy animal-print panties barely concealing her backside. Katie Comeaux, number 2, was nude on her knees, her hands behind her head. She looked to be dancing to some pulsing music in the background, and her pubic hair was trimmed into a neat and thin strip. May Fontenot lay on her back with her legs spread before us, her hands gripping her inner thighs, and touched the tip of her tongue to her teeth. It was incredible stuff, all of it, and spoke to an imagination few of us appreciated at the time.

I squirmed in my seat at the sight.

When we finally got to Lindy's page, there she was, more tastefully rendered than the others. Her back was to the artist, as it often was when she ran, and she peered over her shoulder at us. Her hair, pulled back into a ponytail, traced the soft valley between her shoulder blades, and she was topless. Below this, her gym shorts were pulled down to her knees, as were her panties. The only colors on the page were two bright splashes of blue: her Reebok running shoes.

I would have emptied my pockets for the document.

The boys kept flipping on, though, wondering what new miracles awaited us, and we eventually got to pages where Clay had practiced with anatomy. We saw detailed drawings of erect penises from all angles, numerous workups of vaginas with various patterns of hair. I learned more in those few minutes than in all my previous experience. And since we were currently blind to any other world but this one, none of us noticed Mrs. Berkowitz approaching to see what the fuss was about. Once she did, we surrendered the notebook instantly. We chattered to her of our innocence.

I was never the same after this, nor was Clay.

He was pulled out of school that day and did not return. I don't know what happened to him, whether he was expelled or just could not face us, but we never saw Clay Tompkins again. We talked to people at other schools to see if he transferred, we looked around for him at sporting events and restaurants. Nothing. I long wondered where he went. How does a boy just disappear?

Decades later, I saw Clay Tompkins in *USA Today.* He was living in Seattle and, together with a partner, had started a company that designed video games. It was cutting-edge stuff, the article said, meant primarily for adults. These games are now called first-person shooters and are popular, so I know he makes no end of coin. I hope he's happy. I feel sorry for people like him. He was just a curious boy then, with genuine talent, and his only mistake was expressing it.

But Clay Tompkins had also given me a strange gift, which was the inexhaustible joy of pornography. I was an immediate fan. When I got home that night, I rushed my way through dinner and ran to my room. I got to work beneath my sheets with a pencil and sketchpad and drew Lindy in every way I could imagine. Most of these early sketches were unrecognizable, of course, merely a collage of inappropriate stick figures, but the act of creation gave me tremendous satisfaction. I had her right where I wanted her, I figured, in my room, in my mind, at the tips of my fumbling fingers.

And then, in one of the first rushes of lustful inspiration I would experience in my life, I drew thought bubbles above Lindy's head to get her emotion across.

The things I made her think. The things I made her want.

These would come back to haunt me.

9.

I believe Louisiana gets a bad rap.

I don't want this story to add to it, though I know it will, because people often discount what we say here. We are relegated to a different human standard in the South, it seems, lower than the majority of this great nation, as if all our current tragedies are somehow payback for our unfortunate past. You may hear, for instance, something like, "Yes, it is a shame those folks in New Orleans drowned. But why didn't they just evacuate?" Or, "It is terrible about that boy being shot, but I'm sure you've heard about the race problems there."

Another catastrophe? Another injustice? Forgive me if I don't look surprised.

This bothers me. It bothers everyone in the South.

So, in case you don't yet know, let's get this out of the way.

It's hot here, yes. It rains and it floods.

If you say, "It's not the heat, it's the humidity," it's because you're from some other sunny place where you thought it was hot. It's *both* the heat and humidity. It's okay. You'll survive. There are ways to get along.

One thing you do is amplify the pleasure of meals. Three times a day you sit down with friends or family who, if you're lucky, are often the same. You take a break from the heat. You set a napkin over your lap and you can't believe the utter joy. This tomato might just save your life, the cool fruit of it, that cold beer or iced tea your salvation. This is not gluttony.

You eat this way for a reason.

When everything else is burning, sweating, beaten down by a torturous sun, only your tongue can be fooled. So you tease it with flavors like promises, small escapes from a blatantly burdensome land. You offer it up sharp spices, dark stews, iced cocktails. Anything you can think of to do.

There is a saying in South Louisiana that "when we eat one meal we talk about the next," and this is true. Who wouldn't? In this imagined menu lies a future, a forecasted life, a community, perhaps even a weekend full of cheer and good food. What should we cook on Saturday? you wonder.

Yes, honey, yes, darling, believe me when I say that sounds good. And at the house across the street, a similar family is doing the same. Perhaps a Sunday spent over a pot of beans. A lunch of hot po'-boys wrapped in butcher paper. It is also an unwritten rule that we don't talk politics at the table. This is not because we're dumb or old-fashioned or just too polite, but rather because we see right through it.

Middling stuff, the world. Nothing worth mucking up a fine meal.

And so the soul of this place lives in the parties that grow here, not just Mardi Gras, no, but rather the kind that start with a simple phone call to a neighbor, a friend. And after the heat is discussed and your troubles shared you say man it'd be nice to see you, your kids, your smile. And from this grows a spread several tables long, covered in newspaper, with long rows of crawfish spilled steaming from aluminum pots, a bright splash of red in the blanketing green of your yard. It is food so big it must be stirred with a paddle. You gather around this. You worship it. There is nothing strange about that.

Only the unfortunate don't see it this way.

When I was in my twenties, I had a short-lived friendship with a fellow from Michigan. He had moved here for college, and so I bragged to him the way that all of us down here do, about our food, our hospitality, those mantles we cling to. I invited him to a friend's party in the Garden District of Baton Rouge, a neighborhood full of old majesty and wraparound porches. Our host, one of the cavalry of great unknown cooks in this state, slaved all day over a steaming pot of crawfish. He offered my friend local beer and iced watermelon, anything to ease the day's scorch. Then, when the table was piled high with boiled corn and potatoes, spicy crawfish from a pond not too far away, my friend backed away from the crowd. Dig in, we all said. We'll show you how to peel.

He was polite but did not budge, insisting that he just wasn't hungry.

"Your loss," we said, and we meant it.

Later, in the car, he told me that he couldn't believe I had eaten that.

"They're mudbugs," he said. "You guys were just eating a pile of insects. It's more disgusting than I thought it would be."

I did not begrudge him his idiocy. Instead I explained to him that the crawfish is technically a crustacean, no different biologically than the lobster he'd likely ordered at the finest restaurant in Ann Arbor, the term "mudbug" a misnomer. What he'd witnessed, I told him, was great luxury on a miniature scale.

"All I saw were bugs," he said. "All I saw were drunk and sweaty people, sucking on the heads of dead insects."

This is no small point.

It is this type of wrong-ended telescoping that gets Louisiana in trouble.

When I was a boy, for example, I played football with Randy behind his house. We set up end zones between twin oak trees in the back lot and used rows of bright yellow ragweeds as our boundary lines. We drew up plays by tracing our fingers through the thick grass and imagined scores of rabid fans there watching. We hiked, spun, dodged, and threw tight spirals to each other through the hot and heavy air. We dove and we caught. We scored and we celebrated. On one particular day, Randy punted the ball and it careened off his foot. It hit a tree and bounced into the small swamp behind our properties, covered at the time by a thin layer of green algae. Together we stood at the banks of this swamp, a place our parents told us not to go, and we were wary of snakes. We watched the football float in the still water, a child-sized football, mind you, for we were children, and we knelt in the mud to catch our

72

breath. We tried to think. Before we could devise a way to retrieve it, we saw a nutria, a large swamp rat that looks like an otter, swim up to our ball through the muck. It nosed the thing, watched it spin around in the dark water, and it ate it.

Now go into the world and tell this story.

No one will ask you the rodent's history, how legend has it that they were brought here from Argentina by the McIlhenny family, the founders of Tabasco, to be bred for their fur on Avery Island. So you will not get a chance to tell the epic tale of the hurricane that is said to have followed this event, allowing two of these rats to escape their cages like some brave and famous lovers and start a family in an unfamiliar land. The listeners are not interested in that. They do not see these animals setting off into the wetlands like pilgrims, like our own ancestors, to whom we owe a great debt. Nor will they see the two happy boys like me and Randy in this story, with bright glowing eyes and big hearts, witnessing a spectacle as bizarre to them as it would be to you. Instead, your listeners will only reaffirm to themselves what they previously thought about Louisiana: that it is a backwoods place with huge rats in the algae, some wild nightmare they're glad not to face.

As another example, it once rained so hard in my youth that the swamps behind Woodland Hills backed up. It looked like we lived on a lake. Piney Creek Road itself also flooded, and our proud houses stood like chalets on some muddy gulf. For two days we watched snakes cruise the water. We watched our family dogs splash about like children. We threw fishing lines from the tops of our driveways and we waded with our poles into the lawn when the hooks got stuck on the concrete. We ate canned foods and drank warm Cokes. When the rain stopped, Old Man Casemore launched his aluminum boat right from his carport and trolled up and down the street like our own private Coast Guard, delivering us food that he'd made. Then the water receded and normalcy returned.

I imagine that many children in South Louisiana have stories similar to this one, and when they grow up, they move out into the world and tell them. This is not the problem. It is the way these stories return that dog us, the way they are altered by the outsiders who hear them. A man from California once asked me, for instance, if I rode to school in a boat. A woman from Des Moines said, "What was it like? Growing up chasing gators off your porch? It sounds

74

horrible."

It isn't like that. I promise.

Even in the summer of Lindy's rape, for instance, there was joy.

We played baseball in the street. We chased the ice-cream man from two blocks away.

Lindy was a part of this, too.

In fact, in the weeks immediately following the crime, after the police had made their rounds, the only difference we noticed in Lindy herself was a change in her schedule. No more piano lessons, to my dismay. Lindy went to therapy instead. No more bicycle ride out to the track at five o'clock, but rather a ride to and from the track with her parents. Small stuff. She looked the same to us then as she always had, bright and smiling, although all of this would soon change.

And so, terrible as it was, the summer of her rape carried on, bright and blue-skied, and full of immense pleasure. Even our parents, who had taken the news of this crime and the lack of a subsequent arrest the hardest, eventually came back into the fold, bonded together by the appearance of late-summer whiteflies in the neighborhood.

Tiny and prodigious creatures, whiteflies look like lint.

Alone, they are easily squashed, nothing more than a bit of dust on your fingers. In great numbers, however, they are disastrous, and feed indiscriminately on anything green. They colonize beneath the leaves of the flora available to them and work their tiny jaws to extract sap from the plant. This is not the trouble. The waste they subsequently excrete attracts a type of mold called black sooty, and this name speaks for itself. A dark color grows over the plant life, eventually growing so thick that it divorces the plant from the sun and a botanical sadness takes over. Irises lie down in their clumps. Trees drop their leaves out of season.

So, when Piney Creek Road came under siege that late summer, the neighborhood formed an alliance. Kids sprayed soapy water all over the gardens while their parents called one another to talk about successes and failures, progress and setbacks, any subject *other* than Lindy and the possible suspects in her rape, and were happy to focus on the more manageable problem at hand.

That Labor Day, when the infestation seemed under control, there was a party at my buddy Randy's house, the Stillers' house, and everyone there was in good spirits. Parents drank margaritas and iced beer as their kids ran around like lunatics in swim trunks. Lindy Simpson was there, too, without her parents, who had since withdrawn from these types of affairs. She wore a blue one-piece bathing suit, and I followed her around the yard with a water gun. It was all laughter and cheer until around six o'clock, when we heard a chain saw revving up in the distance and a group of us went out to see.

In the farthest bend of Piney Creek Road stood a common area, a spot of land that was not technically on anyone's lot. It was obvious now that despite their best intentions, no one had taken it upon themselves to treat the large live oak that stood there, and so this tree remained the last bastion of whiteflies. As such, the oak had apparently just given up, dropping all of its leaves on that Labor Day like some defeated sigh. So, while everyone else was at the party, saying good-bye to a summer they'd like to forget, Lindy's father had sprung into action. He wore goggles, shorts, and a T-shirt, and laid into the ancient tree with his chain saw, an act so strangely violent that none of us knew what to say.

Two of the neighborhood men left the party at full trot to try and stop him, to explain to him that the tree was not dead, that it would come back next year, and that he had no right to do what he was doing. Then, when they got halfway up the street, they halted dead in their tracks. It turned out that on closer inspection, these men could see something that we hadn't seen from the party, something that only Mr. Simpson had seen, after the tree dropped its leaves and went bare.

On the third-lowest branch of the live oak, slung around a tangle of sticks, a faded blue Reebok hung from its laces.

So the men returned up the street to us, solemn, and let Mr. Simpson continue his work with the chain saw. When we asked them what they'd seen up there, why they hadn't stopped him, the men put their large hands on our heads as if we were their own sons, their own daughters.

"Let's all go back to the party," they said. "Let's all get something to eat."

So we did, and this is the last day I remember seeing Lindy happy.

Yet it had nothing to do with the sight of that shoe.

No. I admit it.

This time, I was to blame.

10.

In the weeks after it occurred, Lindy's rape was a strange sort of secret.

Everyone in the neighborhood "knew," but I can safely speak for Randy and Artsy Julie and myself when I say that back then, we didn't exactly *know* what we knew. We knew the police had milled around for a bit, sure, we knew that we had each been asked a few simple questions, but since our parents had also asked us to be discreet about the crime (another mysterious word for me in those years) we didn't understand much more than that. We noticed that people now acted differently around Lindy, was all, that our parents lifted their voices when they spoke to her that summer, that they let us stay out a little past suppertime if they saw we were playing with her. "Did you have a good time with Lindy?" my mother would ask me. "It's important that you kids have fun."

All of this just to form my excuse, I suppose, when I tell you the next thing I did.

I was not yet fifteen years old, remember, and in the first week of that school year, my freshman year, when we were all changing back into our uniforms after gym class, a few of the guys began talking of Lindy. As chronicled, many of these kids had their eyes on her since the onset of time, and our entry to high school seemed to give them a courage I was not yet feeling. They passed along rumors like scouting reports in the locker room: about how Lindy had broken up with some boy I knew she never dated, about how one guy had seen her breasts at a pool party that summer. And so, in a burst of self-serving slop I'm still ashamed of, I also offered up what I knew. I said the word low, and under my breath, because that's the only way I'd ever heard it spoken.

Rape.

It was a word that refused to bring me an image, despite my recent relationship with it. In the weeks I'd sat alone in my room, wondering about its dark meaning, I envisioned Lindy suffering strange beatings, but yet I never saw any bruises on her face. In an attempt to increase my understanding, I went back to a poem I remembered reading in school the year before, Alexander Pope's "The Rape of the Lock," and the meaning

80

became even further unmoored. I later looked the word up, just to get a hold of it, in a thesaurus my father had left in his study. I came upon these synonyms:

Plunder. Seizure. Violence.

So, I knew "rape" to ride shotgun with some grand injustice, yes, I was not dim. But I never thought of it in terms of Lindy's virginity, her budding spirit, her body, being slaughtered in a sexual way. I never thought of a thing that could not be made right. All I knew was that the boys in the locker room wanted to talk about Lindy that day and that I wanted these boys to talk to me.

The effect was immediate.

Word shot like current through the high school circuitry. And when approached, Lindy denied it in every way. However, due to the unexpected depth of her bawling, her strange shouting, she was too obviously upset to convince them, and by the time the afternoon bell rang, Lindy had aged right in front of us. Her ponytail looked unkempt and off-center. She allowed notebooks to spill out of her backpack and spoke to no one as she trudged through the school parking lot to meet her mother, who, on this day, was waiting to drive her back home.

Later that afternoon, just before dinner, Lindy knocked on my door. I felt sick when

I saw her through the peephole. All those times I'd lain on the floor and wished for this exact vision to materialize, for her to dismount from her bike and come see me, all the times I'd imagined just what I'd say; these all died, silly and unused, next to the potted plants in the corner.

I opened the door and stood there.

Behind her, I saw purple clouds slide like battleships into position, the evening rain set to get under way. She was barefoot, Lindy, she wore a dark T-shirt over her uniform, and, my God, she was already gone from me then. From all of us.

"Is it true that you're the one who told?" she asked me.

I didn't say anything.

"How did you know?" she asked me. "How did you know about that?"

This was an odd question to me.

"Your parents," I told her. "The police. Everybody knows."

Lindy looked crushed.

What did she think her parents had been doing, I wondered, in the days they went door to door with the cops? Why did she think our mothers brought all that food to her house as if someone had died? I didn't understand it. After all, this was a girl who got ill over the death of astronauts. Couldn't she feel the mourning in her own neighborhood? Or, by this time, nearly two months after the crime, had she just hoped we'd all forgotten?

I didn't get the chance to ask her. Lindy turned and ran away.

She did not speak to me again for a year.

In that year, Lindy tried on different personalities, all of them false and doomed. She began by taking a strange pride in her appearance, as if the secret had never gotten out, and started running around with an elite crowd. She wore large bows in her hair at school and jingly bracelets on her wrists. She sidled up to the most coveted virgins and laughed cattily at any younger boys that walked by. When this did not work, and the virgins crucified her, she quit the track team and grew dark. She listened to the heavy and slow music that older kids listened to, The Cure, Joy Division, and she wore black eyeliner to school. If you saw her away from Perkins in those days it was hanging around in dark places like the abandoned and unfinished dorms of Jimmy Swaggart's disgraced church in Baton Rouge, where we all knew not to go, or maybe hovering on the outskirts of the movie theater, chatting with older boys in combat boots who had no business being there.

None of these disguises suited her.

But in my guilt, in my love, I followed these personalities, too.

I got my mom to take me to a high-end clothing store for Christmas, when Lindy was still in her bows. I grew furious when my mom tried to buy me knockoff Polo shirts and discounted shoes, as if she were out to sabotage me. I became nervous and self-conscious and spent days trying to tie the leather laces of my Timberland loafers in a manner called "the beehive," which I had seen Michael Tuminello, the leader of the Perkins School preps, do. On weekends I stood out by the mailbox in my new pastel getups. I walked up and down Piney Creek Road and whistled, hoping Lindy might see me through her window.

And then, when Lindy went dark, so did I, shunning the expensive apparel my mother had bought for me. Instead I dragged her around to record shops and thrift stores. I got her to buy me skull rings, incense, and black T-shirts with band names I'd seen displayed in the patches on Lindy's schoolbag. She worried about this, I know, but she did not deny me.

Yet my desire to catch Lindy's eye grew

so consuming that I began hating myself and my suburban appearance, as if this was to blame for nearly everything. After a while I even grew to hate my own curly hair, as the rockers Lindy liked all had straight hair, often cut in dramatic angles and gelled. So I slept in baseball caps to straighten my hair out. I used a hot iron to style my bangs. I shaved the sides of my head.

At the height of this period I began to get in minor troubles at school. I stuffed paper towels in the urinals and flooded the bathrooms. I wrote graffiti in Magic Marker on the lockers. Some part of me hoped that if I kept this up long enough Lindy and I might be sentenced to the same session of detention after school, where if nothing else we would be forced to speak to each other in the ridiculous roundtable confessional the teachers made us do. Yet this never happened, and Lindy was able to avoid me completely.

I therefore began to stay up late and sleep little, listening to bands I'd overheard Lindy talk about, and I hated this music. The lyrics were dark and without perspective, wrapped up in melodies that inevitably collapsed, self-aware, on themselves. Even as a kid I knew this. To get into her type of music was to sing along with a man on his death-bed. So that's what I tried to do. I wrote poems about Lindy in red ink. I got an earring. I hit puberty.

All this to say that when Lindy and I emerged from that year, we were changed.

Lindy was now a brooding girl who roamed the halls of Perkins alone. Any friends that she did have were meek things who may as well have been shadows. She shunned bright colors, blue included, and wore only gray boxer shorts underneath her uniform at school. She rarely shaved her legs. She became increasingly obsessed with a band called Bauhaus that I was never sure how to pronounce and scribbled things like anarchy signs on her Chuck Taylor high-tops. She cut her hair to chin length and her bangs traced her soft face like sickles.

She became thin and, most said, bulimic. Rows of small pimples appeared on her chest.

This was a hard thing to watch.

But in the following year, when we were speaking again, when we were close, Lindy explained to me how all this had happened.

She said that therapy was to blame.

Lindy told me that her months in group counseling, something her parents insisted she attend, were the worst thing that could have happened to her. It was worse even than the way her father spied on her at all hours in the year that followed the crime, worse than the way she would see his car sitting inconspicuously in the corner of the movie theater parking lot as she bummed cigarettes off of random guys. It was worse than the sheepish way he would later act as if he hadn't been spying at all, as if he didn't know what she was talking about, when he cruised back around to pick her up at eleven. And it was even worse than the manner in which he eventually collapsed his remorse into hers, begging her to talk to him, and adding complicated locks on their doors.

Because what therapy did, she explained, was introduce her to a world of problems she never would have known about otherwise. The girl who cut herself; she was in her group. The anorexic. The bulimic. The nymphomaniac. They each offered rebellious possibilities to Lindy, which she explored. The girl in her group who'd watched her mother die in an automobile accident that she herself had caused. Now there was a look at depression, she said. The boy who was molested by his uncle. Good grief.

Ultimately, the scope of these ills made Piney Creek Road look obscene to Lindy, she said, the way the blossoms on our crepe myrtles bloomed. The lovely street was like an ignorant joke. Therapy had taught her this, and she wore the lesson all over her face.

So I took on the look of a troubled boy as well. I flipped my long bangs out of my eyes when adults approached me. I quit the soccer team, which I was actually good at and enjoyed, and started playing guitar instead because I thought Lindy might find it sexy. I smoked cigarettes, and later dope, in the Taco Bell parking lot on school nights. I rarely smiled.

But my image was papier-mâché.

You could poke a hole right through me in those years and all you would see fall out were items from Lindy's closet. No blood in me then. Only the one obsessed heart. I stood for nothing. I fought for nothing. Can't you see?

I'm drawing myself as innocent here.

Don't we all?

11.

The third suspect in Lindy's rape was the adopted boy named Jason Landry. One of the slew of children that Mr. Landry and his wife, Louise, fostered on Piney Creek Road, Jason was the only one who stuck around. He'd been in their clutches since he was an orphan, a toddler, and was two years older than me. He was not a pleasant boy by any stretch and, just as the people of Woodland Hills wondered if he could have been involved in the crime, we also wondered why *he,* out of all the children the Landrys cared for, became the constant. Through a little research of my own, I've since learned that it is not unusual for a family like the Landrys to keep one individual child with them throughout their fostering years, to adopt him, so that the other children they host will have a playmate. This is called anchoring, in the literature, and is the benevolent interpretation of this process.

The truth, I believe, in the case of the Landrys, is that Jason was kept around for a different purpose. Erratic and troubled, Jason was used more as a normalizer than an anchor. He was, in the technical sense, a socializer for the other foster kids. To put it more simply, his well-fed existence, no matter its quirks, was empirical proof to the other orphaned children who came in and out of their doors that a life could be made with the Landrys, that you could survive it. This, of course, was also proof to Child Services. So if a young boy or girl felt uneasy during his or her first weeks at the Landrys', if they thought perhaps there was something amiss, Jason could tell them, "Cut it out. Suck it up. This is normal."

A relative term if there was one.

Jason Landry had thin white hair, even in his youth, yet he was not an albino. His eyes were the color of clean river sand and he had gaps between all of his teeth. I have no idea what tribe of man he was birthed from, no idea of his origin. Perhaps no one does. His skin was yellow, in how I remember him now, and he smelled constantly of the cigarettes his mother smoked in their kitchen. He had been kicked out of the Perkins School in eighth grade for reasons that were never disclosed to me — rumors about him and another boy in a bathroom. Rumors that he'd sexually threatened Ms. Gibson, a fragile Spanish teacher who had lupus. And since he did not attend any youth soccer or swim leagues, he did not play with the rest of the neighborhood kids often. Whenever he did, it ended poorly.

Jason once fought with Bo Kern, for example, over a ten-dollar bill they found in the street, and he was beaten soundly. He ran home screaming. Later, when we had finished up that afternoon's game of tackle football and forgotten about the skirmish entirely, Jason Landry returned to us with a knife. He didn't speak to us, or confront Bo, but instead stood on the opposite side of the road and jabbed the knife into a pine tree, again and again. He wore camouflage pants and a green T-shirt as if he couldn't be seen and ducked to the ground when cars passed between us.

This behavior was neither new nor isolated.

Jason was also known to tackle the neighborhood girls in strange ways that they complained about. He would lie on top of them a bit too long, perhaps. He would press himself against them. Artsy Julie held sticks in her hand like a crucifix when Jason appeared. Lindy refused to let him cover her on pass plays. Whenever we rode go-karts around in the summers, Jason would beg us for a chance at the wheel. When we would finally relent, he would take off down the road and not return. He had inexplicable scars, shaped like dimes, on his back.

Some days, when he was trying to be friendly, he'd pull out clumps of his thin white hair and say, "I bet you can't do that," and we hated him. It was easy to.

Even before Lindy's rape, his behavior looked like evidence.

Yet one day, or perhaps on many days, in the year before the crime, I sat with Jason Landry on the top of the hill behind his house. He lived next door to Randy, two doors down from me, and we rested our backs against a steel storage shed. I have no idea what brought me there that afternoon. What level must the boredom have reached? We picked at the grass, dug around at the dirt, and played with roly-polies that curled fearfully in our hands.

After a while, Jason nudged me on the shoulder and pointed out into the woods.

"Jackpot," he said.

At the edge of the trees stood a dog, peeking around the corner at us. I have no idea the breed. It looked like it lived in the swamps, if that were possible, as its fur was matted with mud and its rib cage visible against its skin. One of its ears was also forked, apparently from some scuffle long ago, and hung awkwardly from the side of its head. We watched it trot from tree to tree.

Jason reached underneath a tarp.

"This is what I've been waiting for," he said.

"What are you doing?" I asked.

"Relax," Jason said, and pulled out a rusty tin bowl from the shed.

He then got up and proceeded to dig through the garbage cans in their driveway. He produced several scraps of food, some pork bones, chicken skin, some old pasta, and walked the bowl of food out into the grass, where he called to the dog, although he didn't have a name for it. "Here, mutt!" he said. "Come here, you dumb hound! No one's going to hurt you."

I remember the high sun on that day; the oak shadows raked across the lawn like stripes. "Whose dog is that?" I asked. "Where does it live?"

"It's nobody's dog," he said. "It's just a lousy cur. It digs through our trash and shits in our yard. It drives my dad nuts. He spends all day looking for it."

I watched the dog approach us, stopping every few paces. It looked like a worried soul with its tail tucked between its legs, and Jason laughed at its posture.

"Come here, you stupid mutt," he said, and rattled the bowl in his hand.

"Why don't you tell your dad you found it?" I asked. "You guys could keep it."

Jason looked at me like we had just met.

"That's not what he wants to do with it," he said.

I could fathom no other option.

"I'll keep it, then," I told him. "We could give him a bath."

"You better not touch my fucking dog," Jason said. "I'll kill you if you touch it."

It was hard to tell if he was serious. That was perhaps the defining characteristic of his personality. Jason Landry had a way of making you feel uneasy, as if you never really knew who you were dealing with. When you shared a laugh together, for instance, and he seemed a normal boy, he would then repel you with some phrase not likely to come from a child — a threat of premeditated violence, a vulgar joke. And these moments would create in you a sense of distance, chasmic at times, that you knew better than to try and bridge. In this way, Jason was at least predictable in his unpredictability, and so I was never truly afraid of him the way I was of Bo Kern, who was all action and little talk. Still, I surely didn't trust him.

So, I stood up off the grass while Jason coaxed the dog to, and I tried to prepare myself for some emergency. Jason set the bowl on the ground and backed away. He made kissing noises with his mouth.

"Come on," he said. "I'm not going to hurt you."

The dog trotted a wide perimeter around us. It sniffed at the grass and inched closer.

"Eat, boy," I told him. "Get you something to eat."

"That's right," Jason said. "You better eat up while you can."

The dog nosed the bowl and then slowly, carefully, lifted a piece of meat with its mouth and began chewing. It licked like a beggar at the bones.

"That's a good boy," I said.

Then, after the dog began to look comfortable, after it really began to dig in, Jason ran toward it.

"Get the hell out of here!" he yelled. "Go on, you stupid mutt!" He kicked at the dirt and clapped his hands. "Go on!" he said.

The dog paced around in confused circles. "You worthless stray!" Jason said. "Get the hell out of here!" He picked up a stick and threw it at it. He waved his arms in the air. He kicked over the bowl of food. The dog then sprinted away into the woods, whimpering, with a noticeable hitch in its hind leg.

"Stupid mutt," Jason said. He then tipped over the garbage cans in their driveway. He spread out the trash like it had been rifled through.

"What are you doing?" I asked.

"We better get out of here," he said. "My dad's going to be pissed."

So I followed him. I made no stand about the dog.

Again, this is no hero you're talking to.

On our way back toward the street, back into the world, Jason stopped to dump over a bowl of antifreeze that had been placed near their garage. We watched it stain the hot asphalt green.

"I just saved that dog's life," Jason said. "Where's my parade?"

I later stood with Jason Landry in the woods, all in this same year, maybe this same day. Who knows? My memories of the neighborhood keep no calendar but one: before Lindy's rape and after, and this was before. That I can tell you.

We had been exploring, Jason and I, cutting trails through the brush with machetes and trying to find a good place to build a tree house. We wanted it to be a sturdy place like a fort, we decided, a place we could hole up in if there was ever an invasion against the neighborhood. We talked about finding a tree so thick that we could bore a tunnel right through its middle and into the ground so that, if the fort was ever surrounded, we could escape and pop up on the opposite side of our unsuspecting foes. In the meantime, we agreed to stock up on things like spears and Coca-Colas and bows and arrows. We should make sure the fort had windows to shoot out of, we said. Maybe dig us a moat.

This was just boy talk, the American standard.

I'd had conversations like this with Randy as well. We'd tromped the woods like scouts do. But with Jason, the tenor of the conversation was different. When he talked about Russians falling from the skies, or packs of rabid wolves descending on us from the forest, you got the sense that Jason was serious, and prepared for their inevitable appearance.

So, when Jason sized up a tree, it was technical. He would pick at the bark of it, stomp his foot on the ground as if listening for something, and then construct the fort in his head like some primitive engineer. His eyes would scamper up the trunk where a ladder should be. He would lay 2×4s out like a deck. He'd envision impenetrable walls with long slits to fire weapons from and, when he was finished, you could almost see him all alone in his safe house, rain falling on the tin roof overhead. Then, after he was satisfied, and the place fully built in his mind, Jason would take the stance of a sniper. He'd hold an invisible bow in his hand and pull back the arrow and you could watch his eyes trace a figure in the yard below him, a large and lumbering creature that Jason had waited all this time to face.

"That's right," he would whisper. "Just a little bit closer."

And with his left eye closed, his body carefully positioned in his fort, Jason would not miss.

He made me swear this location to secrecy.

"What about Randy?" I said. "He'll want to know."

"Is he any good with weapons?"

"I don't know," I said.

"Tell him if you want," Jason said. "But if anyone tells my dad, I'll kill them."

"What about Lindy?" I asked him.

"Good point," he said. "I guess we will

need someone to repopulate the world."

"Right," I said. "She's not like that."

Jason laughed and tore a big chunk of bark off the tree to mark the fort's location.

"What?" he said. "You like that slut?"

"Don't call her that," I said.

Jason laughed again, genuine and deep, as if truly tickled.

"Come on," he said. "I want to show you something."

So, sweaty and freckled with bites, we walked back through the woods to his house.

A piece of the puzzle about to connect.

12.

When we arrived at Jason's house, his father was picking up the trash cans I'd seen Jason overturn. He was grumbling to himself, a blue sweatband around his head and dark prescription glasses concealing his eyes. Again, was this all the same day? Was this a pattern? How much time could I have shared with the Landry boy? The specific truth is impossible to mine for you here, except for what I know the large man said.

"You boys see a dog running around out there?"

"Don't you think I'd tell you if I did?" Jason said.

"Don't be smart," Mr. Landry said.

Jason held up his palms like an innocent. "What?" he said. "We didn't see anything, did we?"

Mr. Landry looked at me.

"No, sir," I said.

Jason led me into the garage and, as soon

as we got out of sight, he did a little dance of joy. He gave me a high five. He had just won a round of some oedipal game he'd created, I imagine, and he shot his father the bird with both fists. *Fuck you,* he mouthed. *Fuck you!*

We entered his house through the back door, and the place was as dark and quiet as if nobody was home. We then walked to the kitchen to see his mother sitting silently at the dim breakfast table, cigarette smoke lifting from her hand without drama. To the left of her sat the foster girl Tin Tin, a sickly thin child of mixed origin. She was quiet, unresponsive, and did not last long at the Landrys'. When she heard us enter the room, she stared in our general direction like the blind might. This was one of the few times I ever saw her.

Jason's mother, Louise Landry, was not an attractive woman, although she may have been, had everything in her life been different. But in the world in which I knew her, she wore her hair in a tight braid pulled over her shoulder and to the front. She had deep wrinkles near her eyes, spoke in a rasp, and picked at the gray-and-yellow ends of her braid while she smoked.

She was from a large Pentecostal family in rural Mississippi, if you can believe what my memory tells me, and she'd left both that brood and that religion when she married her husband. As such a strange pair, the giant and his country wife, the neighborhood often speculated about the Landrys' courtship. It was rumored that he was once her psychiatrist who stepped over the line, or that he had kidnapped her off her farm in Tupelo, or that she was sold to him by some righteous cult.

At large, we were afraid of them. We didn't bother to ask.

Back then, our only evidence to the character of Louise Landry was that she rarely ventured outdoors. Whenever we saw her, she was toting an obligatory plate of deviled eggs to a party in the neighborhood. Then she was sitting out on the back porch, drinking coffee and smoking cigarettes in her long denim skirt as the rest of us swam. She kept little company, and she and her husband showed no public affection that I ever saw, neither to each other nor to Jason, nor to any of the other children they currently held in strange hospice. So, if you didn't know, you would be hard pressed to guess that they were a family. The only time they spoke at these functions was after Mr. Landry had too much to drink and began blustering about local politicians, or making inappropriate comments to the women and children.

To Artsy Julie once, she told me, at a Fourth of July party when she was twelve:

Come over here, girl. Let me get a whiff of you.

But we will deal with him later.

As far as Louise goes, my mother claims that she tried to befriend her for years, all to no avail, especially in the days that followed the fights we'd hear on our back porch. She'd invite her to luncheons, to play tennis, to go shopping, anything she could think of to get her out of her husband's earshot. But every attempt at friendship was met with the same response, my mother said, delivered to her in Louise's Mississippi hill-country accent, when she'd furrow her brow and say, "Now, Kathryn. Don't be silly."

Kathryn, my mother's name. After all these years, it's still strange for me to think of her as a person. An adult. Separate from me in the world.

Yet there was no doubt as to the distance, the separation, between the Landry household and my own. It was not just the darkness, the foster kids, the history; it was also the tension. When Louise saw Jason and me tromp into the room, she snapped as if caught. "What have you boys been doing?" she said. "Jason, what's going on?"

"Nothing, *Louise,*" Jason said. "I was just going to show him my knives."

"Did you change your sheets?"

"I'll do it later."

"But you won't, will you?" Louise said.

Tin Tin laid her head on the table as if falling asleep.

Jason grabbed the back of my shirt.

"Come on," he said, and I followed him toward his room.

Jason didn't bother to flick on any lights as we navigated the cluttered living room and passed into the narrow hallway. And since our house and the Landrys' house were both designed the same way — four-bedroom, three-bath ranchers, large and functional, with windows galore — I recognized the fact that this could easily be my own home we were skulking through. Their den was simply set up in the opposite direction, their fireplace laid in a different brick. Instead of the scented candles my mom kept aglow on the end tables, they had ashtrays, overrun with spent butts. All the same. Totally different. How easily, I wonder now, could we have switched addresses and been changed?

When we passed what in my house would

have been my older sister Hannah's room, Jason stopped and pointed at the door. "That's the mother lode," he said.

I looked up to see a series of latches on the door, each run through with a combination-style Master lock.

"What's in there?" I said.

Jason smiled his gap-toothed smile.

"Wouldn't *you* like to know?"

I then followed him into his room, where he finally turned on the light.

"Pretend to be doing something," he said. "Tell me if *Louise* comes."

Jason walked into his closet, got on the floor, and riffled through the dirty clothes.

I looked around his room. It was full of posters that seemed too young for him. Nothing embarrassing, exactly, but apparently decorated years prior and never thought of again. There were Transformers posters, Winnie-the-Pooh posters, and the wallpaper had a border of clowns. His chest of drawers was also something like I might have, pasted with Star Wars and Hot Wheels decals, while on his desk stood a small fishbowl, murky and green. Its only inhabitant was a dead tetra, molting in a castle.

I sat down on Jason's bed and watched him fiddle with a knife in his closet, prying open a panel in the wall, and I felt something cold begin to seep through my shorts. I put my hand on the bed and it was wet. I stood up and wiped my hands on my shirt.

"Why is your bed all wet?" I said.

"Shut up and listen for my mom," he said. "Play Nintendo or something."

I walked over and flicked on the small TV screen in the corner. I pressed the power button on the Nintendo. As the television warmed, and the images came to, I heard his mother walking down the hall.

"Jason," I said, and she walked in.

She held a bundle of sheets in her arms.

"What are you boys doing?" she asked. "Where's Jason?"

Jason walked out of the closet with the knife in his hand.

"What are you doing in here?" he said. "This is my room."

"You know what I'm doing," she said, and walked over to his bed. She pulled off the sheets and crumpled them onto the floor, exposing a plastic mattress with a large circle of dark yellow in its center.

"Get out of here, *Louise,*" Jason said. "I told you I was going to show him my knives."

"You can do that while I'm here, can't you?" Louise looked over at me. "Is that really what you two are doing?" she asked.

"I was just playing Nintendo," I told her.

So Jason feigned a presentation as Louise changed his bed. He brought out a box full of knives, some Swiss Army, one Rambo, and a slew of bowies. He pulled them out of their leather sheaths and used the blades to cut the thin hair on his arms.

"Look how sharp," he said. "Imagine what this one could do."

"This one has a bottle opener," I said.

"You just don't get it, do you?" he said.

Louise then finished with the bed and gathered up the soiled sheets. She stood in the doorway and watched over us. "How's your mother?" she asked me.

"Fine," I said.

"That's good," Louise said. "Has she been dating?"

This was a while after my father had left us, a couple years, and I knew that she had. Men called our house on the telephone and my mother told me they were just plumbers or electricians but then had me hold the phone for her while she went into the other room to pick it up. She'd also begun sending me over to Randy's to spend the night when she went to "dinner parties" and "socials," and I'd later watch through Randy's bedroom window as these men brought her back home around ten o'clock or eleven. They often sat in the idling car for several minutes and on some occasions walked together to our front door, where I could see these men kiss her hand, her cheek, perhaps touch her hair before leaving. She never told me their names or what they did on their dates or in their cars or what she thought of them. I don't blame her for this.

Some things are better left unsaid.

"I don't know," I told Louise, but I suppose I'd waited too long to respond.

"She's a lucky woman," she said, "to get a fresh start like that. You tell her that when you see her. You tell her how lucky she is."

"Okay," I said, and Louise walked out of the room.

Jason slammed the door behind her.

"Open that door!" she said.

"Make me!" Jason yelled, and offered me another high five.

"Showtime," he said.

I sat down on the corner of the bed as Jason retrieved a manila envelope from the hidden compartment in his closet.

"Check this out," he said, and sat next to me.

Jason unclasped the envelope and revealed a stack of professional-looking photos in black and white. "You like that Lindy girl?"

he asked me. "Take a look at this."

He began riffling through the pictures in his hands, all of which I immediately recognized as photos of the neighborhood. There were pictures of women walking with strollers down the sidewalks, a photo of Mrs. Kern pulling weeds. I saw pictures of Artsy Julie doing cartwheels, a candid shot of my mother driving down Piney Creek Road in her car.

"Wait," I said. "What are these?"

"My dad left his office door open a few months ago," Jason told me. "I nabbed what I could."

"The locked door?" I said. "What's in there?"

Jason looked up at me. "You want to see the good ones or not?"

"Okay," I said.

Jason separated a stack of about ten photos from the bunch. He quickly looked them over and then handed the stack to me. "Merry Christmas," he said.

These photos were a dream.

And the subject, of course, was Lindy.

The first three shots were of Lindy laid out on a blanket, sunbathing in the front yard like she sometimes did. Lindy leaning back on her elbows. Lindy looking up at the sky. The photos were all taken from the same angle, but zoomed at different distances, as if the artist had taken his time. One shot of just the collarbone, I remember, the straps of her childish bikini. The next group was of Lindy on her bicycle, a slight grin on her face as she hopped a small bump. Then the flex of her thighs as she reverse-pedaled to stop. The frame of the bike between her legs as she stood atop it, no longer riding, and talking to someone off camera. This was a perverse miracle, I knew. But I didn't care.

"Who took these?" I asked.

"Don't be an idiot," Jason said. "Hurry up. No time to jack off now."

I flipped through the next few photos and they were all of equal value.

Lindy in a handstand. Lindy singing to herself as she walked.

What words, I wondered? What thoughts? How could a boy like me know them?

"Can I keep this?" I asked.

"You perv," Jason said. "You're just a fucking perv, aren't you?"

I was thirteen years old at the time. I didn't even know what that meant. Chalk it up to another time he put a distance between us.

But after much begging, Jason told me I could keep the photo of Lindy singing

110

because it wasn't in his regular rotation. He warned me not to get it all sticky. He made me promise to return it the minute he asked me to, and he was serious.

"If my dad finds out you have that," he said, "he'll kill you."

I was willing to take the chance.

This was Lindy we were talking about. For once I was not afraid.

With her photo in hand, her mysterious song in my grip, his father would have to sprout wings to catch me.

13.

Perhaps growing wings is what fathers do.

Maybe it is written somewhere that, at an undetermined time, every father will feel an ache in his back. He will sleep uncomfortably, tossing around in bedsheets that used to feel warm to him and soft. He will spend his private time craning his neck toward the mirror, trying to catch a glimpse of what's been itching him lately, perhaps only two small nubs at first, right on his shoulder blades, and later the look of two feathered joints. I can't imagine the fear in these men. I can only imagine their choice. A creature with wings must use them, of course, or else go the way of the dodo.

So these men finish up that last cup of coffee. They wait until no one is watching.

They take to the sky.

Like Lindy's father, for example, who sprouted his wings far too late. He became an unfortunate hawk, the poor man, circling the blue above Lindy's head from the night that she was raped until the moment she left him. He was a strange sight soaring over the movie theater parking lot. A distant squawk from the branches of Piney Creek Road. All of this to ultimately become a rueful and bitter bird, a tattered and woeful-looking thing plucking out his own feathers when he finally returned to his perch and found Lindy gone.

But he is not the only example.

The terrible Mr. Landry is who I'm thinking of now, sitting squat and thick-winged on the storm gutter of his dark and musty house. He was like a fat owl who allowed none to pass, a hunter with a head that spun completely around. And yet the true danger of men like him is that they are so still, so quiet, that you forget that they're out there until late at night, perhaps, when you are waiting for something to cook on the grill or enjoying a peaceful time with your family. It's in times like these when you hear the owl's call and it chills you, like a voice at the far end of a tunnel. *Who cooks for you?* the owl says. *Who cooks for us all?*

This is a question left unanswered until it's too late, because predators like him are mere shadows gliding across the dark lawn. In your ear, maybe, the suspicion of wind.

Then you are gone, swooped up and eviscerated before you reach the birds' nest. Make no mistake. He will chew you up in this place, the owl will. He will cough out your spent bones.

All of this imagining just to get around to my own father, I suppose: a canary who felt a need to escape his clean wire cage. A man who, like so many others, flew the very coop that he himself had made.

How else to describe it?

Thin and tall, my father started going bald before I knew him.

In the pictures I've seen from right after my birth, from the hospital, his thin hair is swept neatly to the side and gelled, already concealing the truth of him, I suppose. And there are people out there who will claim to remember moments like these, when they were just an infant in their father's embrace. I have friends who've told me stories from when they were one or two years of age, and recited to me the tender beauty of it.

Impossible. Ridiculous.

I was ten years old when my father left, and I have few substantial memories of him living with us at all, as if it was in fact his departure that flipped on the switch of my consciousness. Maybe some vague image of the two of us washing his car, sure. Maybe the both of us standing by the pool in our swim trunks. Still, these visions were likely given to me only by the old photos that my mother kept in our albums. Nothing real in them. No connection to the moment as it happened. I understood that.

Yet, as if to convince me otherwise, my mother would often say things like *Surely you remember the time you two fell asleep in that hammock? Surely you remember when you caught that catfish at False River? Surely you remember horseback riding with him, snug in the same saddle, at that business convention in Butte?* I didn't. *Listen,* she'd say, *surely that pool party where he taught you to swim?* No. *The time you locked yourself in his car while he was washing it?* Not at all. So *Here, here,* she would say, and scramble around for the album. *Let me show you the pictures.*

Yet the closest I ever felt to my father in the years right after he left us were the times I would walk through a department store, dragged along by my mother on a shopping trip after school, when we would pass through the men's section on our way to the mall. The smell of shoe leather. Yes, there was something in that. The whiff of a specific cologne. There was memory there,

115

too. So I would raise my head vaguely at these scents, something deep in me stirred, and look around.

I would expect nothing. And I would receive it.

But it is too easy to crucify men like this. If every disappointed son and daughter got their shot at revenge, I imagine, there would be only a handful of men above fifty left walking the Earth. Who would be president? Who would we blame? So what we must do instead, when we deal with our fathers, is stick to the facts. When the legions of us (and there are legions of us) stitch back together the men who once held our mothers, who once made them promises they surely intended to keep, we must not let emotion get in the way.

So I can tell you this. My father was a realtor.

Having a hand in the suburban sprawl of places like Woodland Hills, he was wealthy by the time he hit forty. With this wealth came the American Dream as it existed in the 1960s and '70s. The big house. The three children. The country club. The tennis wife. The Mercedes.

Then, the brightly colored wings.

My father's feathered pair led him out of our picture window to a familiar place not

116

too far away — the Fairview Golf and Tennis Club, where he perched on top of a cash register manned by a perky eighteen-year-old girl.

Laura, a name that has been forever soiled for me, was blond and flawless.

A freshman biology major at LSU at the time, she must have found something scientifically interesting about the canary that appeared on her register whenever she worked. I can't blame her for this. Her job at the club, I'm sure, was unfulfilling. The bird's song, I know, was persuasive. He was, after all, a salesman.

There's no mystery as to how these things happen.

And other than those times when she innocently provided me with golf balls at the driving range, with sno-cones at the club's snack window, my first real contact with Laura was in 1990, about five years after my father left us. This was during the time that Lindy was not speaking to me, the tail end of that dreadful year of silence, when my mother called my father back to duty. He'd moved to a small town called Prairieville, Louisiana, since their divorce, a place maybe fifteen minutes away from Baton Rouge that was just beginning its own housing boom, but he might as well have moved to Wisconsin. I rarely saw him, and when I did it was for some holiday or special occasion where there was enough distraction (presents to be opened, a cake to be cut, a song to sing) to keep us from talking deeply about anything. I didn't know what he thought of me in those years and I didn't know what to think of him. I knew only that he'd hurt my mother and my sisters, and that he'd hurt me. Yet I had no idea how to change any of that. What child does? So, I didn't try.

Instead I spent my energy on things I believed I could change, like my appearance, and like Lindy's opinion of me. This preoccupation led my mother to confess to my dad that she'd become worried about the music I listened to, the way I moped about the house in black T-shirts. She told him a boy needs a father around, and that the holiday visits and gift cards stuffed with money were no longer cutting it. So my father showed up one Saturday morning.

I should have seen it coming, as my mother had been cleaning house for a week. She'd gone to the beauty parlor and gotten a new haircut. She'd woken up early that Saturday and walked through the house fully dressed, dusting end tables and putting on mascara in the reflection of the kitchen window. I ignored her, of course, and was so unprepared for his arrival that when his Mercedes pulled up in our driveway, I almost didn't recognize it.

"Okay," my mother said. "Okay okay okay."

The two of us watched him through the kitchen window, now bald as a stone and looking fit, as he walked up to the front door like an appraiser. He stopped and kicked at a piece of the walkway that had apparently come loose since he'd last seen it. He stared at the roof as if checking for damage.

We opened the door without waiting for a knock, my mother and I, and he said, "Hello, Kathryn. Hello, son."

I'd like to think now that I returned him a zinger.

I'd like to think now that I was fully aware of his lack of interest in me as a teenager, and that I was angry about how easily he'd released me from his daily life. "Hello, sperm donor," I should have said back to him, or, "Hello, ghost." But in reality, I only remember feeling awkward about my strange and new hairstyle when my father first saw me, the way I'd shaved the sides of my head to impress Lindy. I remember feeling uncomfortable in the new rock-and-roll clothes I'd been wearing since Lindy went dark, too, about the silver hoop earring in my left ear, and about the way I hadn't really thought of my father in months.

And so I only said, "Hey, Dad."

His plan was to take me fishing. He said he knew a place.

My mother had already packed a bag of outdoor clothes, unbeknownst to me, culled from some laundry she had been doing, and mentioned to my father that she was planning on cooking a roast that evening. "I'll have it stewing in the pot all day," she said. "If you'd like, you could eat dinner with us when you get back."

My father patted me on the shoulder and said that he was taking me for the night instead. He said we had some serious bonding to do, and not to expect us back until we'd caught every single fish in Louisiana.

"Oh," my mother said. "Okay."

After all those years, she still loved him. All three of us knew it. So, no need for me to recount for you the look I saw unfold and lie dead in her eyes when she realized that yet another meal she'd imagined between them would have to be eaten alone.

My father and I spoke little on the way to the place. It was nearly a three-hour drive. He asked me about soccer, which I told him I'd quit. "What?" he said. "You're the best player they've got. I thought you loved soccer." He was right about this. I did love it. But that seemed irrelevant compared to what I thought Lindy might like in those days. So "I don't know," I told him. "I guess I kind of grew out of it." My dad looked somewhat disappointed to hear this news and, as if to change the subject, asked me about girls. I told him there was one girl who was all right, but she had some baggage. "Well, there you go," he told me. "That's all you need is the one, right?"

My father smiled blankly as he said this, and I guess this was my trouble with him.

Was he stupid?

This is a legitimate question not often asked about fathers.

To the outside world, I know the answer was no. Here we were trucking down the highway in a Mercedes, a couple of expensive fishing rods bent like hooks in the backseat, an ice chest I could hear sloshing around in the trunk. He wore a nice collared shirt, some khaki shorts, and a pair of tan leather boat shoes with the laces tied up in the beehive fashion I'd tried so hard to master without him. So here was a man who balanced his checkbook. A man who knew which fork to use when. He told jokes and shook hands and sold homes for hundreds of thousands of dollars, all evidence of a person with an active and working brain.

But to me it wasn't so simple.

And in order to stick to the facts, I'll try not to dwell.

All you need is the one, he'd said to me, his own son, a child of divorce.

What was I left to think? Was this a man who didn't understand irony? Was this a man so devoid of perspective, so unaware of the craters he'd left in his wake, so oblivious to the fact that I *knew,* that my sisters *knew,* that everyone *knew* what he'd done, that he thought a comment like this was acceptable? *Really?* I'd wanted to ask him. *All a man needs is the one?*

Or was the truth of it more depressing than that?

Was he a man neither smart nor stupid, but merely unremarkable? Was he the most inconsequential kind of man, the one who just says something because it pops into his mind? A man who attaches no meaning to his thoughts, to his voice, or to his present situation, all so that he can seem quick-witted and steady? Was he the type who, time after time, has trouble recalling the most important things he's said to you, things he promised you, because he was actually somewhere else when he said them?

When he took you by the shoulders and said, *Listen here, son. I'm not going to leave you. I'm not going to hurt you. Nothing's going to change.* Was he a man who was already gone?

I knew the answer even then.

So, the facts.

I smelled that good cologne in the car. I saw my chin in his profile.

He asked me how my sisters were doing, a common refrain when we spoke.

"Tell them," he said. "Tell them I've been meaning to call."

And because of moments like this, because of the way I often imagined a better version of him lurking quiet and remorseful beneath the surface, all my spite toward my dad would turn to pity one day. A day we'll get to soon enough.

As for this day, we drove to a place called Cocodrie, a fishing village near the Gulf of Mexico. We passed rows of wooden camps built on pilings and finally cruised into a parking lot paved in oyster shells. We parked by a dock.

We had a good time, I guess, for an hour or so, casting artificial baits toward the grasses opposite the old dock, yet we caught nothing. And after a while, a carload of young men pulled into the parking lot.

These were guys in their mid-twenties who reminded me of Robert, Alexi's old boyfriend, in that they wore LSU baseball caps and T-shirts with the names of various campus bars like *The Chimes* and *Murphy's* on them. And since I had recently posited myself as a rebel of sorts, a troublemaker at school, these fellows looked like clichés to me now. They were good old boys with similar sunglasses and haircuts, everything that Lindy's music raged against.

"Hey, fellas," my father said to them, and they returned to us the same, unloading ice chests and fishing poles out of their trunk. One of these guys pulled out a portable radio that was playing Run-DMC's "Walk This Way," which I liked at the time but wouldn't admit. He walked up next to me and threw a line out into the water.

"Anything?" he asked me.

"Nothing," I said, and glanced back to see my father talking to a few of these guys and laughing, leaning on the hood of their car and drinking a beer. I rolled my eyes at him, embarrassed that he would assume some camaraderie with people half his age.

And then, as is often the case when fishing, my lack of concentration earned me a strike and a redfish turned over the top of my bait. I saw the black spot of his tail fin rise from the water and, like a novice, I yanked my line right out of his mouth. The bait shot back toward the dock and hooked itself into my jeans.

The guys had a good laugh at this, my father included, and mimicked my panicked reaction. "Take it easy, sport!" my dad said, and raised his beer at me.

I turned back to the water.

"*You* take it easy," I said, and the guy standing next to me heard.

"Hey, little man," he said. "He doesn't mean any harm."

I shot this guy a ferocious look. "You don't get it," I told him. "That idiot's my dad."

The guy laughed.

"I know who he is," he said. "He hangs out at my apartment, like, every day."

14.

Laura showed up shortly after.

She wore a faded Tri-Delta sorority T-shirt over a green bikini top and stepped out of the backseat of a car with two other girls just as sun-kissed and heart-crushing. They sported pink cotton shorts with dolphins on them, flip-flops that exposed their painted toes. They had just conquered and finished up college, you could tell, and the world was in front of them. And in the moment before I recognized Laura, the second or two it took, I had already bent her in every pleasurable shape imaginable to me. I was a pubescent boy at the time, remember, my mind a brothel, and nothing more. And now that I've had the years to think on it, I wonder if part of my initial attraction to these sorority girls was that they fit the shape I'd once imagined Lindy would grow to. Back when she was ponytailed and athletic, when she was bright and popular,

I'd envisioned the two of us one day lying naked and spent in my disheveled mess of a dorm room. I'd forecast us some glowing and all-American future.

But due to the crime against her and the enormous guilt I'd felt about it, the way I'd followed her into this thrift-store posture of suburban rebellion, I knew that I was already cut off from these twenty-something debs in their blossom. And, therefore, when I saw them arch their backs from the car ride and wave their half-empty wine coolers at the boys who had met up with my father, I realized how ugly I must already look to them, and I wanted them all the more for it. So I will spare you the many nights that followed this, when I fantasized mightily about my father as some quivering cuckold to me and his college-age sweetheart.

Instead, I merely watched as he and Laura greeted each other, hugging nervously, and I acted as if I couldn't care less. I turned my back to the whole scene and eventually heard them approaching behind me, their steps amplified on the oyster-shell parking lot.

"Are you sure it's okay?" I heard Laura whisper. "Glen, are you sure?"

"It's fine," he told her. "Hey, son," he asked me. "You remember Laura."

I looked back at them, my hair hanging over my eyes.

My father had his hand on Laura's back, up near the shoulders, like she could be some friend of the family, some aunt I hadn't seen in years, someone he cared for.

"Hi," Laura said to me, gently. "It's been a long time. It's good to see you again."

"Yeah," I said. "It's a real Kodak moment."

And then, in one of the few times something lucky happened to me in those days, that redfish gave my bait another strike. I looked back to see my line moving away in the water.

"Oh, Glen," she said.

"It's okay," he told her. "He's just got a fish."

The two of them walked up to the dock and stood beside me.

"Bring her in, son," my father said. "Don't lose her."

Then, as if there was nothing else to say, they watched me fight it.

You should know:

Louisiana is the Sportsman's Paradise.

This is our state slogan.

We have it on our license plates here, our billboards. And though I'd normally felt separate from this as a child, though I'd

128

been the type to stay silent as people talked about shooting a deer or blasting baited ducks from the sky, I felt I understood it all then. Because when I was engaged with that redfish in Cocodrie, the rest of my world fell away.

The fish tugged at the line with an urgency I'd not expected. It was a heavy thing, dashing around for its life down there, and it cared nothing about my awkward situation on the dock. It would happily pull me in the water and leave me for dead if it could. It would drag me beneath some ancient and salt-bleached stump. I had no other choice but to fight it. Don't you understand? Life is complicated.

It's a form of joy to have no other choice.

So, I set the hook. I dug in. The span of our fight would be a respite, I knew, from the people standing behind me, from my worries, from every place I did not want to be. As long as that fish wanted to get away, and as long as I was unwilling to let it, we would have each other.

I could therefore imagine people with big problems seeing this type of sport as a paradise. A wife sick at home, perhaps, a paralyzed child. I could see why these husbands and fathers would venture out in cold mornings to drink coffee in a duck blind, why they would revel in being single-minded. Why they would designate entire days to this pursuit and how these days could turn easily into seasons. I began to feel Louisiana itself making sense to me, in a way it hadn't before, and yet finally landing that redfish, the first trophy I'd ever captured, felt like an ending rather than a beginning.

The fish was a beauty and I was congratulated. Water dripped from its skin.

Then it was weighed and gutted.

After this, the sun fell and my father's friends did not leave.

It turned out we were all staying at the same camp that night, and the details of how this came to be were never mentioned. I had several ways to interpret their presence, of course, but none of them mattered. All I knew was that my father, when given the opportunity to be with me, to set me straight in life, had chosen to sacrifice nothing. He had altered no plans, nor did he consider the wild impropriety of this situation from my point of view. Rather, when told by my mother that I was in trouble, that I needed his help, he chose to simply endure me for an evening.

And since this is not about me, since the goal is to uncover what happened to Lindy,

I'll spare you the total depression of this event. Just know that the night fell to heavy drinking for my father and his cohorts, and then to poker. In times they forgot I was there, the young men and women kissed one another openmouthed at the table. They hit up my father for beer money. Laura remained nice enough, and my father, in his own version of therapy, I suppose, drank several bourbon and Cokes out of a Styrofoam cup.

When they later turned up the music and took to dancing in the wood-paneled cabin, I slipped outside, unnoticed, and walked to the far end of the pier, where I skipped oyster shells like rocks into the still and black water. After an hour, I heard someone walking up to me. It was my father. He stood underneath a floodlight and steadied himself on a wooden beam, his shirt untucked.

"Hey, son," he said. "Everything all right out here?"

I looked at him but said nothing. He shifted his weight from foot to foot and slapped clumsily at a bug by his ear. I could hear music still playing in the cabin, the swell of girlish laughter.

"It's dark out here," my father said. "There's bugs."

We stared at each other for a long time. And although scenes like this now strike me as heavy and important, replaying like loops in my mind, I had no deep thoughts on this occasion. I instead listened to fish moving in schools along the shallow banks and watched my father try to stifle his hiccups. After a moment, one of his friends returned from a beer run and the glow of headlights lit us up on the dock, where I imagine the two of us standing there in the spotlight looking totally unrelated, as awkward as strangers in a hospital elevator. We both blocked our eyes from the glare, and then it got dark again. I could hardly see.

I heard my father take a deep breath through his nose.

"I'll take you home in the morning," he said.

"Okay," I said.

I eventually fell asleep on a pull-out couch and my father passed out on the front porch of the stilted cabin, sitting in a lawn chair with the Styrofoam cup in his hand. Laura slept alone in her room.

The next day I pretended to feel sick.

I barely spoke to anyone and feigned sleep the entire ride home. My father, now sober and guilt-ridden, tried to explain life to me in the car, to give me some eloquent bit

132

about how love finds you when you're not expecting it, how it doesn't bother with age or situation, and how it doesn't always play fair. He told me repeatedly to take good care of my mom because she was a special woman he would always love, and she deserved the best. He continued to talk even when he thought I was asleep and yet surprisingly little was revealed. Or perhaps I just didn't listen.

I had my reasons.

Earlier that morning I had overheard him tell Laura that he was just going to drive to Baton Rouge and drop me off and that he'd be back to the camp that evening. I heard him tell her that she'd done great, that I was just an angry teenager, and that they would have some "real fun" upon his return. So I had heard enough, to be honest. I had nothing to say.

When we got home, my father told my mother that something was wrong with me. He said he would call her later that week to check up, but that he had an appointment to get to that afternoon and couldn't stick around. My mother, we both could tell, had been crying.

"Kathryn," he told her, "don't be so dramatic. He might just have a cold or something. I tried talking to him, but he slept the whole way home in the car."

"Glen," my mother said, "that's not what makes him sick."

My mother looked over at me and, for the first time in my life, I did not recognize her expression.

"You need to see something," she told him. "You need to see what I found in his room."

15.

I've imagined this day to death, the day I became a suspect.

In the first version, a child's version, my mother is a wreck. As soon as I left the house with my father, she cried over a teapot. She cried over her laundry. She took off her fancy clothes and put on pajamas, poring over old photos of my father and me. She thought about us entirely, and wondered why men act the way they do. She still considered me a good boy in this fantasy, the same swaddled infant who once nestled up to her breast in the delivery room, and so she planned out my meals for the upcoming week. She tearfully sliced up that roast so I could have sandwiches the next day. She double-checked to make sure we had the potato chips I liked. Then she walked into my room with a load of freshly folded clothes under her arm and, by total accident, stubbed her toe on a wooden box underneath my bed, with a latch on it that I had mistakenly left unlocked.

In the second version, the one that came to me when I grew up a bit, I see my mother as a complicated person, a woman lonely and in need. In this version she recovered quickly after my departure and suddenly saw her empty house as a palace where she could finally rule. She poured herself a glass of wine before lunch. She lay on the couch and unbuttoned her blouse. She fell into adult dreams and dialed up her numerous gentleman suitors to say, *I'm here, now, I'm alone, I'm normal for a change.* And whether they came over or not, whether she took out her frustrations in a way that so many of us would, this is beyond the reach of our business. But after night came, and she was alone again, she stumbled tipsily into my room. She dropped some half-folded laundry on the floor and, exhausted, decided to make a pillow of my black T-shirts and baggy jeans that now smelled of fabric softener. And then, before passing off to sleep, she noticed a box beneath my bed with a latch on it that I had mistakenly left unlocked.

In the final version, the one that still comes to me intermittently, in times when I want to feel innocent, my mother began snooping as soon as I walked out the door. She did not wait to see me wave to her from my father's Mercedes, nor did she even bother with cooking that roast. Instead she stomped straight into my room and flung the clothes out of my drawers. She dumped my schoolbag out on the desk. She flipped through my notebooks. She called up Randy and Artsy Julie to grill them about my character. She stood on footstools and riffled through the items at the top of my closet. She looked underneath my mattress. And just when she was about to give up, when she was a second or two from realizing that my rebellion was only a quick rite of passage, nothing to be alarmed about, she sat on the floor to assess the damage she'd done. Then, out of the corner of her eye, she saw a box underneath my bed with a latch on it that I had mistakenly left unlocked.

Regardless of how it all happened, what she found in the box was this: five poems; twenty-seven pornographic drawings of Lindy and myself; a green bracelet made by Lindy's Christian pen pal in Jamaica; two hair barrettes; six pages of pornography torn from a magazine called *Cherry* that a guy named Ronnie Gibbs had brought to school; seven wallet-sized school photos of Lindy (two with her face cut out and pasted to the aforementioned *Cherry* pages); the condoms and sex pamphlet that my mother herself had given me; four mix tapes; a small bottle of Astroglide personal lubricant (half empty); six packets of vending-machine condoms with names like Mud Grips, French Tickler, and Lambskinz on them; the photo of Lindy singing to herself as she walked that I'd gotten from Jason Landry; a page ripped from the back of my yearbook that Lindy had signed for me in the seventh grade that read *Hey you! Have a great summer! Hugs, Lindy* (the *i* dotted with a heart); a pair of cheap plastic binoculars; and, finally, unfortunately, a blue Reebok running shoe.

Most of these items had easy explanations. I dabbled, for instance, in poetry. The majority of my verse was so vague, however, that if it weren't for the accompanying visuals, my mother likely couldn't have pegged my muse. One poem I remember was called "106 Steps" and detailed the amount of walking it took for me to get to Lindy's house. *Step number six, I bet you taste like Pixy Stix,* and so on. Lindy's name was never mentioned, of course, as I substituted words like *heaven, nirvana,* and *paradise* for the Simpson house. It was awful stuff.

Another was called "Roses in My Hand" and made a series of veiled innuendos about every red part of her that I would like to touch. I wasn't trying to be coy, though, I was just a kid to whom everything seemed unclear. I wanted to fondle her *heat,* her *aura,* her *soul,* none of which I'd physically know how to locate if she allowed me. The last one I remember was written in violet Crayola for effect and was titled, simply enough, "My Blood Is You."

This was not so bad. I've heard more malice in pop songs.

Much of the incriminating memorabilia could also be explained by my habit of pacing the sidewalk in front of Lindy's house. This was fairly innocent stuff as well: the barrettes, the green friendship bracelet that had unraveled and fallen off in the rain. Surely a boy can't be blamed for that. Think of men who walk along the beaches in sunglasses and full-brimmed hats, scouring the sand with metal detectors. These are not felons. Think of our parents, even, holding on to some gold-plated brooch their mothers once wore, or stowing away a box of ribbons their father garnered in war. We are all small historians, aren't we? We are all private treasure hunters, every one of us. So what was I supposed to do when, after the crime, I happened upon that lone Reebok sitting in a pile of trash at their curb?

Yet I was no fool. The homemade pornography was hard to defend. Stick figures or no, the lusty intention was there. My erotic thought bubbles had recently evolved into diatribes, as well, bursting out of Lindy's head as she knelt in front of me on a piece of construction paper torn in a fit from my school binder. She spoke in long sentences in these scenes and said things like, *I have always wanted this since that time you tackled me last summer.* Or, *This is the way I like boys to give it to me.* Or, in the one I really regret, when she was on all fours, screaming, *Yes! Please! Again!*

I had no excuse for such things.

And even then I understood the despair that must have sunk into my mother's bones when she saw this. I also understood the way this discovery must have recast for her the conversation we had with the police officer in our living room, when she realized, in other words, that this box may have already been sitting there silently, beneath my bed, when I performed so innocently for the Simpsons. What was she to do with this idea?

I didn't ask.

Yet it all looked so devilish out in the light,

my private collection, where it was never supposed to be. This was especially true of the way I had pasted Lindy's face onto the torn-out pages of those magazines. Heaven help her. There she was, glued to the page, disembodied and smiling innocently for the school photographer as she unknowingly bent over some enormous penis or pinched her nipples with a trail of semen on her breasts. The poor thing. I see that now.

I didn't know what I was doing. Please understand that. I don't want this confession to lose you. No boy knows what he is doing when he first stumbles upon masturbation. We become amateur inventors, we gawky and lunatic teens, and Lindy was simply the stuff of my workshop, of my laboratory. And I've spent years wondering how different my life would be if I was like the millions of boys who hadn't been caught, if I was like any other normal person who had the privilege of privacy, if I'd have been able to keep these fantasies locked up where they should be, in my mind, in my heart, with no empirical evidence to speak of.

But who am I kidding? I've never been any good at keeping things locked away.

Look at me now, for instance. Look at me telling you, of all people.

Yet the real problem, it turned out, was not the pornography, which my father laughed off when she told him. Nor was it the Astroglide lubricant that, in a fit of unbelievable bravery, I had purchased at the K&B Drugstore within biking distance of my house. Nor was it even the rambling poetry or mix tapes I had made but never given to Lindy, nor even the blue Reebok, which I was able to explain to her in the way I have to you.

No. The real problem was the pair of binoculars, and the photo I confessed to her came from the Landrys'. These items brought repercussions. Our home was never the same.

16.

The binoculars first:

In 1988, the year before Lindy's rape, the Landrys fostered a young criminal by the name of Tyler Bannister. He arrived shortly after Tin Tin's quiet and unexplained departure and was sixteen, the oldest child they'd ever fostered. As it turned out, his years of bouncing from one family to another had done to him what it did to many other young boys in that limbo and made him distrustful and cruel. His presence in Woodland Hills was unwelcomed. There were several reasons for this.

Tyler Bannister introduced a new set of problems to the neighborhood that the younger kids, myself included, had yet to develop. And since we were already dealing with our own budding messes in Bo Kern and Jason Landry, his sudden appearance seemed overkill. He brought to our streets the knowledge of drugs and vandalism, and he did not even look like a child. He kept his head shaved bald in all seasons and had blue tattoos on his wrists, neck, and ankles. He once claimed he'd done these to himself with a needle and Bic pen. Another time, he said they'd been put there against his will. He was a perpetual liar. All we knew for sure was that one of these tattoos, crudely drawn but recognizable, depicted a boy with a gun in his hand. Another was of a dark blue cloud with a lightning bolt through its center. And the one on his neck, just below his right ear, was of a bird with one wing.

In the times he found his way into our yards, Tyler told us stories we weren't prepared to hear. One I remember about his exhausting sexual relationship with the middle-aged mother of a previous foster home. He talked about how she "loved it up the ass" and about how she would come into his room and give him blowjobs when the father fell asleep. Another anecdote of the way he once put a lightbulb into the vagina of a girl he shared a group home with. We rubbed our eyes and couldn't believe it. "Chicks are freaks," he told us. "Don't let them tell you any different."

But Randy and I, and even Jason, who seemed totally enamored with Tyler, remained skeptical of some of these stories. They were so wildly inconsistent, so foreign from our experience on Piney Creek Road, that we had little to say in response. When he told us of letting a black guy touch his penis so he could score some blow, for instance, we just covered our faces and thought, *What in the world is blow?* We were too nervous to ask. Or when he told us that he'd once lived with a band of gypsies who pimped him out for sex in the back of the Kmart parking lot on Plank Road, we thought, *Hey, that doesn't sound so bad,* because all we heard was the sex. But the devil was in his details. "It was the truckers that were the worst," he told us. "Just the smell of their nuts."

Luckily for us, other stories cast doubt on all this grotesquery.

Like when he told us about his real father, his biological father, who he said was abducted by aliens right in front of him. He told us they were nothing like you saw in the movies, "none of that bigheaded little-green-men shit." He instead said they looked like trees and squirrels and "all this stuff you see around you." We laughed at this thought. "Laugh all you want," he said. "It's not so funny when it happens to you."

Everything had happened to him.

His mother, he once told us, sold him to the circus to pay for doctor bills. Another time he said she died while playing William Tell with some famous actor. "I won't even tell you which one," he said. "There's no point. That guy's got serious hush money." But he'd also once told us his mother had fallen overboard off a millionaire's yacht and was lost at sea, which confused us, and that she was probably just raising some other guy's kids now, all "amnesiaed out." He figured she might come looking for him one day, but he wasn't holding his breath. Still, Tyler liked to spray-paint his name on things, he said, "in case she ever wakes up from her coma."

The boy's dreams were all over the map.

Despite the inaccuracies of these stories, however, there was nothing confusing about Tyler's actions. Although he was there for only a few short months in the year before Lindy's rape, Tyler carried out an impressive campaign of terrorism and left a permanent mark on Woodland Hills. He destroyed mailboxes with homemade explosives and M-80 fireworks that he had apparently stockpiled. He stole all the street and yard signs in the neighborhood and stuffed them into the storm drains along Piney Creek Road. We found this out weeks later when it rained and we flooded, the Parkers' long-lost "It's a Girl!" yard sign suddenly bobbing its head out of an open manhole. He toilet-papered houses and salted yards. He graffitied images that matched his tattoos on the light poles and oak trees. He let neighborhood pets out of their fences. He stuck garden hoses through open car windows and turned on the water. He also smoked the first joint I had ever seen, sitting in my backyard.

This was a big day. I had been outside playing with a remote-control car my mother had bought me as a surprise. It was a complicated machine called The Hornet that we'd struggled to put together. It ran on expensive yellow-coated batteries that you had to recharge every night, and the motor required constant maintenance. It had become a thing I hated in many ways, as it was too fast for me, and rarely worked when I wanted to play with it. My mom took me to a store called The Hobby Hut most Sundays to get it tuned up, where she talked to the guy that owned the place as I fiddled around with airplanes made of balsa wood. When we got back home I would take The Hornet out in the street and try to drive it, where it would crash and roll over on the pavement. Inevitably, these times would end with some wire burning out and a puff of smoke curling up from the battery.

"I'm sorry," my mother would say. "I should have gotten a different one."

"Don't say that," I'd tell her. "I love it."

On this particular day, I was out in the backyard, running the car on the grass, where it was slower and more manageable, when I saw Tyler and Jason walking around in the woods. They came up to me, smiling and out of breath, and Jason said, "We just saw two frogs getting it on in the creek. Tyler blew them up with a firecracker."

I laughed and struggled with the remote control.

Tyler watched me for a moment and then removed a bag of weed from his pocket. He sat on the grass and began expertly tossing out seeds and rolling it up in some papers.

"Now we're talking," Jason said, and rubbed his hands together.

Tyler flicked open a Zippo and lit the joint that I honestly thought was a cigarette.

"You smoke?" I said.

"This place is so fucking boring," Tyler said. "What would I do if I didn't?"

I sat next to them in the yard and made the car do loops around the trunk of an oak tree. The scene was quiet but for the buzz of the motor.

"See what I'm saying?" Tyler said, and offered me the joint.

I told him I had allergies. I told him I "just say no."

"Don't be so gay," he said.

"He's not gay," Jason told him. "He's got a hard-on for the Simpson chick." He made stroking motions with his hand. "He jacks off to her like thirty times a day."

"I do not," I said.

"Then where's my picture?"

"I don't know," I said. "I forgot about it."

"Right," Jason said.

"What fucking picture?" Tyler said, pulling a bit of dope off his tongue.

Jason told him the story.

Tyler smiled until he found out where the picture had come from, the locked room inside their house, and then he took on a look I'll never forget. It was intense and solitary, and he looked pained, as if balling his mind into a fist. He held the joint beneath his nose like it was a precious thing. He breathed in the yellow smoke.

"You going to share that or what?" Jason said.

"Why should I?" Tyler said, and he didn't.

He instead removed a couple of M-80 firecrackers from his pocket and lit the fuse of one with his joint. He threw it toward my racer. It missed but blew up a clod of dirt by the tree stump.

"What the hell?" I said.

"Those Hornets suck anyway," he said. "The batteries are always burning up."

Was there anything he didn't know?

"Still," I said. "My mom gave it to me."

"I'd give it to your mom," he said.

"I would, too," Jason said.

"I'd give it to your little girlfriend, too," Tyler said. "Lindy what's-her-name. I'd give it to her right there in her room with all those stuffed bunnies and New Kids on the Block posters."

"What are you talking about?" I said. I was enraged.

The idea that this vagrant stranger would know the specific contents of Lindy's room was outlandish to me. I deemed it a preposterous lie and threw it into the same stinking pile with his other monstrous tales. Because the truth was, despite our entire youth together, our series of glowing summers, I had never been inside Lindy's room. I'd imagined it, sure, down to what I thought would be a green-and-white checkered bedspread draped over a white wrought-iron bed frame with white rose inlays next to a white wooden desk with colored construction paper fanned out on

150

top of it beside a series of fluffy white pillows that Lindy would lie upon while talking on the phone beneath a white bulletin board lined with blue first-place ribbons that her parents had tacked along the edges in neat rows above a pink tape deck on the nightstand where my mix tapes would one day go beside a white bookcase full of yearbooks and picture albums that stood above a shaggy pink rug beneath a heaven of glow-in-the-dark star decals she had pasted to a white and latticed ceiling fan that was constantly turning.

Sure, I'd imagined it all. But I had never seen it.

"Like you've been in her room," I said.

"Dumbass," he said. "You don't have to go *in* it to see it."

The both of them laughed.

"This guy just doesn't get it," Jason said.

"Do I have to teach you fucks everything?" Tyler said. "Come on."

Tyler then spat on his wrist and extinguished the still-burning joint, an act that looked immensely heroic to me, and one that I myself would ape barely a year later. He got off the grass and told me to grab the Hornet so we wouldn't look suspicious.

When we got to the street, he instructed me to steer the car toward Lindy's house as we followed behind it. "All right," he said. "Check out three o'clock. The oak tree by their driveway."

I looked over to see a tall water oak sitting alone in the space of grass between the Simpson house and its driveway. It stood about thirty feet high and had branches that Lindy could likely feel if she leaned out of her window just so.

"You notice anything about the trunk?" he said.

The trunk of the tree was warped and knobby, like many of these oaks are known to be. I saw a knot in its trunk about chest high, and I immediately knew what he was getting at. The thing had the look of a foothold.

"One hop on that knot, one jump to that branch, and bingo," he said. "You've got an eyeful."

"That is so wicked," Jason said.

"It's all right," Tyler said. "How long can you watch some teenybopper talk on the phone?"

Forever, I thought. I could watch into a time with no end.

"The real action is at that house down the street," Tyler said. "The one with the fat wife."

"The Mouilles'?" I said. "Isn't she pregnant?"

"Do I look like a doctor?" Tyler said. "I just call her Tons of Fun. I mean, that lady likes to *fuck.*"

As we stood there, lost in our own fantasies and looking anything but inconspicuous, Lindy came down her driveway with the bike at her hip. She was wearing green running shorts and a pink tank top, and I felt hugely guilty when she saw us standing in the road in front of her house, talking about how to spy on her. Her bronze and muscular legs. Her fit hips. Her smile. It was all too good for me.

"Hey, dorks," she said.

"I was just playing with my car," I told her.

"Hey, girl," Tyler said. "Where do you think you're going?"

"To the track," she said.

"Why don't you come hang out with us?" Tyler said. "We'll show you ours if you show us yours."

Lindy scrunched up her face.

"Gross," she said. "Like you have anything I want to see."

"Oh, *I've* got something," Jason said.

"Shut up," Tyler told him. He smiled at Lindy. "They're just kids," he said. "They don't know what we've got going on."

About this time, Dan Simpson, Lindy's father, drove up Piney Creek Road in his silver-and-blue station wagon, just getting home from work, I suppose. We stepped out of the road and he rolled down his window by turning a crank with one hand while awkwardly trying to wave at us with the other. I waved back. After he pulled into the driveway, he stopped his car next to Lindy and said, "What's on tap for today? We breaking the four-minute mile?"

Lindy smiled and walked her bike a few feet closer to his car as they casually re-hashed what all of us already knew, where she was going, what time she'd be back, who she'd be with, and we all laughed sarcastically when Mr. Simpson used his horrible Italian accent to say, "Just do not-ah be late, *mi amor,* because tonight I make-ah the famous Steak Simpsone Pizza-iola!" He then kissed his fingers as if to say *delicioso!,* waved good-bye to all of us, and drove his car into their garage.

Lindy straddled her bike, smiling ear-nestly, as if that particular meal actually did sound good, and lifted the kickstand with her foot. She looked back at us, and then at Tyler specifically, as if she'd forgotten he was there.

"Shouldn't you be out robbing old ladies or something?" she asked him.

Tyler laughed. "Maybe I will, *mi amore.*"

"Good, then," Lindy said. "At least you won't be bothering me."

Lindy then stuck out her tongue and took off down the sidewalk on her bike. She pedaled hard with her rear end up off the seat in a way that I now realize, in my worst moments, seemed to me some juvenile invitation. Tyler grabbed the remote control from my hand and made The Hornet follow her up the road. He was an expert driver, it turned out, and almost caught her.

"You shouldn't be so mean," he called to her. "I know where you live."

Lindy flipped us the bird as the car squealed up the sidewalk behind her until it finally died and sat still, out of radio range. We watched her ride out of sight.

"You should totally nail her," Tyler told me. "She's too bitchy for me."

I had no reply.

He handed me back the remote control, now useless, and said, "Let's go check on that fat chick. There's this great row of shrubs right outside their window. She goes nuts before her husband gets home. Uses all sorts of toys and shit. I'm telling you. Don't let chicks tell you any different."

So the two of them walked down the road and I chose not to follow.

Instead I walked the path Lindy had taken and picked up my car, the battery now smelling of smoke. I thought I could smell something else in the air that day, too, however. A whiff of her, maybe. The way we leave a trail. I stood there for a long time.

And although I still think of Tyler Bannister often, I saw him only a few more times after that day: once when I was standing in the darkness beneath Lindy's oak tree and holding that pair of binoculars in my hand. I heard rustling up in the branches, some soft grunting, and the clink of a loosened belt buckle. "Get the fuck out of here," he hissed.

So I did, and Tyler disappeared from the Landrys' about a month or so later.

He was gone before Lindy's rape. He was never a suspect.

17.

As for my candid photo of Lindy, the explanation would have to wait.

A strange stretch of time arose between the day my mother discovered the box beneath my bed and the day it was all finally dealt with nearly a year later. And although I'd hinted to her of the dark room where the photo had come from, she did not immediately take this issue up with the Landrys. She instead grounded me indefinitely, told me to stay away from Jason, and grew preoccupied with the other disasters that came to define her.

The first one was subtle.

In the wake of her discovery, my mother had contacted Peggy Simpson, Lindy's mom, and the two of them became close friends. I was so mortified by the idea that my mom would spill my secret fantasies to this woman that when she first invited her over, I did all I could to sabotage it. I greeted Mrs. Peggy at the door. I was extremely polite. I offered to pour her some coffee, fix her an iced tea. My mom knew what I was up to when I pulled up a chair beside them at the kitchen table. What child, she understood, would desire this type of company? She looked at my odd haircut, the ring in my left ear, my pale arms. She saw no child at all anymore, I suppose.

But my mother didn't understand my keen love.

I'd confessed it to her, all right, when I first tearfully defended those items she found in my box. But how does one relay this giant emotion? I didn't have the vocabulary then. When I told her, for instance, that "Lindy is all that I think about," my mom said, "I can tell. You ought to be ashamed." Or when I said, "No, Mom, I love her!" she said, "What I've got in my hands is *not* love, son. What I've got in my hands is obsession."

I couldn't argue with that.

Still, there must have been something in that initial conversation about love that gave my mother pause. I mean, I must have said something that stuck. I know this because when I stood in the living room eavesdropping on their conversation, thinking my chance of happiness with Lindy doomed, I heard Mrs. Peggy say, "He's a good boy, Kathryn. You have to be so pleased," and my mother took a long time to respond.

What must have gone through her mind at that moment? I wonder.

Surely she stood on a precipice.

Could she empty out my box for this woman, who had already suffered so much? Could she show her those school photos of her young daughter, prematurely pasted onto the adult world? More so, could my mother call her own parenting into such dubious question and risk whatever credibility she might have? Was there a part of her, in other words, that felt as if we had hidden evidence from the police? Did she feel some sort of guilt now, some sort of responsibility for the crime, just by giving birth to a boy who could have these thoughts and then so joyfully entertain them? It was more complicated than I understood at the time. Because she had to know that if I was truly innocent, if my raging obsession for a girl who'd recently been raped was mere circumstance, as she hoped it was, could she possibly say about her son what could not be unsaid?

I got my answer, I believe, when I heard my mother continue the conversation.

"Tell me, Peggy," she said. "How's Dan?

How's your husband?"

"He's a goner," Mrs. Peggy said. "He never sleeps. He blames himself. We all do."

"I understand," my mother said, and took a long and deep breath. "So, any leads?" she asked. "Any developments? Or would you rather not talk about it?"

"Nothing new," Mrs. Peggy said. "Lindy remembers so little, and pressing her for details only makes it worse. She locks herself in her room. She barely speaks to us. I wish Dan could understand that, but you know how men are. He just wants to fix everything."

"It's strange, isn't it?" my mom said. "I mean, about men. You'd think they'd realize they wouldn't have to fix so much stuff if they didn't go around breaking it in the first place."

The two of them shared a knowing laugh about this and I could picture them each sipping their drinks and smiling, considering the ridiculous men in their lives, and wondering how we ever got along without them. Then, when this light mood passed over, Mrs. Peggy took a deep breath. I could hear it from around the corner.

"The police have basically stopped calling," she said. "Part of me is thankful for that."

"Thankful?" my mom asked.

"Is that horrible?" Mrs. Peggy said.

Her voice sounded suddenly small and fragile. "Am I horrible for just wanting it all to be over?" she asked.

I heard my mother moving around in there. I pictured her perhaps leaning forward to look Mrs. Peggy in the eye, to touch her knee. "No," I heard her say. "No, you are not horrible. Let's talk about something else, okay? Let's talk about whatever you like."

"Okay," Mrs. Peggy said. "That sounds nice." Then, after a while, she said, "But what do I like?"

I went to my room after I heard this. I felt somehow pardoned.

I felt protected.

Still, I consider this friendship a disaster because of the way it affected my mom. She gorged herself on empathy for the Simpson girls from that day forward. Whether this was out of some brand of guilt introduced to her by the contents of my box, or just a remarkable aspect of her character is beside the point. My mother spent countless days with Mrs. Simpson in the following months: shopping with her, drinking coffee on the front porch, talking on the phone late into the night, and even accompanying her to a therapy group for parents.

Each of these excursions left my mother exhausted with grief, as there was no end to Mrs. Simpson's remorse. It even began to show on my mother's face when she would return home to me in the late afternoon, where she would lie on the couch and stare at the ceiling. I'd watch her kick off her shoes, rub the palms of her hands against her cheeks.

"Mom?" I'd ask.

"She's just such a nice person," she'd say. "The poor, poor girl."

I never asked to which Simpson she was referring.

Regardless, the second disaster was the reappearance of my bumbling father. Our unfortunate trip to Cocodrie and the ensuing discovery of my box had apparently struck some sort of paternal nerve in him, although it was obvious he didn't know what to do with this emotion. So he began to stop by sometimes after he had showings in Baton Rouge, usually not for long, just to check on us and maybe fix a dripping faucet in the guest bathroom. He had only one "important" talk with me during this time, regarding my behavior, when he sat me down in my bedroom.

"Look, son," he said, "I know this is

uncomfortable, but you really freaked your mom out. She's a little worried you were holding out on her when the police came over."

"I know," I told him. "She doesn't trust me anymore. I can tell."

"It'll pass," he said. "That's the thing about women. Everything with women takes time."

"I just wish I would have locked that stupid box," I said. "I wish she wouldn't have come in my room."

"I told her that," he said. "I told her every boy on this block probably has a stack of porn in their closet. That doesn't mean anything. I'm not sure if women understand that. We're wired a little differently, you know, men and women. A boy's got to have privacy. If it wouldn't have been the Simpson girl, it probably wouldn't be so bad."

"I never wanted to hurt her," I said.

My father laughed.

"No man ever does," he told me. "That's why I'm not worried about you. That's why I told your mom not to worry about you, too. Because the person who did that to your friend was *not* a man. He was an animal. You understand that? You *are* a man. That's the difference."

I thought about this for a long time. An

enormous part of me wanted to believe him.

"What are you saying?" I asked. "A *real* man only hurts women by accident?"

"Bingo," he said.

I felt some nameless air clear between us. But this was as far as we got.

His growing presence in our house did not seem to me the return of anything comfortable. I instead felt crowded out by the obvious playacting we all began doing. I was supposed to be happy he was back, I understood that, and I tried to be, though I felt a more pressing need to protect my mother, who took it all so seriously.

After he would leave in the evening, sometimes staying as long as supper, I'd often hear my mom analyzing his every gesture on the phone for Mrs. Peggy. His smile. The way he complimented her chicken. He remained with that Laura, she knew, but still.

"They always say that if you love something," I'd hear my mother say, "set it free."

She'd sip her wine and listen.

"That's right," she'd say. "If it's truly meant to be."

Nobody else saw it this way.

When my sisters would call home during this time, the first thing they'd ask me was, "Is Dad over there again?" and if I said

"No," they'd say, "Thank God. Let me talk to Mom."

And thinking back on it now, I suppose that even she had glimpses of the farce of it all, the idea that two people can ever "go back," because on nights when they returned to familiar marital flirting, scooting around each other in the kitchen, I'd later hear them fighting as he walked out the door.

"It's all or nothing," she'd say. "You can't just do what you want."

This was a concept my father did not understand.

So, he continued stopping by, sometimes bringing over bottles of wine and videotapes he'd rented from a store that a friend of his owned. The night that remains the most vivid to me was centered on the movie *Airplane!,* already a decade old at this time and, to my father, a classic. He had nearly all of the lines memorized, and he and my mother would laugh at jokes I didn't get. This was adult stuff here, this movie, despite the tame rating and childish props, and it operated on a level for them that I was unable to access.

When a particular scene in a disco came on, for instance, they lapsed into utter flashback. My father paused the movie and said, "Come on, Kat. I know you haven't forgotten my patented lightning-strike move." He got up from the recliner and cleared a space on the floor. He shot his pointer finger up toward the ceiling.

"Sha-zam!" he said.

"Oh, lord," my mother said and laughed. "Don't remind me."

This, however, was his mission.

My father grabbed a record off the shelf and played it. He let their story unravel.

"You wouldn't know by looking at us," he told me. "But your mother and I used to tear up the dance floor."

"We took one disco lesson," my mom said. "You hated it."

My father smiled and took her hand. He pulled her off the couch. "Come on," he said. "I don't remember it like that."

The album he played was something by Diana Ross, I believe. It held no magic for me.

Still, I watched the two of them dance.

My father pulled my mother close to his chest, his necktie loose. He tapped his foot to the beat. "Ready?" he said, and spun her awkwardly around the room. My mom laughed and pretended to be embarrassed by it all, saying she couldn't remember the steps. This was apparently true, as the next

166

few minutes devolved into nothing more than repeated lightning strikes by my father, which neither of them tired of.

I started off to my room.

"Hey," my mom said. "You could learn something here. You may not know it, but your father's always been an excellent dancer. That's one of the first things I noticed about him."

"Is that right?" my dad said.

"You know it is," she said.

I fell asleep that night with the music still playing, their sporadic laughter sliding underneath my door, and when I woke up the next day I, as per my usual ritual, looked out of my bedroom window in hopes of a Lindy sighting. This was like breakfast for me. Sometimes I would see her in a bathrobe and slippers, going out to get the morning paper for her father, although this hadn't happened in months.

It also didn't happen this day.

Instead I saw my father's Mercedes still parked in our driveway. It was as strange to me as a desert landscape. I felt transported. And I would be lying if I said that I was cynical to it all at that moment. My sisters may have been if they'd seen it, but, like my mother, I suppose, I still had the tug of a dreamer inside me.

So I hurried up and got dressed. I thought perhaps a small piece of life fixed and began to shuffle all the old memories of my father into a pattern more pleasing to me than what I'd carried for so long. He was not altogether a bad fellow, I thought, when you looked past a thing or two. A real man, after all, never means to hurt anything.

I smelled coffee when I entered the living room.

I fancied bright presents under the tree.

Then, when I got into the den, I heard the lock on the front door turning. I walked into the foyer to see my father still wearing the clothes he had worn the night prior, his tie now slung over his shoulder. He held a cup of coffee in his hand and his shoes were untied. A key ring dangled from his pinkie finger.

"Dad?" I said. "What's going on?"

He didn't even look at me.

"Where's Mom?" I asked him. "Is everything all right? Surely you're not leaving."

He had no answers to these simple questions. So, like the man I knew, he said the first thing to come to his mind.

"Son," he said. "Please. Don't call me Shirley."

Then he walked out the door.

The two of us back to square one.

I spent the rest of that morning picking up empty wine bottles and washing their dirty glasses from the night before. I couldn't stand to look at the stuff. My mother stayed alone in her room until supper that night and didn't speak much when she emerged. This type of thing became a habit of hers, staying in her room and crying, as the biggest disaster of all came next.

18.

The death of my sister split my world open.

This occurred on April 6, 1991, and marked the beginning of the end of me and Lindy's year of dreadful silence. It also left my mom ruined.

My specific memory of this event, however, is hazy. This is not something I'm proud of.

All I recall is being home alone one Saturday morning. My mom was off at the mall, shopping for clothes, getting a haircut, who knows. I was barely sixteen years old at the time. I didn't have a car. At approximately ten o'clock that morning, the phone rang and a woman asked me if my sister Hannah was home. She was not. Hannah was twenty-seven. She had an apartment on the other side of town. I told the caller as much. A series of subsequent calls then trickled in, all by a woman with the same voice who asked me if my parents were home, and how old I was.

I suspected a scam.

"Don't call back here," I told her.

"Please," she said. "Just take down this number for me."

I didn't bother.

And since this was a time before cell phones, I have no idea how my parents received the news. I only remember one final call, from my father, who told me there'd been a car accident. He then told me he was picking up my mother to go to the hospital because she couldn't drive herself.

"Is she okay?" I said. "Is Mom okay?"

"No," he said. "It's not your mom. It's Hannah."

"What's going on?" I said. "People keep calling for her."

"Just stay there," he told me. "Don't go anywhere."

This was as much as I got.

The next few hours were spent in itchy solitude. The phone continued to ring, yet it was never my parents. The voices instead morphed into aunts and uncles and grandparents who were cagey and guarded in what they said to me, prefacing it all by asking what I knew. I told them the greatest truth.

I knew nothing.

When late afternoon came I saw my family drive up to our house, all sitting together in one car, and this remains to me the clearest image of the event. My father drove the Mercedes with two passengers in the backseat, and I watched them pull into the garage behind the house. It took me a long time to understand who these people were; such was the distance from the last time they had looked like a family. In the car sat my mother and my other sister, Rachel, a person I realize I've not even mentioned by name before now.

There's nothing behind that. We simply weren't close then. This is nobody's fault.

A decade older than me, Rachel was already off to graduate school in Lafayette at that time, an hour away from Baton Rouge, and so a large amount of thought went simply to what she was doing back home. It made no sense. I watched her help my mother out of the car, and this took some effort.

My mother looked like a stranger at that moment and, in truth, it would be a long time before I saw her beautiful again. Her back was hunched over. Her face was slack and wet. If I had the ability, I could draw her for you, her sad figure, still crystal clear in my mind. But I don't. Just know that my sister was also disheveled and upset, and that my father looked composed as a robot.

This is what gave it away. I bawled before they told me the news.

My final memory of that moment is of burying my face into my father's stomach and crying until I made his shirt wet. After this, a large chunk of time disappears.

When I think back about this scene, most of my thoughts go to why I chose *him* to cling to. What must my mother have thought? What did I say to console her? Was I so selfish that I thought only of myself? When I try to remember the specifics, it seems that I can only hear my mother in the background saying, "I'm sorry, son. I'm so sorry," but why would she be apologizing to me?

This is a time I want back.

Yet I can only flash forward to that evening, when a stream of relatives began rushing through our front door. Old friends of the family. The people of Woodland Hills. And then, worst of all, there was Hannah's inconsolable fiancé, a man we called Finally Douglas.

I didn't really get this joke back then, likely because, as a teenage boy, I didn't much care. But I understand now that the nickname Finally Douglas was a compliment to this man named Douglas, a sigh of relief on my mother and Rachel's part that Hannah, after a number of bad relationships, had finally found a person who treated and loved her in the gentle way that all good people recognize. They were to be married in October of that year at a plantation called Magnolia Mound, a beautiful stretch of land in the northern part of Baton Rouge.

And now this.

And to further establish my credibility, I will confess to you the unfortunate truth. I don't remember much about Hannah. When I think of her now, all these years later, I think only of her death, and the details go like this:

On a bright and blue day, she was sideswiped by a gray pickup truck while backing out of a shopping center on Jefferson Highway. Her neck was snapped. She was pronounced dead on arrival. She didn't feel any pain. I heard this phrase again and again.

Still, I have to wonder about the accuracy of these things.

How much of the truth was I spared? In turn, how much truth am I sparing you?

If she was dead on arrival, for instance,

why were they at the hospital so long? Why didn't they call me? The common rumor passed around at her wake was that she had been pulling out of an ice-cream parlor when the accident occurred and that she still had a bit of her favorite, double chocolate fudge, on her lip when she passed. She died happy, people said. It's hard to imagine a better way.

I clung to this for years.

But now I think about the time of the first phone call, ten a.m., and wonder what kind of ice cream is sold at that hour. I understand that I could easily flip through the phone book and call the place where it happened. I could casually ask when they open. I know this.

But I refuse. I want to rely on my memory. It's important that you understand this. What else, besides love, do we have?

That said, when I think deeply about Hannah, only a few scenes arise from the rummage. They are of no obvious consequence. One from when I stayed the night at her apartment where she and Finally Douglas made us veggie pizzas. We played Sorry! and watched *Dune*. I didn't understand a bit of it. I recall no particular conversation. Most vivid to me is that she had a small table in the corner of her living room that doubled as a chess set. You could lift the top of the table and store the marble pieces beneath. It was made of a dark lacquered wood. There you go.

Thank you, memory.

Another time, in her senior year of high school, when she was listening to music in her room. I was only seven years old, yet I remember walking in to see her staring at herself in a full-length mirror, wearing a green cap and gown for her upcoming graduation. The record she was playing was by a band called Madness, a song titled "Our House (In the Middle of Our Street)," and the album cover, which she had tacked to her wall, depicted the band members all huddled together and smiling, their heads framed behind the rack of a billiards table. The song was loud, and Hannah was smiling. She saw me in the mirror and turned around. She held out her arms.

"Hey," she asked. "Does this thing make me look like a wizard?"

I wish these memories were more vivid. I wish there were more of them.

The one I cherish most took place in a time I can't quite finger, though I now imagine it to be during the Finally Douglas days. I was in my room, where Hannah had come to sit on my bed and ask me something. A favor, perhaps, a question, an invitation; I don't remember. All I know is that her hair was long and dark brown. It was straight, unlike mine, but she had done something to curl it this day. It twisted in soft columns on her shoulders, and she fiddled with it as she spoke. She smelled of perfume and wore a white cotton sweater with blue jeans, a turquoise necklace. The sweater was made of thick braided ropes and hung loose around her neck and shoulders. I've since gotten the impression from my family that Hannah was somewhat of an artist, a freer spirit than the rest of us, and so I imagine this sweater being fashionable at the time. I have no idea what information was exchanged between us.

I only remember that when my sister got up to leave my room she was happy, and her life was good. I know this by the slight flourish she gave to her exit, reaching up to tap the top of my door frame as she entered the hall. I clearly recall the playful little hop she gave to this gesture, the way I heard the thin bracelets on her wrists jangle, and the obvious manner in which I loved her.

So, after she died, I endowed this scene with great power.

When I would sit alone in my room in the year that followed, pretending I didn't hear my mother and sister sobbing in the spaces adjacent to me, I would stare up at that spot on the door frame. I thought about the impulse that makes a person go out of their way to touch a thing like that. It must be joy. It must be some sort of deep satisfaction. It must be peace.

Don't tell me any different. I am happy with memory here.

The reality, however, is that this event laid waste to my family.

My mother became a person whom I could no longer understand. Yet she was never neglectful of me in the years that followed. She instead became overly gracious and forgetful of nearly all my flaws, and, in truth, she may have erred in this way. With everything else turned sour in her life, I suppose she needed to believe me an angel. I only wish I could have provided.

What else is there to say?

My sister Rachel was also changed. She dropped out of graduate school and moved home for a year. And although, as a family, we'd always been quietly Catholic (going to Mass on the holy days, attending Sunday school if nothing else was going on), my sister Rachel found Christ in bold and permanent ways when Hannah died. It was infuriating to me at the time. The random death of an innocent person seemed to prove to Rachel that God had a plan for everyone, while it poisoned for me the idea that there could be a God at all. So, I antagonized her by picking fights about all the obvious religious hypocrisies, like how a Christian God could doom people to hell because of where they grew up, like how he could unleash disease and war on those who had not sinned against him, et cetera, and although I was mainly just trying to pester her, although I was mainly just jealous of the way I would see her and my mother hold hands to pray at the dinner table, I believe I was also teetering on the brink of true faithlessness in those years, as many teenagers do, and it scared me.

Sensing this, Rachel began to leave little prayer cards on my pillow. She hung a poster above our breakfast table that had a lone set of footprints in the sand and began to speak almost exclusively in religious clichés. She talked about God "closing doors while opening windows" and "carrying us through the hard times," while her favorite phrase of all became "everything happens for a reason," and I found her impossible to talk to. I think now, of course, that I was simply afraid of her faith and the strength it took for her to have it. It was much easier for me to be angry about Hannah and about God and about the state of my family, which, in those years, seemed to be shrinking.

And then there was my father, as well.

He had not been on good terms with my sisters, Hannah especially, since the divorce, and this made the timing of her death, from his point of view, particularly torturous. And even though this always made sense to me in a generic way, the way the two of them didn't get along, I didn't find out the real reason until many years later when I learned that Laura was an acquaintance of Hannah's, and a member of the same sorority Hannah had quit. This cleared some things up for me. Although I'd always understood that Laura was young, it was not until I received the image of her possibly standing beside my sister in that same green cap and gown that I felt it sink in. Perhaps they had chemistry class together. Perhaps they once shared a whisper about the same handsome guy.

Worse than that, when my mother pictured my father with Laura, when she thought about their sex, perhaps she could muster only a version of Hannah still in her diapers, some hard candy stuck to the front of her shirt. How deeply my father's character must have changed for her. How strange he must have looked. What kind of man could be with a girl, after all, who would let an old man like him touch her? Worse, even, what kind of woman could my mother be, who'd let this old man back into her bed?

Such were the troubles on Piney Creek Road.

All told, Hannah's death had made each of our faults obvious, and in the end, this ate my father up. Years after this, once my father and I could drink together and he considered me a man, when we grew to be friends, he would sometimes lapse into a deep and momentary despair. And it came only upon the mention of Hannah.

"I can't even talk about it," he'd say, and then he'd ask me how often I spoke to Rachel.

"Just like you," I'd assure him. "Mainly on the holidays."

"I don't understand it," he'd tell me. "Why won't she love me like you do?"

What was I to say? The man asked only answerless questions. He still does this.

So, I have always considered him punished.

But the ultimate truth of this event, I suppose, the real reason I've led you here, is to explain to you the most unexpected conse-

quence of Hannah's death.
It brought Lindy closer to me.

19.

The event was called the Spring Bash.

This was still 1991, the month that my sister died, and I'd been out of school for two weeks, dealing with funeral stuff and moping around the house in black T-shirts. Hannah's death had provided me with the ultimate excuse, I suppose, to act as selfishly as all teens want to act. I ate Burger King every day. I stayed up late watching pornography that came fuzzy and scrambled through the small television in my bedroom. I slept at odd times, sprawled out on the sofa, and I imagine from the outside I probably looked troubled, perhaps even depressed and devastated, but the truth is, I didn't feel that way. When I look back upon that version of myself, a lanky kid in ripped jeans watching *The Price Is Right,* a kid annoyed at the voices of neighbors visiting with my mom in the kitchen, I think that little was deep in me then. I was just lonely.

I was just lazy. I just didn't want to deal.

Still, my mother insisted I go.

It had been arranged, unbeknownst to me, that I would escort Artsy Julie. In the years since our early youth, in the time since she'd so blissfully tossed clovers at the bed of moss, Artsy Julie had changed only in physical ways. This was not a bad thing. Still, she'd gained some weight to become a girl that people would backhandedly compliment as "big-boned," but she was not at all unattractive. Her only failure was that she seemed to have been birthed in the wrong decade, as she was clearly a hippie in bloom. She put flowers in her hair at school, drew things like unicorns on her notebooks, and read thick novels of heroic fantasy. I saw her once, for example, sitting in a circle of pimply boys at school, playing Dungeons and Dragons at a lunch table. She pumped her fist when she rolled a certain number on the ten-sided die. She pretended to sprinkle magic potion all over her mashed potatoes. She seemed to be having some genuine fun. We were in high school at the time, though, and this, of course, was social suicide. If she had been popular, I suppose that all this independence may have looked hip to us. But she was not.

She wore the wrong type of shoes with

her uniform, made excellent grades, and told what seemed to be inside jokes that nobody shared. Her hair was black and long and often unwashed, and her hairbrush left tracks where she combed. Her sole earrings, I remember, were green plastic butterflies. She gave us so little to work with. Artsy Julie, however, had also become buxom in the turn of her freshman year, the top of her plaid jumper suddenly chock-full, and so she was not altogether ignored.

She picked me up for the dance in a green and ruffled dress, more uncomfortable than even I seemed to be in my blue blazer and polka-dotted tie, and we gave each other corsages. Our parents made a big deal of this, taking our picture in various poses both in and outside of the house, and we made faces to screw up the photos. My mother still has these pictures, framed and hung up on the wall, and it's like I travel back in time when I see them.

When Julie and I arrived at the dance, a band was already onstage playing cover songs like "Brown Eyed Girl" and "Mustang Sally," and she acted as if she'd landed front-row tickets to the Stones. She left me alone and danced wildly by herself in front of the stage for hours. She took up a massive amount of space, moving dramatically, as if summoning up some tribal god. In times the music swelled, she would be joined by more popular boys and girls who danced with irony, but she never engaged them. This was a personal thing for her and, despite the way she was skewered for it socially, or perhaps because of it, I always admired her for this. She was a person who, as long as I'd known her, seemed able to do what I could never do, and simply not give a shit. Her hair, done up by her mother in sparkly braids and green barrettes, was fallen by the fourth song. She had sweat stains on the belly of her dress. I finally spoke to her during the intermission, where she was guzzling punch at the snack table.

"You having fun?" I asked her.

"I'm so thirsty," she said.

That was as much as I got.

As soon as the guitarist finished up his cigarette outside the auditorium and climbed back onstage, Artsy Julie was gone, using her high heels to play air drums before the music began. A few guys came up to me as she did this and patted me on the shoulder. "Smart move," they told me. "Those ta-tas are amazing." So, in this way, I learned that Artsy Julie wasn't unwanted. She had her own thing going on and, truth be told, I was not unaffected by it.

What's most important here, though, is that I learned something about myself at this dance as well. Apparently, the death of my sister and my ensuing absence from school had granted me some type of celebrity. Guys who never spoke to me much before this, good-looking guys who played football or ran for student government, gave me a thumbs-up. Girls who rarely acknowledged me behind them in hallways or in Latin class asked, "Are you coming back to school on Monday?"

I told them, "I guess so," and they said things like, "Good."

I imagined a couple of reasons for their change.

The first arose from the strange look in their eyes when they approached me. I could tell they were dealing with unfamiliar emotions here, unfamiliar emotions for teenagers, anyway, all headlined by a feeling of pity. In each of their awkward handshakes or polite questions, I felt that I could see right through their eyes and into their kitchens, their dining rooms, where their parents had told them about what happened to my family. And when they first shook it off as something completely irrelevant, I could see their parents slowing down to emphasize the tragedy, perhaps pointing

187

over at their own siblings, or maybe even at-
tempting to explain to them the devastating
depth of parental love and what the loss of
a child would do to them personally. And
then, through the earnest timbre of their
voices, I imagine these kids got it for a
second. I think that perhaps there was a
minute or two when their young hearts collapsed heavy inside their chests. Not for me,
necessarily, but rather for the glimpse of
their own mortality as a thing they'd not
considered before, a wobbly house of slick
cards. Still, since none of these friendships
stuck around, since none of them galvanized
into anything more than that initial gesture
at the dance, I've come to suspect a different reason for their concern toward me during this time.

The Perkins School was a private school, I
remind you, a small community, and we
were seen by the rest of Baton Rouge as
some sort of paradise. In this way, we were
often scorned by outsiders as spoiled kids
who had no idea of reality, even by those
parents who would have sold their homes to
afford their children a shot at this haven. So
it was important that we lived up to the
hype. To sit in a classroom with a desk left
empty by a kid in some sort of turmoil, in
some deep depression, did not fit the bro-

chure. The silence that followed my name during roll call, for instance. The empty space on Mr. Taylor's wall where my history project was due to be tacked up. All these things were unacceptable. It was therefore critical I get back to school on Monday, you understand, so they could forget what my tragedy had tempted them to learn.

Yet not everyone played this game. Lindy, for instance, offered me no condolences.

She arrived late to the dance with a guy named Matt Hawk. He was a senior at McKinley High, a public school known to be rough and tumble. It was the type of place we Perkins School students made fun of, not out of snobbery, necessarily, but simply to assuage our own fears about how long we would last at a school where fights broke out at recess, where smart kids got jumped in the bathrooms.

And since McKinley had no sort of dress code, our own private-school attempts at rebellion seemed foolish in their presence. I was big trouble at Perkins, for example, because my bangs fell over my eyes. I had a hole in my left ear. Matt Hawk, on the other hand, had a silver bolt pierced through his eyebrow. He had a black ring through his nose. He was punk in a way that no Perkins kid would ever have the courage to be, and

189

even his hair, thick and tall and unkempt, looked as if nothing could tame it. And at the far end of his muscled arm, the arm of a future mechanic, perhaps, a woodworker, he had a series of black leather bracelets. Beside these bracelets, he had a strong-looking hand mapped in veins. And worst of all, on this night, inside this hand, he held Lindy's.

Lindy wore a dress I can best describe as gunmetal blue, and she was stunning, although she'd done her best to hide this fact. She wore dark eyeliner, combat boots, and had her hair pulled back tight and severe like some depressed artist. She had regained a little weight in the recent months, though, and, thankfully, no longer had the look of a bulimic waif. Still, her jaw was sharp and defined. Her anger was striking and impenetrable. Her supremacy was, to me, so obvious.

She and Matt Hawk spent the evening standing in the corner of the auditorium like judges. They looked much older than we did. And I suppose the other girls, although they made fun of her behind her back, were jealous of Lindy for this catch. I watched random groups of them approach the couple cautiously, to shake Matt's hand, to remind him that they'd met before, but

190

he acted aloof. The chaperones, you could tell, were as displeased as I was by his presence.

How did Lindy even meet this guy? I wondered. How much of herself did she give him? How much of her life had I lost that past year?

I couldn't keep my eyes off her.

In a break between the music, she and Matt snuck outside with the band, and when they returned, they giggled with each other as if stoned or high on cocaine. A group of Perkins School jocks soon became aggravated by Matt's attendance, as well, and circulated the idea of beating him up in the parking lot, as if letting him know about territory. This fantasy was short-lived, however, as even the strongest among them likely imagined being caught alone in a movie theater parking lot by vengeful public-school gangs. In this place, we knew that there would be no survivors. Still, we talked tough, as kids do.

The rest of the Spring Bash was uneventful.

I pretended to have a nice time while watching Lindy. (She tried, once, to get Matt to dance to a Guns N' Roses song. She went to the bathroom three times. She hugged him around the waist, which he shrugged off.) The only other thing I really remember about this dance is seeing Randy, whom I had since drifted away from (he'd become preppy and athletic), slinging his date over his shoulder during a cover of "Pretty Woman." He looked happy in this pose, and I was pleased for him. I wished him well.

Then, before the dance was officially over, the cool kids began filing out. We, Artsy Julie and myself oddly included, had been invited to an unchaperoned after-party and, as is the case with everything in high school, this is when things got interesting.

20.

The party was thrown by a girl named Melinda Jones. Her family, even by Perkins School standards, was filthy rich. Her father was a lawyer and state politician, and this position had apparently granted him immunity from all things, including parenting, so Melinda's mansion was considered by us to be little more than a well-furnished brothel. Understand, of course, that this was all rumor to me. I'd never been there before this night.

So, I was excited.

Artsy Julie and I piled into a car with four other kids and, before we were even out of the gymnasium parking lot, warm twelve-packs of beer were pulled from beneath the seats, joints rolled up and lit in mere minutes. I indulged. Artsy Julie, on the other hand, seemed immune to it all and politely declined both the booze and drugs as if she had no interest. She was wet with perspiration, happy and sober, and I could smell her sitting next to me. She stuck her head out the window and lifted her heavy hair from her neck. I felt oddly jealous of her, curious about what went on in her head. What did she think of me, for instance, when we were kids on Piney Creek Road? What did she think of me now? What did she think about anything?

I didn't ask.

In fact, by the time we arrived at Melinda's house, I'd almost forgotten about our date entirely. The reasons for this were predictable and obvious. I was sixteen years old. My sister had just died. Lindy would be at the party. I was unhappy. This one night, I figured, could be the exception.

Similar to the way we used to race across campus as eighth graders, trying to form some sort of reputation, I fantasized that I could plant my own stake in the ground at this event and establish myself as a wild man of sorts, perhaps someone even a bit dangerous, someone like the older boys I had watched at Perkins who became famous as "partiers" and who girls like Lindy (I hoped) gravitated toward almost unconsciously. Someone, I knew, very much like Matt Hawk.

So when we entered the party, I scouted

for trouble.

In the living room, expensive couches and antique end tables had been placed against the walls, where some boys I didn't recognize were setting up instruments. People lined the staircase to the second floor and watched them get organized. They had amps, mics, drums, and guitars, and things looked promising. In the kitchen, half-empty bottles of booze covered the marble countertops and, scattered around the tiled floors, a series of ice chests sat stuffed with every cheap beer you can imagine. Natural Light. Miller High Life. Old Milwaukee. One chest, in particular, was full of Rolling Rock and the bottles inside that open chest glowed like emerald treasure. I grabbed one, drank it with a thirst I didn't recognize in myself, and felt brave. I then grabbed another bottle, as to look perpetually double-fisted, and walked outside, where people were standing around a swimming pool and smoking cigarettes, some inhaling, many not.

Parentless and free, we were beginning our trek into pandemonium that night and everyone knew it. We stood around, drinking in our nice clothes, not yet soiled, and stared at the shimmering pool like the finish line we knew it would be. I spoke to people

I rarely spoke to and began intentionally slurring my speech to get the word out. When people asked how wasted I was, I told them, "I'm just getting started," and they were encouraging. I smoked dope out of a two-foot bong in the pool room. I lied and told people that I had pills I wanted to take but left at home. I used words like "quaaludes" that I didn't know the exact meaning of and tried to establish some semblance of mystery. When I heard the music crank up inside, I raised my bottle in the air and stood like a statue. I wouldn't let anyone talk to me until the song ended. I then paid a guy five dollars for a pack of his cigarettes and lit one after the other, exhaling as often as possible through my nose to look tough, to look as if nothing could bother me.

Within the hour, everyone was hammered.

Boys began to wrestle around in their suit coats, and girls flirted with guys who were not their dates. A series of dramatic and complicated high school plotlines soon twisted through the house and, amid the madness, a Jack Russell terrier (Melinda's, I'm guessing) swam in the pool, nipping at the discarded corsages that floated like candles at a Chinese funeral. I watched two guys climb up on the roof. I saw a girl fall into the bushes. Then, through the large picture windows that faced the pool from the den, I saw Lindy and Matt Hawk walk inside.

As any person in love would do, I threw some immediate and irrational thought toward what they had been doing in the past hour (they fucked in his car, she blew him in the driveway, they shot up drugs in some public-school bathroom), and the worst in me came out. I declared myself officially wasted and began stumbling around. I imagined myself a bigger person, physically, and fantasized about bedding down any girl that dared look at me. This was not entirely an act. Since I rarely drank at that time, the beers had made my face numb and emboldened me. I walked inside and watched the band.

I'd taken up the guitar myself since Lindy went dark, remember, and so I spent a few songs sizing up the guitarist. And although it is not in my sober nature to boast, the truth of the matter is I could wail. Such was the end result of many nights spent alone with my guitar, aping the songs I imagined Lindy listened to, the result of myriad fantasies of myself center stage with Lindy in a spotlight before me. I was a true Artist in this regard, I suppose, as all people are when they spend time alone with their heart and mind and try to bridge the great distance between them.

So when the band looked like they were about to take a break, I asked the guitar player if I could sit in for a song. He asked me if I could really play or if I was just wasted and I said something asinine like, "Does the pope shit in the woods?"

"If you break any strings," he told me, "I'll kick your skinny ass in front of your date."

"Relax," I told him, and did a few impressive scales to put him at ease.

Then I searched the crowd to find Lindy.

When I saw her, she was standing in the corner and arguing with Matt, who looked like he might as well have been waiting around at a dentist's office. His boredom was well rehearsed and unshakable, and Lindy was becoming animated, drinking something out of a plastic cup. She looked already drunk, and this pleased me.

I turned to the band, cranked up the amplifier, and played the first few notes of the Guns N' Roses song "Sweet Child O' Mine," the one I'd seen Lindy attempt to get Matt to dance to at the party. The band recognized the song, like everyone our age did, and picked up the beat. When I turned back toward the crowd, the song coming together better than even I had hoped, I saw Lindy looking at me. She'd cocked her head to the side like a dog sizing up a stranger and there passed between us a moment, I believed.

Then she turned back to Matt.

This gesture only fueled me, however, only gave shape to my thoughts, and I played better than I had ever played before. We sounded like professionals, and I was lucky that the drummer and singer were skilled. There is no better gift to a boy alone in the world with a guitar in his hand, that I can promise you. So, I set the volume at ten and let my hair hang over my eyes. Kids sang every word in robust chorus as they beat their leather shoes on the stairway banister and played air guitar with their dates. I saw Randy peek his head around the corner of the kitchen and salute me with a bottle of rum. I looked back at the drummer, who smiled, the bassist, who nodded, and, as the window to the backyard became crowded with harkening faces, I collapsed inside of myself for the solo.

In the place I found there, in the world I imagined, Lindy was filling up with wonder about me. How had the boy she had known as so meek and so shy in her neighborhood grown into this man now before her, playing a song that she loved? How had she neglected the obvious similarities between them? How had she not noticed that he could be all things to her, dangerous if she wanted him to be, sweet-hearted when she needed him?

Even more so, how had she been so foolish as to let other men know her, when the one that knew her first had not wavered? How? I saw her wonder about herself in this place. Why?

Why not?

This was my fantasy.

The reality is that when I opened my eyes, the house was rocking. Kids were hopping up and down in place as the singer began unleashing Axl Rose's trademark lamentations over the song's swelling composition: *Where do we go?* Axl sang. *Where do we go now?*

At that age, it was the best question we'd ever heard.

So I stood firm on the plush carpet and delivered to my peers what they wanted. I flexed every muscle I had. Finally, as the song was coming to a close, I saw Lindy dancing by herself, her date now disappeared as if I had driven him off my land, and I urged the band to play one more measure, for good measure.

They understood my desire and we rocked it.

God, yes.

This is Romance. This is Memory. This is the good stuff.

It did not last long.

21.

After the song, I spent a short time as a hero.

People came up to me and shook my hand. They poured me warm shots of vodka and tequila, which I drank. I'd become a mark of the evening, it seemed, a signpost, as in my bravery I had boldly proclaimed into the microphone that every Rolling Rock in that house was now mine and that only the foolish would try to stop me. As the evening progressed, kids asked me what number beer I was on and the answer bloated. I ended up in the second-floor game room, playing pool with a girl I had never seen before and constructing a pyramid of green bottles on the top of a pinball machine. It was well past two a.m. at this point and the lot of handsome young boys at the dance had aged into exhausted-looking businessmen, their ties loose around their necks, their hair skewed. I was legitimately drunk, for the first time in my life, and wondered how I'd ever been satisfied with anything else.

Back downstairs, the band had finally quit playing and the atmosphere was now a jumble of things: a drunkard banging on the drums that had been left there, a girl screaming at her date, and the blare of a Michael Jackson record. Kids had long ago begun to smoke cigarettes in the house as well, ashing into porcelain vases, and so the upstairs game room had the feel of a bar. Four or five guys played Nintendo on the large projection-style television on the far wall, and Trent Wilkes, a heavyset boy who played offensive tackle, was passed out underneath the pool table. Every once in a while I'd hear someone howl for no reason. It was that kind of night. Things felt great up there.

Then Lindy walked in and everything changed.

She stood in the doorway of the game room and steadied herself.

I had no idea what had passed in her life since I played my song for her, since I'd become a man on the scene, as I'd done all I could to act tough and ignore her. Still, I had the feeling that it hadn't gone well. My evidence to this effect was that her dress was now covered in stains where liquor had been spilled — Jägermeister, maybe, or some thick and brown beer. A black smudge of mascara beneath her eye now lent her the look of an athlete. She scanned the large room as if she'd forgotten why she'd come up there, and then, finally, she looked at me. She smiled.

I smiled back.

"Hey, you," she said, and there it was, the end of my loneliest year.

I'll spare you from all flights of fancy that you can assume took charge of me at that moment: our heartfelt confessions, our long conversations about star-crossed love and epic misunderstandings, how we'd wasted so much time without talking. None of those possibilities came true.

Instead I will only give you the words:

"Hey, Lindy," I said.

She took a long time to respond.

"Look who it is," she said, and walked toward me. Her combat boots were untied. She gave me a hug and I felt her falling into me, pressing herself against my chest for balance, and I inhaled a scent I did not recognize as of yet. It was a scent I would later come to know in college: the syrupy breath of a drunken girl, the not yet ashen smell of a freshly smoked cigarette. At the time, however, this scent was a rich mystery, and I enjoyed it.

I helped her gain her balance, and looked into her eyes for the first time in a long time.

Unfortunately, I saw little there.

Lindy was present, undoubtedly, standing right there before me, but nothing in her countenance attested to this fact. Her eyes, instead, scanned my face benignly, as if considering a child's drawing held up by a magnet on the fridge. She smiled, sure, but I had no idea at what. When I think back about her now, she reminds me of so many other women I would know only briefly in life, only drunkenly, and I suppose this night is the reason I never ventured to know them any longer. Because when I later saw this same look in other women — pitiful, vulnerable, immediately attainable — I knew there would be no future between us.

As for Lindy, she stumbled, caught her balance, and squeezed my arm.

I flexed my biceps like an idiot in love.

"Look at the rock star," she said.

"Who, me?" I smiled and, behind me, I heard someone say, *"Please."*

I turned around to see the girl I'd been playing pool with rolling her eyes at Lindy and waiting for me to take my turn. This gesture seemed impossibly crude, grossly ignorant, but it was just one of many vulgarities the kids in that room offered forth. The guys on the sofas were watching us, too, I realized, and also making fun of Lindy. She was a mess, there was no doubt. In hindsight, I suppose I should have taken this as a sign that I should be escorting her to the bathroom, washing her face with a warm cloth, and caring for her. Instead I wanted only to talk with her, to be with her, and I wanted this desperately. As such, I made numerous mistakes.

I said the first thing that came to mind.

"Where's cool guy?" I asked her. "Where's Matt?"

Lindy screwed up her face like she didn't know who I was talking about. She then twisted her body around to scratch some sort of itch on her back and stumbled forward again. She pushed me against the pool table and spilled red juice on my shirt. She held my arms again and we laughed.

"I know you," she said.

"I know," I smiled. "I know you, too."

"No," she said, and took a low tone. "I mean, I know what you do."

I felt panicked as to what this could mean. Still, I acted coy about it all. I tried to be flirtatious. "You know what I do?" I said.

Lindy nodded.

"What's that?" I asked.

Lindy leaned in close to me and lingered there. She stood on her tiptoes to speak, her face right next to mine. I felt her hot breath in my ear.

"Let's go somewhere," she whispered.

I was unprepared for this request.

"What do you mean?" I asked her.

Lindy looked at me again, not directly, but in the vicinity in which she thought my face ought to be. She then smiled dumbly, a million miles away, and leaned in to whisper again. "I know you want me," she said, and I felt her lips on my neck. "Let's go somewhere."

How can I explain the utter disappointment?

It wasn't so much that Lindy was on to me that made her remark so depressing. The secret, after all, was not well kept. I'd done what I could in that year to let her know of my affection. I'd let the word slip out to friends in random conversations about who we would like to bed down, who deserved the attention of our awkward desires. I'd also dressed like she had and trotted the sidewalk in front of her house like some doomed C student in a teenage love film. I'd sent Mrs. Peggy, her mother, home with my kindest regards. And although she didn't

207

know this, although it's possible she may not have known *any* of this, I'd also spent countless nights perched in a tree outside her house, watching her shadow play opposite the closed white curtains of her bedroom and praying for her to open them.

All I'm saying is this: if there are vibes in this world, I had sent them.

So, it wasn't that she'd busted me.

It was instead the obvious way in which she didn't understand what she'd uncovered.

"Let's go somewhere," she'd said, as if it were as simple as that. "I know you want me," she'd whispered, as if "want" was the same thing as "need."

I did what I could to stall.

It didn't go well.

"No, I don't," I said.

Lindy put her hands on my stomach. She leaned against me as if she was falling asleep.

"Let's you and me go," she said again.

"Lindy," I told her, "I think you might be drunk."

This was the wrong thing to say.

Lindy stood up straight and glared at me. She squinted her eyes as if someone had turned on the lights. She said, "Are you fucking kidding me?"

Lindy then pushed herself away and wheeled toward the other kids in the room. I saw a purple hickey, the shape of a continent, on her neck. She looked furious and petty in this pose, and a blue vein rose in her forehead. She pointed at me. "This guy," she told them. "This guy watches me all the time. You can't trust this motherfucker."

"Lindy," I said. "What are you talking about?"

Lindy glared at me, and I wonder, even now, if she felt she'd finally cleared the air between us. If maybe the *real* reason she hadn't spoken to me in all that time was not only because I'd spilled the beans about her rape, but also because my adoration had become too obvious for her to bear. There's nothing worse, after all, is there, than having to endure a love that you don't return? So maybe she thought outing me might do it, might finally cut me off from her completely, might end whatever admiration I'd held for her for so long. She stood before me after she'd said this, panting, and waiting for my defense.

I didn't get a chance to reply.

In the background, one of the guys sitting on the sofa said, "Go home, you drunk bitch," and the room filled with laughter.

At this, my heart broke for Lindy — it died for her — for the first of two times that night.

Lindy scowled at these guys, a couple of jocks who had long ago written her off as some skank, I suppose, some girl who deserved nothing but scorn, and she threw her cup across the room at them, splashing red juice on the pool table. This gesture had no effect. The guys just laughed more deeply and turned their attention back to the game.

Lindy stomped out of the room.

"Why do you talk to that slut?" one of the guys asked me.

"Don't call her that," I said, and stood there energized, ready to defend her again.

They had no interest in debate.

So, with nothing left to do, I let my mind implode around what had just happened. I'd wanted to run after her, of course, to clear things up. In fact, I'd wanted the whole scene to be played over again. And the truth is, at that moment, when I was sixteen, if I could have done it all over again, I probably would have reshuffled the scene to end with me and Lindy kissing in the backseat of a car, in a bathroom, or maybe wrapped around each other on the very pool table upon which she had pressed me. I wondered angrily why I had let that opportunity slip out of my hands, and couldn't fathom how another would ever appear. So I threw my pool stick onto the table and went into the bathroom, where I locked the door behind me.

I raged in this place.

I threw around inconsequential things like toilet paper rolls and toothbrushes, yet couldn't bring myself to do any real damage. I stood for long minutes in front of the mirror, cursing at my pimpled and drunken face. I spat in the sink like a tough guy might do and recognized little about my own reflection. You fucking sissy, I called myself. You fucking loser. Yet I felt no connection to these words as I said them, no connection to anything at all.

Eventually, this anger waned and I grew hopeful.

After all, she *had* spoken to me, had she not? She had expressed some desire, no matter how drunkenly, how clumsily. Surely that must mean something. I began thinking about the number of guys at that party and why, out of all of them, she had chosen me. Even as a teenager I knew how alcohol was said to let loose your most sunken desires. So maybe there was something behind it all to believe in? This was not outlandish. Alcohol had also given me the confidence to play for her that night, to pick up a stranger's guitar and let fly. This type of stardom was mere fantasy before this party, before the booze, and so maybe her display in the pool room was similar. Perhaps she *had* been watching, all those days, as I walked the sidewalks of Piney Creek Road. Maybe she, too, had just been waiting for the right moment to speak.

Yes, I thought, *all of that.*

I washed my face in the sink. I rinsed out my mouth. I tidied up the place. And when I emerged from the bathroom, the party was over.

A few stragglers still lounged around on the leather recliners, but the only noise I could hear now came from outside, where I later learned a fistfight had broken out over Matt Hawk making out with somebody else's date. So I stumbled through the filthy house, full of adrenaline, and ran into a guy I used to play soccer with.

"Have you seen Lindy?" I asked him, and he laughed.

"Last time I saw her," he said, "she was standing over there, trying to make out with Chris Macaluso."

"What?" I said. "That's impossible."

Chris Macaluso was an average kid. He

sat the bench on the basketball team. I remember an anecdote about his parents not letting him drink Cokes. All this to say that he was nice enough, I guess, but a mere afterthought on the high school landscape. So this was no small blow. Surely my friend's eyes had deceived him. Surely he'd mistaken some other drunken beauty for Lindy. Surely all was not lost.

I did what I could to erase this image from my mind and walked outside to smoke the last crumpled cigarette in the pack I'd bought earlier that night. Here I saw the swimming pool, shimmering and littered with garbage, and at the far end of the pool, I also saw Lindy. She was sprawled across a lawn chair, passed out cold. Nobody else was around.

I figured this was my chance.

I walked over to her and pulled up a seat.

There, with just the two of us, I was finally allowed to study Lindy's body.

Her legs, still muscular and lean from her years of running track, from her former joys on Piney Creek Road, from youth, were strewn to the sides of the chair. Her arms were flung over the rests. She looked as if she had been dropped there from a great distance, and her hair covered most of her face. As I scanned her body I noticed that the hem of her dress was lifted well above her knee, exposing her inner thigh, and I saw in this place the tail end of what looked like a scar.

I checked the area around me to make sure I wasn't being watched, that this wasn't some dubious setup, and it was not. My only company was the Jack Russell terrier, who was now turning in circles on the edge of the diving board, waiting for a party that wouldn't return. So I looked back at Lindy's thigh, the ripe muscle, the soft skin, and, in an act I'm not proud of, I leaned forward and nudged her dress farther to the side with my hand.

It was there I saw a series of razor-thin scars, whiter than her already white skin, which stopped just an inch or so below her black panties. What kind of pain causes a person to do this? I wondered. In what room of her house did it happen? On what day had I seen her walk out her front door with perhaps a small hitch in her step, a thin line of blood on her shorts?

Without thinking, I began to touch the scars gently with the tips of my fingers, and they felt like twine in her skin. They were softer than all else I knew. So I petted them. I counted them, and the number was four. I then began to wonder what these thin scars might taste like, what their texture might do to my tongue, and in a moment of sheer terror I looked up at Lindy. It struck me again that this might be a trap. That soon people would come out of the bushes: my mother, her parents, the cops. It struck me that she could still be awake.

She was not.

Instead I noticed that she must have been passed out for some time now, maybe from the moment she'd left me upstairs. I knew this by the way people had had fun with her, shoving empty bottles and spent cigarette packs in the top of her dress, where they had undoubtedly taken pictures for posterity.

But there was something else, too.

In their fun, someone had written in black marker on Lindy's face. I could see the edges of it beneath her mussed hair and immediately knew this wasn't the good-natured stuff we'd done to one another at sleepovers, where kids drew clown noses or whiskers on the first person to fall asleep. It was nothing as innocent as that. Instead, after I gently brushed her hair from her face, I saw that it was just a simple word, scribbled in all caps across her forehead that read:

FAKE.

Upon seeing this, my love for Lindy multiplied itself in brand-new ways. I felt sorry for her and I felt destroyed by her. I felt angry at whoever did this and guilty that I'd only just now noticed it. I wanted desperately to continue touching her and yet I also wanted to laugh at her, to say something cruel like *Look what you got by not loving me.* Instead I pulled the dress back over her thigh.

I felt ill.

Behind me, I heard a kid crank up his car stereo in the driveway. I heard teenagers laughing and drunk, singing along to the song that I recall as being "Fuck tha Police" by the rap group N.W.A. Soon, Artsy Julie came around the corner and looked at me. She seemed to find nothing strange, nothing meaningful, in the way I hovered over Lindy. She merely relayed to me the fact that our ride had left us and she was going to walk home. She said a neighbor had just come out in their bathrobe and told us they were calling the cops. She said the whole thing was stupid.

"Okay," I said. "I'll catch up with you."

I looked back at Lindy, knowing that if no one else intervened she would be nudged awake when the cops got there, that she would be described in police blotters as "unconscious" and "underage," and so I tried, to no avail, to rub the black marker from her forehead. I licked my thumb and scrubbed at the ink like a parent. I used my nice dress shirt, my tie. Nothing I did could erase it, and nothing I did woke her up. So I lifted Lindy by her shoulders and dragged her behind a large clump of azaleas blooming hot pink at the far corner of the yard.

I laid her softly on the lawn and saw the moon show up on her eyelids, still painted a glittery silver, and as I stood there watching her eyes move frantically beneath them I imagined that she was busy watching the stuff of an entirely different world in some deep and restless dream, and then I went home.

I ran home.

22.

What followed Hannah's death and the Spring Bash was a summer of visitors, the clearing of Bo Kern's name from Lindy's rape, and the arrest and public scandal of the serial killer Jeffrey Dahmer. Also, the heated sound of Lindy's breath on my telephone.

The visitors came mainly in the form of remorseful and well-intentioned family members who, like my sister Rachel, I suppose, sensed some invisible SOS coming from my mother that I was too young to pick up on. When I think back upon it now I can see it, of course, the way it took all of my mom's energy to act happy in my presence, the way she, too, had become more religious and more shy. The way she now drank coffee from a chipped mug with the words "Today is the first day of the rest of your life" on it. But, I didn't appreciate nor even understand it all then. I was just a simple American teen at the time. I was in love with an unlovable girl.

The visitors to my house were mainly cousins, aunts, and uncles, and old friends of the family who came over in shifts to have long grave talks with my mother in the den. They would often stay the night, the weekend, some part of them glad, at the least, to be giving my mother something to do. My father had been generous, or court-ordered, depending who you ask, by leaving us the house and paying alimony and tuition, et cetera, and so my mother had gotten a part-time job selling purses at a department store just to keep busy after the divorce, but she quit this job when Hannah died. She now woke up only to look forward to going back to bed, it seemed, graciously providing me with meals in the interim, and spent her afternoons sitting alone in odd rooms of our house as if trying them out. Still, she never complained to me. She never asked for my help.

Yet I would be reminded of my mother's sadness, her poor state, when the women who visited would call me to their sides and touch my shoulders, compliment me, and tell my mother how handsome I was becoming. Or when the men who accompanied these women would sit next to me on the sofa, watch some television, and finally say what seemed to take an enormous amount of courage for them to utter. Something like, "She was a special girl, your sister."

Or like when my grandfather, my mother's father, once said to me, "It's not natural, you know, burying a child. It makes me worry." This was a man who had lost his own wife, my grandmother, to a massive stroke when I was only a toddler. This was a man who'd seen half his squad die in World War II and tattooed their first names on his bicep. "What you need to understand," he told me, "is that your mother really needs you now."

"I know," I said.

But what was I to do? Wash the dishes? Mow the lawn?

There was no putting back what had been taken, and it was perhaps only this specific knowledge that the increased bustle in my house afforded me. Because, more than anything, what these people made clear was that the tragedy my mother was suffering through was unattainable and unknowable to me, no matter my close proximity to it. It was something not even the visitors could fathom, they told me — the loss of a child — and they were parents themselves. And, ultimately, this sense of futility made me feel more separate from my mother than close to her.

So, I thought, what chance did I have to fix her?

However, this summer was not entirely without promise or excitement. I found myself forever affected by my uncle Barry, for instance, my mother's brother, who I had seen maybe once before in my life. He showed up at our door unannounced one hot Friday with a beat-up suitcase and Dodge Charger and said he only planned to stay for the weekend. Yet in the month that he lived with us, confusing our quiet house with his frequent laughter, with the classic-rock albums he played in our living room, I grew up in complicated ways.

This was the stretch of time from June to July, when the heat of Louisiana bears down on all living things, and I had not spoken to Lindy since the dance back in April. Some part of me hoped she would call me, would thank me for not taking advantage of her, and would confess that it wasn't just drunk talk that made her want me that night. I was afraid that if I approached her, however, I would find out the opposite of all this was true. I therefore spent my days inside mainly, playing Super Mario Brothers and strumming my electric guitar with the amplifier turned off. And when darkness came I spent the evenings in my sister Rachel's room watching shows like *Blossom* and *Full House* on a small television she'd brought home from Lafayette.

She was now only watching things with "good Christian values," she said, and so whenever she'd leave the room, I'd switch her small television over to trashy shows like *Married with Children* or *Geraldo* just to annoy her. I suppose I wanted her to worry about me at this time, to pray for me. If not that, I figured, what else would we talk about?

Hannah was not an option. We talked enough about her without words. She was what Rachel dropping out of school to live in her old room said, what my sitting beside her watching TV said. What our mother shuffling past us down the hall said, and what the quiet closing of her bedroom door said. That was enough conversation for both of us.

Yet we had plenty to talk about when my uncle Barry arrived, and, in this way, he was a welcome distraction. In his early forties at the time, my uncle Barry was mysterious to me, as were his actions in general. He was a handsome man, as I remember him now, but he did not comport himself in this way.

He kept a blond stubble on his chin, had an unkempt thatch of the same color hair on his head, and always looked to me as if he had just stepped in from the rain, like the wind was blowing where he had been. I remember him wearing nothing but khaki shirts and blue jeans, like the perfect mix between a big-game hunter and an out-of-work carpenter, and I also remember that he carried with him an old Duncan yo-yo. It was a sturdy yellow thing that he often took out of his pocket to care for like ancient gentlemen did their pocket watches. This only added to the mystery.

Yet all I knew for sure was that he'd married a woman a few years prior that none of our family knew very well. She'd come into his life and assumed control, my mother said, in the way a business manager does when trouble arises. They'd moved out to Utah, Nevada, and then Arizona, following her work as an assistant professor of drama. And since Barry had never been one to hold down a job himself, this type of life suited him. In fact, he seemed agreeable to nearly any situation.

When we showed him the small room in our house where he would be staying, for instance, my father's old study with a pull-out couch, he kicked up his feet and shut his eyes and said, "When I close my eyes, it's like I'm at the Windsor Court." Or when my mother initially asked him why Sharon, his wife, hadn't come along, he just smiled and said, "Now, Kit-Kat [his name for my mom], there'll be plenty of time for that later." Yet I never heard him bring it up again. He also, as far as I could tell, didn't bring up Hannah's death. There may have been conversations about Hannah that I wasn't privy to, of course, heartfelt and adult stuff that passed between him and my mother, but somehow I doubt it. Just his presence alone was his condolence, it seemed, as if to say, "Hey, sis, you know it's bad if I'm here."

He did a lot for me, though, during this time, and maybe that was his mission all along. I've never asked my mother about this, if maybe she'd secretly called him to duty the way she'd done my father the year prior, and I won't. But he quickly became a friend of mine that hot summer, when I'd drifted away from so many others and still wasn't speaking to Lindy, the one I thought of most often.

From the moment my uncle Barry walked in the door, I felt the two of us to be in on a secret together. There was something about his face, I suppose, his enormously blank and unassuming smile, that attracted me. He made me feel unafraid of the world and, in this feeling, let me realize how afraid of the world I truly was. When my mother was tense and unapproachable, for example, he'd do things like joke with her that he and I were stepping out for cold beers when all we'd really do was sit on the front porch and talk. I'd watch him unfurl his Duncan and let it spin an inch above the ground without ever pulling it up and I felt older around him, without feeling the discomfort that I did around other men of his age, like my father. When I later told my mother about this, after he'd left and I complained to her that I wished that he'd stayed, she said this was likely because Barry himself had never grown up, that he was still probably about my age in his mind.

Her evidence to this effect went unspoken, unexplained, but I saw it in the way she rolled her eyes whenever I recounted an anecdote of his, like the time he ran a friend's car into a ditch in El Paso and then, trying to pull it out, crashed a forklift on top of it. Or the time he said a parakeet followed him around for a year, perching on his shoulder and being protective of him for no discernible reason. Or the winter he spent in Alaska, where he said the dogs were

225

all beautiful and the women all rabid. These were just a few of his improbable stories, mind you, yet my mother acted unimpressed by it all.

Still, my uncle Barry had lived what seemed to me this enormous and unpredictable life, the exact opposite of what a teenager feels, and I came to idolize him. And although my mother told me to take everything he said with a grain of salt, I never doubted his tales the way I did those of people like Tyler Bannister or Jason Landry or even my own father, really, because he was not trying to be funny or cruel or impressive when he told them. Instead he recounted these stories as if they were still as surprising to him as the day they had happened. "I couldn't believe it, either," he'd say, "but there I was."

Yet there were some days on the porch when a car would pull into our driveway and Uncle Barry would leave me to go talk with the man that drove it. Often for only a minute or two, sometimes laughing, other times exchanging what appeared to me to be only a handshake, and other times banging his fist against the car as if in pain. When I asked him about this, he shrugged the visit off as being that of an old friend, somebody telling him about a possible job.

And since Barry was a handyman of sorts, he often disappeared for days, working on "construction jags," as he called them, because the suburbs of Baton Rouge were booming back then. I spent those days without him feeling especially lost and confused, like the only sane man in a house full of crying women. What made this all worse was that when Barry returned from these jobs he would always act more philosophical and resigned. A woman would drop him off in our driveway, never coming inside the house, and I'd ask him who she was. "Who, her?" he'd say. "That was mistake number three hundred and eighty-four."

I laughed at this until I realized that the next time it was mistake number three hundred and eighty-five, then eighty-six, and so forth, and I got the feeling this was an accurate count. And during these times our jovial talks on the porch would stray from the visible things around us to questions that had no obvious origin or answer. He would sit for long minutes, crickets calling out in the distance, and utter what seemed to me to be impossible truths. One, I remember, about sleep and love.

"Do you like to sleep?" he asked me. "I mean, do you like to just lie in bed all day?

Maybe spend a whole weekend just sleeping?"

"Not really," I said. "I mean, I don't think so."

"Me neither," he said. "So, here's the deal: what you need to do is get you a woman who loves to do that. Because if you like to sleep all day and so does she, then y'all won't ever get anything done. But what's worse is if neither of you like to sleep, if both of you can't stand lying around idle."

"Then what?" I asked him.

"Then you're never in bed at the same time," he said. "Then you end up like me."

I had no idea what he meant by this, as being like him appeared to me a wonderful possibility. Still, at that moment he seemed to be working out some problem in his head that had nothing to do with me or my mother or Piney Creek Road, and he looked sad. So, I said naïve things. I tried to be encouraging.

"I'm sure it's different for different people," I told him. "I mean, I'm sure sometimes everything works out all right."

"Nope," he said. "That's the thing. Love is always the same for everybody."

This, you must understand, was the opposite of all that I'd heard. I'd watched movies where the goodhearted got together.

I wrote love poems to a girl who wouldn't speak to me. I believed, without sarcasm, in soul mates. I was a private-school kid in America, by God, and felt that nothing was off-limits to me if I tried. True love and happy marriage and healthy children were inevitable.

"Love's the same for everybody?" I said. "That's depressing."

He sat around thinking about this.

"I think you might have misread me," he said. "Let's put it this way: are you in love with a girl right now?"

I smiled, or maybe I grimaced, and this gave it away.

"Okay," he said. "All I'm saying is this: that girl you're in love with right now, you're *always* going to be in love with her. In some way or another. Her or someone else just like her. Love never changes. You might be fifty years old and find yourself doing the craziest things for a woman who you think is nothing like that first one, but she is. There will always be some connection, I promise. Love *never* changes. So the trick is to pick a good one to start with. If you do that, then there's nothing depressing about it."

I leaned over in my chair and thought about this. I put my elbows on my knees like an old man on a fishing pier.

"But what if you *don't* pick a good one?" I asked. "What if the person you base all your loves on is the wrong one?"

"Well, then," he said, "you end up being what they call the vast majority."

I looked at the house across the street and two doors down from us and didn't say anything for a while. My uncle handed me his old Duncan yo-yo.

"Go ahead, man," he said. "Talk about her. I'm listening."

23.

It is easy to gloss over agony.

They say this happens with women and childbirth, when they experience pain off the charts. Ask them how it feels during the process and you'll get daggerlike stares, answers in a sailor's vocabulary. Ask them a few months later, when they are holding the child, or after they've put him or her to bed, and they'll say, "I remember it being bad, but not *too* bad." Then give them a second, wait for a smile.

This is not the only example.

Even when we talk about youthful summers and strange uncles and front porches, it's easy to not recount the many hours we spent furious. In my case, I'd written Lindy a flurry of passionate and apologetic letters, never mailed. I'd tried to cut my own thighs with a Swiss Army knife but gained neither pleasure nor scars from the experience. I'd dialed up teen help hotlines in the middle of the night that we'd been given by guest lecturers at my school. "What is your emergency?" they'd ask me. "I don't know," I'd say. "Do I have to have an emergency?" and they'd be quiet until I hung up. I did things like push-ups when I couldn't sleep. I thought, constantly, of Lindy.

Yet when I found myself asked to actually speak of her I realized how long it had been since I had. My uncle Barry was looking for a simple description, I'm sure, maybe just a name and a face, but the task seemed impossible to me. And if it had been my mother or sister who'd asked me to talk about Lindy, I would have ignored them. But with Barry, a person who didn't know her history, our history, and who didn't know that to speak of her was to speak of a before and after, of two lives wrapped into one, I felt I might as well tell the truth.

"There's this girl," I told him. "And when I look at her, I don't know what to do."

Barry smiled as if he understood, as if he'd known this exact feeling himself. He leaned forward in his chair. "Well," he asked me, "what do you *want* to do when you see her? Let me guess: cook her a steak? Protect her from danger? Rip off her bra?"

"I don't know," I said. "All of those things, I guess. But I think what I'd really like is to not have to do anything. I'd like to just kind of stand there and look at her, maybe, watch her laugh. Maybe she could tell me something funny."

"Okay," Barry said. "Then what? I mean, that's just a start. What comes after that?"

"I don't know," I told him. "Then maybe she could tell me something sad."

"Ouch," he said. "You've got it bad."

"She never talks to me," I said.

Evening soon fell on the porch that night, and we first knew this by the way we began to scratch at our ankles, wave at mosquitoes buzzing our ears. Next door to us, we saw the Stillers' floodlights click on automatically. We heard a neighbor pull their trash out to the curb. Finally, the sky began to purple.

"Listen," Barry said. "I wish I was even half as smart as you when I was your age. Back then I thought the way to pick up girls was to rev a car engine and stuff a sock in my jeans."

"Does that work?" I asked him. "I'm willing to try anything."

"Yeah." He smiled. "It works, but not in the way you want it to. It's like turning on a bug zapper. You get a lot of action, but all you're zapping is bugs."

I unfurled the Duncan and let it spin. Its

bottom ticked the concrete slab of our porch.

"When it comes to women," he told me, "what you want to do is just like you're doing. When you get a chance to talk to this girl, just be there and listen. Don't believe all that 'you gotta be tough' or 'you gotta be sensitive' shit. Just let the girl think whatever *she* wants to think. If you do that, then the good ones will see something good in you and the bad ones will see something bad. See what I mean? You're a blank canvas. Let them do the painting. Just don't go prancing around like some phony. It's like my buddy Carl. He wears this toupee and it looks all right. But when he picks up a girl and she likes him, he's miserable."

Barry looked off in the distance like he was thinking fondly about Carl, some friend of his from where? What state? What life? I didn't know.

"Why?" I asked him. "If Carl's getting all the girls, then why is he miserable?"

"Because," he said, "he knows one day she's going to want to hop in the shower with him. What's he supposed to say to that? There's not a woman on Earth who respects a man that won't take a shower with her."

"Really?" I asked.

"I think we're getting ahead of ourselves,"

234

he said. "Pull up that Duncan."

So I did, and then I spun it again.

"Did it always work out for you that way?" I asked him. "I mean, just letting them see what they wanted to see?"

My uncle Barry sat up in his chair and checked his watch. He scratched his chin. I think now that he was likely wondering what time it was in Arizona, a few zones over, and what his wife may have been doing at that hour, but I didn't consider it then. "No," he told me. "It doesn't always work out that way, because *we're* painters, too. I mean, we can be wrong about them like they can be wrong about us. I guess that's what complicates it. We're not perfect, either."

This comment made sense to me, yet I'd no clue how to use it to my advantage. It ultimately sounded like all the other advice about love sounded to me in my teenage years, like it was pointed in some different direction or meant for someone else. *Just be yourself,* they all said. Yet there I was, *myself,* and I was miserable.

"So," I said, "I guess all you're saying is that I should be careful."

"Nah," he said. "You're going to love who you love. Being careful won't solve anything."

And it was after this that we saw a strange thing.

Across the street and two doors down, Mr. Simpson, Lindy's father, stumbled from his driveway and onto the Kerns' front lawn. The sun was still low in the west and gave everything an ominous glow, the last moment of clarity before dark, and there was no mistaking that Mr. Simpson was drunk. His feet crossed before him as he walked and his arms looked loose in their sockets. His head hung heavy. We heard him yell Bo Kern's name.

I knew this meant trouble.

When no answer came, Mr. Simpson picked a small piece of loose concrete off the sidewalk and threw it through the Kerns' dining room window. My uncle Barry stood up from his chair. "Stay here," he said. But I didn't.

Instead I followed him at a trot up the street, where we saw Bo Kern and his father barging out of their house, examining the damage, and then turning to Mr. Simpson. The dynamics of the whole affair were so abnormal for Piney Creek Road that I didn't understand a bit of it. All I remember is that Mr. Simpson looked nothing like the man I'd seen happily drinking Kool-Aid on his front porch those years before, the one

I'd seen tightening up the seat on Lindy's bicycle and giving her a good-bye kiss before her daily trip to the track. The man I watched now was anguished and he cursed venomously at Bo and his father, slurring his words past the point of comprehension. Still, we all knew the subject was Lindy.

As it turned out, Mr. Simpson had never gotten over his suspicions about Bo, despite the number of times Bo had been questioned, and, for some reason, on this night in 1991, two summers after the crime, he had made up his mind to deal with it. He was awful and raging and yelled primarily at Mr. Kern as if Bo wasn't there. "Your boy's going to prison," he spat. "I'm telling you right now, I aim to kill him."

Mr. Kern stood in a crooked manner. He was a person we rarely saw in places other than Bo's football games, and I'd never even heard his voice before. All I knew was that his story was a sad one, as he'd crushed his hip in a fall at work years earlier. And when he walked in front of his son on that night, the limp from his work accident was obvious. He told Bo to stay calm and spoke deliberately, as if he was in control, as if the last thing any of us wanted him to do was raise his voice.

"Dan," he told Mr. Simpson. "This is a

grown man you're talking about. And he's sober and you're drunk. So I suggest you go back to your house before the whiskey says something you might regret. We can all talk like men in the morning."

Behind him, Bo Kern was turning in circles. He had the body of a tree trunk, and the brain. He put a wad of Skoal in his cheek. "Goddamn, Simpson!" he yelled. "We've been through all this a million times! I wasn't even home when that happened!"

Still, Mr. Simpson carried on as if he was alone in the world, and I suppose he was.

He pointed at Bo. "That boy is a felon!" he said.

Mr. Kern shook his head and started back to his house. "All right, Dan," he said. "Go ahead and tell him that to his face."

So Mr. Simpson did, and it was only a matter of seconds before Bo Kern knocked him to the ground. He cracked him twice, that I saw, with his fists, and Mr. Simpson was reduced to a puddle on the lawn. Bo Kern stood up, crazed. He spat black tobacco on the grass as a way of controlling himself. What he could have done to Lindy's father that day, my God. What his strength could have done to any of us there in the neighborhood. I'm sure he realized it.

He kicked at the grass and looked over at

my uncle Barry and me. "She ain't even got no titties!" he told us. "What would I want her for, anyway?"

And with this simple statement, as odd as it seems, Bo Kern's name was cleared from Lindy's rape. The obvious sense it made, coming from Bo, and the dumb earnestness with which he said it made all of us, probably even Mr. Simpson included, finally believe him. I never heard anyone mention him and Lindy again.

After Bo left, slamming the door behind him, my uncle Barry and I ran up to Mr. Simpson. He was sobbing on the lawn. I'd never seen a thing like this, a grown man crying, not even at Hannah's funeral, where my father sat as still as the furniture. There was only one other time, I suppose, decades later, when I helped a buddy take his dog to the vet to be put to sleep. We sat in the car for a good half hour after they said their good-byes, the man and his dog, his throat clutching and jerking with grief. On the lawn that night, Mr. Simpson did the same.

"She's my daughter," he cried to us. "She's just a kid. What am I supposed to do?"

We had no answer for him.

The three of us squatted there for a while, my uncle and Mr. Simpson complete strangers, until we heard the low whine of the mosquito-abatement truck coming through the neighborhood, spraying chemicals from the back of its bed. I looked up and saw the Simpson women, Lindy and Mrs. Peggy, watching us from separate rooms of their two-story house. My uncle Barry noticed them, too, and when he saw that I was smiling at Lindy, he shook his head for me to stop. When I glanced back, Lindy had closed her curtains.

So, we helped Mr. Simpson to his feet. We dusted him off.

My uncle Barry looked upset about all of this mess, like he knew the whole story about Lindy's rape and her father's decline, though I don't believe that he did. Still, that was the thing about Barry. You just got the feeling that whatever was out there in the world, no matter how great, no matter how awful, he had seen it. I admired this about him.

"Go on inside," he told Mr. Simpson. "Have one last drink but no more, and get to bed. You can't fix it all tonight."

Mr. Simpson stared at the two of us, his lips and nose already swollen, and he nodded. Then my uncle Barry tapped me hard on the shoulder and we set off across the street. We passed right in front of the mosquito-abatement truck and covered our mouths with our shirts. We waved at the driver.

When we got to the porch, I said, "Holy shit."

I'd never seen anything so exciting as that.

My uncle Barry took me by the shoulders. His voice was urgent and sincere.

"I want you to listen to me," he said. "I know that girl over there makes you want to be in love and get married and be a grown-up, but what you saw just now, that's what being a grown-up is. That man out there crying on his lawn. So you just do what I told you and be yourself. I'm serious. Don't wish any time away."

"Okay," I said. "I won't."

"Let's not mention this to your mom, either," he said. "She's got enough to do without worrying about the neighbors. Now, come on," he said, "let's get in the house before we're both gassed."

Once inside, my uncle Barry and I slunk off to different spaces as if it were midnight, though it was barely suppertime. After we eventually ate, saying nothing to each other while my sister Rachel droned on about some new organ they had gotten at church, I went to my room and got in bed. I slept poorly, thinking about that choking sound

Mr. Simpson had been making, crying like a man does, and I had a dream that night that would reoccur many more times in my life, one where I am driving a car with no steering wheel but rather a large set of strings coming out of the dashboard. I feel the tires sliding all over the road in this dream, sending me in and out of oncoming traffic, and the only method of navigation available to me is a tangled mess of twine in my lap. I pull one string and the radio comes on. Another string and the wipers wave. I push on pedals that have no effect. And in the dream that night, the first dream, my uncle Barry sat beside me in the car but said nothing. He looked as if he thought I was doing a perfectly fine job of driving, as if he trusted me with his own life, and this made me feel worse. And as the years have gone by, the passengers sitting beside me in this nightmare have changed, but never my total surprise at the strange problem I've inherited, and never my inability to solve it.

When I woke up the following day, my uncle Barry was gone.

For some reason, I wasn't surprised.

I could tell he'd been shaken by what he'd seen in Mr. Simpson's eyes the night prior, but I hadn't the tools to assemble the connection between the men then. It wasn't until a week had passed and I'd bothered my mother so much about Barry's departure that she finally told me some things I didn't know. The first was about the man who used to pull up in our driveway to talk to him about work. And what she told me was that Uncle Barry's wife, Sharon, had been cheating on him, and that she'd gotten pregnant from some other guy, a professor in her new department in Arizona. And so the man Barry was talking to in our driveway was a liaison for a private investigator in Arizona, my mom said, who Barry had hired to give him all the details of what she was doing while he was away. The whole scenario seemed improbable to me, and so weak-minded of my uncle who I adored that I was upset with my mother for even suggesting it. I didn't believe her.

"How did he have the money to pay for all that?" I asked her. "Isn't that expensive?"

"He didn't have the money," she said. "That's why he left. That's why Barry is always leaving."

"But that doesn't even make sense," I said. "Why would he want to know the details if he already knew she was cheating on him? That just sounds like torture."

"It's love, honey," my mom said. "It's

complicated."

"That's stupid," I said.

"It is," she said.

My mother was telling the truth. I've yet to meet a person who didn't become a stranger to themselves in love, at one time or another. And since I often saw kindness in my uncle Barry, since I saw something close to a boy like me in his eyes, I knew that he was likely as confused by his actions as I was. The random women who brought him home, the awful spying, I've no doubt that he is still surprised that these were choices he made, that he was even the least bit involved in these things. Like he always told me:

"I couldn't believe it, either. But there I was."

I've yet to see him again.

All this to say that what my uncle Barry displayed for me that summer was just how strange and complicated adults are. As a kid you assume you know them because you see them often, and because they care for you. But for every adult person you look up to in life there is trailing behind them an invisible chain gang of ghosts, all of which, as a child, you are generously spared from meeting.

I know now, however, that these ghosts

exist, and that other adults can see them. The lost loves, the hurt friends, the dead: they follow their owner forever. Perhaps this is why we feel so crowded around those people who we know have had hard times. Perhaps this is why we find so little to say. We suffer an odd brand of stage fright, I think, before all those dreadful eyes. And maybe that's what my uncle had noticed about Mr. Simpson on the lawn that night of the fight. Maybe in my eyes, a child's eyes, it was just the three of us squatting in the grass. But, to those two men, the lawn appeared to be full of bodies, full of the people they'd made mistakes with in life now tethered to them and ill-rested and serving no purpose but to remind them of the one awful thing: that life is made up, ever increasingly, of what you cannot change. One man's daughter. Another man's wife. The song plays on.

Yet all I know for sure is that two days after the fight on the lawn, our telephone rang.

It was Lindy.

24.

This was late July of 1991 and although he'd left, my uncle Barry's scent was still in the house. Our phone had been ringing so often from people looking for him — creditors, his wife, her new man — that I'd come to ignore it. Then, after a particular ring, my mother called me into the kitchen. She held the phone to her shoulder. "It's Lindy," she whispered, and the look in her eyes was so hopeful. "Are you two talking again?"

"I'll pick it up in my room," I said.

Little need to explain the panic that shot through me.

The year Lindy and I had spent not talking to each other felt insignificant compared to the concentrated silence that followed our interaction after the dance that spring. Who were we now, I wondered, since she'd whispered something seductive in my ear? How much did she really know about me, about my feelings? Was that a night she even remembered? Or was that finally the real Lindy I had spoken to at Melinda's party, the one who'd sought me out and pulled me close?

I had no idea, and so I agonized over the event in a manner so complete that I'd begun to wonder if it had ever really happened. Had I felt her hot breath on my cheek? Had I held her up from falling? Had I touched the soft scars on her thighs? Had I carried her? Hidden her? Saved her? Understood her? The opposite of this seemed more likely to me now, as if I'd never known Lindy Simpson at all. I wondered, for a moment, if I would even recognize her voice.

I picked up the phone in my room and waited until my mother hung up. Then I stood there with the receiver in my hand, looking at myself in a full-length mirror. I saw a skinny thing in ragged shorts and a T-shirt. I looked nervous and unprepared. I smiled as if Lindy might see me. On the other end of the line, I heard music playing low in the background.

"Hello?" I said.

A long silence passed between us.

"Yeah," Lindy said. "So, I'm supposed to apologize about my dad."

Although I recognized her voice immediately, although I likely could have recited nearly everything she'd said to me in life, I had no clear idea of what she was talking about at that moment.

"Apologize?" I asked. "For what?"

I could hear her flipping through radio stations. I imagined her rolling her eyes.

"I don't know," she said. "For my dad being pathetic, I guess. For the other night with the Kerns. My mom made me call. I think she's going to leave him."

"Shit," I said. "Your poor mother."

Lindy laughed when I said this, a surprising sound I hadn't heard in years. It must have surprised her, too, as she cut it off like a switch.

"What?" I said. "Why did you laugh?"

"Nothing," she said. "I'd just forgotten what a fucking weirdo you are."

"I'm weird?" I asked her.

I thought this might be a good thing.

After all, this is what I'd been going for. This is why I wore black T-shirts and ghoulish jewelry and shaved the sides of my head. This is why my bangs hung over my eyes. This is why I was likely unattractive to all but one particular type of girl, one with issues, one with problems.

I smiled. "What do you mean I'm weird?"

"You sound like an old grandma," she

said. "*Your poor mother.* Who says shit like that?"

This was not the weird I wanted.

"An old grandma?" I asked. "What did you expect me to say?"

"For starters, idiot, you don't have to act all sad. It's not like *your* parents are splitting up."

"My parents already split up," I said.

"Oh, yeah," she said. "Still."

And then nothing.

I waited for Lindy to say something more, but instead she turned up the music on the radio. The song she'd settled on was heavy and growling, and I was humiliated not to know it. If only I could tag the opening bars. If only I could sing along. That would be something. I expected Lindy to turn it back down so we could talk, but she didn't.

"Still what?" I said, and thought I heard her voice. "Did you say something?"

On the radio, the song went into its chorus. It was all sloppy chords and high screaming, and Lindy spoke to me over the blare. "Yeah," she said. "I said you're not supposed to be all concerned about my mom. You're supposed to be upset because it means we might be moving."

I froze at the words.

"Are you serious?" I asked.

"No," Lindy said. "It's all an elaborate joke made up just for you. We spent months on it."

She was being sarcastic and making fun of me, but I still thought quickly about grabbing that moment to spill my whole heart, about apologizing for all I had done to her, about letting her secret out and denying her at the party, and maybe even about loving her since I was eleven years old. Then I recalled what my uncle Barry had said to me about just *listening* to her whenever I got the chance to, just being there for her, so I did.

I stood tall and mute. I waited for her life to open up to me.

"Look," Lindy said, "I was supposed to call and tell you that, and I did, okay? I'll talk to you later."

And that was it. She hung up.

I walked to my window, the phone still at my ear, and stood there. Lindy's house had green shutters. Someone had hung a rug over the rail of the front porch. The blinds were all drawn. I leaned my head against the glass.

"Lindy," I said. "What song was that you were listening to?"

The line went dead.

I spent the next hour in my room devastated.

I'd no idea how to conjure a Piney Creek Road without Lindy and therefore worked so hard at discrediting the notion of her moving that I became positive I'd misheard her, or that maybe everything would be okay between Mr. and Mrs. Simpson, and I promptly began to imagine ways I could make this happen. I could send flowers to the house for Mrs. Peggy. I could type love letters and sign them *Your Husband.* I could sneak into their home and steal the booze from their cabinets. Or, maybe I could just burn the Kerns' house to the ground, make them leave the area to clear up Mr. Simpson's mind. What was that thing that Superman did, where he spun the Earth backward to go back in time? Or what if Lindy could just stay with us if her parents moved away? This was not such a crazy idea. She would be a senior this year. No need to uproot her now. There are sometimes complicated issues with credits transferring, with nitpicky technical stuff. What a shame that would be if she had to repeat a year due to a preventable technicality. I hate to even think of it, the poor girl. Of course, we'd be happy to take her in. Yes, yes, I decided. It's all settled, then.

This thought excited me to such a degree that I began to imagine Lindy walking into my room on accident, wearing an oversized T-shirt and panties, having just woken up on some aimless weekend morning. I stood in front of my bedroom mirror and assumed several poses that I imagined she might like to surprise me in. I took off my shirt and flexed my pale stomach, trying to look sexy. I hooked my thumb into the top of my shorts and pulled down the waistband. *Oh, Lindy,* I said. *I didn't see you standing there. Sure, come on in. It's no problem. Just close the door behind you. Yes, of course.*

You can lock it.

When I finally emerged from my room I was ecstatic with fantasy. I saw my mom and Rachel folding clothes in the den and thought my mother also looked happier than I had seen her since before Hannah's death, humming a bit to herself as Rachel spoke. I wondered if she was starting to feel better, or if maybe my uncle Barry's departure had finally allowed her to relax, and I tried to sneak past the two of them, still flush from my phone call.

"What are you grinning about?" Rachel asked me.

My mother looked up at me and smiled.

"Did you have a nice chat with Lindy?"

she asked. "I'm so glad to know you kids are talking again. She is such a sweet girl. She's had such a hard time."

For one second I considered answering my mom honestly, telling her first about the fight on the lawn, and then about what Lindy had said about her parents' troubles and possible split. I realized, though, that this news would do nothing but sadden my mother, not only because her good friend was perhaps losing her husband, but also because this meant that the reason Lindy had called was *not* to make peace with me, not to be close to me again.

This was important.

If Lindy and I were friends, if we were close, if it looked like our relationship was anything more than a one-way street, my mother would not have to worry about what she had seen in my lockbox. It all made sense to me then. Even though we never spoke explicitly about the rape anymore, and even though she never directly accused me of it, the hopeful look I had seen in my mother's eyes when Lindy called had proved only one thing: she still hadn't made up her mind about me.

My name had yet to be cleared.

It then broke over me how hard that span of silence between Lindy and I must have been for my mother, and it made me ashamed. Even when I think of this now, it depresses me. How many hours had she worried about things she didn't need to? How much pain had I caused her when she still had my father to deal with? When she still had Hannah to mourn? When she still had so much life left to live without either of them?

I couldn't bear to think of it.

I still can't.

So, "Yeah," I told her. "We had a good chat."

"Good," my mom said, and winked.

Behind her, Rachel lifted up a pair of my ratty jeans. "Why do you dress like such a thug?" she asked me. "Are you trying to look like a skater or something? Do you even own a skateboard?"

"I don't know, Rachel," I said. "Are you trying to look like a lumberjack?"

This comment didn't come out of nowhere.

Rachel had changed since Hannah's death, in more complicated ways than I understood at the time. Her increasing preoccupation with Jesus and prayer made sense to me, but not the way this had aged her from a decent-looking coed into a frumpy thing that wore sweatpants and flannel shirts. I suppose that Rachel felt as if caring about her physical appearance suggested she was not thinking about the right things in the wake of our tragedy, not asking the right questions, not facing the truth.

She may have been right. She has always been a good person.

"He's not a skater," my mom said. "He's a rocker. A guitar-playing rocker. Isn't that right, honey?" My mother was being kind, but I was immediately annoyed. Parents have that special skill of making the truth, no matter how benign, an embarrassing thing. We all know this.

"That's not what I am," I said.

"Well, what are you, then?"

"I don't know," I said.

"I know what he is," Rachel said, and then mumbled under her breath, "He's a sinner."

"Rachel!" my mom said.

"What?" Rachel said. "We're *all* sinners, Mom. We all could do better."

And with that, my mother deflated right in front of us. She looked immediately sad and exhausted, and although we all knew Rachel hadn't meant to upset her, it didn't matter. In those days, my mom was always one memory away from being devastated, one conversational turn from a brutal remorse. I believe she might still be this way.

I believe everyone might.

Rachel said, "Okay, Mom. I'm sorry," and continued folding my jeans.

I then walked past them both and into the kitchen, where I felt genuinely starving for some reason, all full of energy and strange hope. I dug around in the pantry, searching for anything to eat, and had designs on becoming a healthier person in life, working out at the gym, and maybe even looking buff the next time Lindy saw me. I could spend the rest of the summer training, I figured. I could convince Lindy to start running again like she used to, this time with me, where we would stop to rest on the track at our school. Where I could pull off my shirt because of the heat and be proud when Lindy stole glances at me, or when she leaned into me jokingly, at first, and then placed her hand on my chest, on my stomach, on my thighs.

Why not? I had just heard her voice on the phone.

She had dialed my number. She had thought of me.

She had said, "I'll talk to you later."

Anything was possible.

So, I made a double-decker sandwich and sliced up a cucumber. I walked back to my room with the plate stacked high and a bag of chips between my teeth. As I passed through the den, my mother was quietly organizing the laundry she had folded, her face resigned and grief-stricken. Rachel was quiet.

When I got to my room, I heard my mother say: "I don't care how you kids dress, Rachel. To me, you'll always be angels."

25.

I was no angel.

Yet in the summer of 1991 it became easy for mothers and fathers to feel blessed by their children. All over America, parents looked at their kids for a minute longer than they had just that spring. They forgave them of minor transgressions. They stole moments to hug them tight in the grocery store, at the swimming pool, to study their profiles and feel proud. The reason for this was simple. On July 22 of that year, every mother and father learned of a place they hadn't considered before, a small dot in the northern part of our country known as Apartment 213, where dwelled the rapist, serial killer, child molester, cannibal, and necrophiliac named Jeffrey Dahmer, a man who was somebody's child.

A little perspective:

On the night of Dahmer's arrest in late July, while I likely sat atop my comfortable bed in my enormous suburban home scribbling a list of pros and cons about calling Lindy back — cons: she won't answer; pros: she *will* answer — an African American male named Tracy Edwards ran terrified through the streets of Milwaukee, Wisconsin. Earlier that night, Tracy had accepted an invitation from an articulate blond man who was interested in taking pictures of him. The man had been generous with Tracy all evening, buying him drinks and complimenting his physique. They flirted in a manner that made Tracy feel good. And even in the car that night, on his way to this man's apartment, Tracy Edwards likely felt that this was something he deserved, the simple excitement of another person's body, of his touch, of a stranger's mouth pressed against his own.

However, by the time I had decided to call it quits in Woodland Hills, to wait perhaps one more day before gathering enough courage to speak to a girl I had known my whole life, Tracy Edwards was sprinting through the streets of another neighborhood, one thousand miles north of me, with two swollen hands; one from being handcuffed and the other from punching that same blond man who, minutes before, had swung at him with a butcher knife. He waved frantically at passing cars. He called out for help. And since Tracy Edwards was a black man in a rough part of Milwaukee — one with a handcuff on his wrist, no less — he drew the specific attention of two police officers on their patrol. They got out of the car and ordered Tracy Edwards to the ground. They steadied their pistols and radioed dispatch. They thought he might be a prisoner escaped.

"You have no idea," Tracy told them. "You have no fucking idea."

And they didn't.

It was only by following procedure that they allowed the blubbering Tracy Edwards to lead them back to Apartment 213, where they found the well-spoken blond man he had described to them, living in a place that smelled of rotting meat. As Tracy pressed himself to the wall and shivered, the articulate blond man calmly explained to the officers that he and Tracy had been drinking and were in the midst of a lovers' quarrel. He then graciously offered to go to his bedroom and retrieve the keys to the cuffs they'd been playing with. And, by casually following him to this place, one police officer noticed strange pictures on the walls: photos of naked men, dozens of them, both before and after they had skin.

He reached for his gun.

In the kitchen, his partner yelled out, "There's a goddamned head in the fridge!"

Our country was never the same.

Don't get me wrong. At sixteen, I wasn't saddened by any of this. Even though I had come to know a thing or two about death myself, my heart did not immediately go out to the victims' families. I still thought of death as something that happened only accidentally or naturally, only to Hannah and the old. I didn't consider what it must have been like to be the mother or father or brother or sister or friend of one of Jeffrey Dahmer's seventeen murder victims. I had no capacity, nor did I even try, to imagine these people coming home to this news while they still had stacks of hopeful leaflets on their desktops:

MISSING: Matt Turner.
MISSING: Oliver Lacy.
MISSING: Tony Hughes.
LAST SEEN: smiling.
LAST SEEN: out with friends.
Understand, please, World:
THIS IS MY SON.

At sixteen, I also didn't consider the trauma of the policemen and women forced

261

to work this case, opening Dahmer's closet to jars of genitalia preserved in milky formaldehyde, to severed heads with holes drilled through the skulls while the victims were, Dahmer later confessed, still alive. To be a cop on this beat? To take each photo off that man's walls and label it? To give it a name? For your day's work to be devoted to testifying to the fact that *this* happened, that *this* was real, that *this* was a part of humanity? How do you go home after that? I didn't even think of it then. All I knew was that this monster was the talk of the world, and I wanted to be a part of it.

So, I picked up the phone.

It had been more than a week since Lindy called to apologize, and I'd thought of calling her back in nearly every hour that passed. I just needed a reason, I figured, to actually dial the number. I just needed a talking point, something other than me, something other than *us,* and what I got was a national tragedy. As more and more details emerged — the bone shrine Dahmer had built in his apartment, the meals he had made of the dead — the story seemed to me as good of an opening line as any.

Her mother answered.

"Hi, Mrs. Peggy," I said. "Is Lindy home? I was wondering if she was watching all this

Dahmer stuff."

"I'm so glad you called," she said. "Lindy hasn't left the TV in days."

And so it began. Lindy and I talked all that night.

To be fair, it was hard not to be morbidly curious about what we, as people, were now publicly shown to be capable of. Sure, there was the horror of it all, the sadness, but it was easier, especially as a teenager, to disconnect yourself from that entirely and simply gawk at the total abomination of a man in a solitary apartment. As a nation, it consumed us. That next year, by sheer co-incidence, a film about a cannibal won an Academy Award. Jeffrey Dahmer's father agreed to write a book for big money. The media ate it all up. People acted shocked.

Lindy, however, was not.

In our conversation that night, Lindy spoke in a way I hadn't heard her before. She didn't sound like the broken girl I'd seen at school that past year, who said acidic things to other people while chewing her thumbnail. Nor did she sound like the drunken girl I had held at Melinda's, who whispered to someone far away. She also, I had to admit, did not sound like the young athlete I'd chased around my block those years back, laughing to herself about how

263

quick she was, and how slow the safe world. There was nothing bubbly in her voice anymore, nothing as innocent as that.

"You know," she told me, "it's all the cops' fault. If they just did their jobs, then the last, like, eight murders wouldn't have even happened. Did you know that, at this point, Dahmer was killing a guy what, like, once a week? Fucking their corpses? Eating their brains? Doing whatever he wanted? How hard is that to figure out? Cops are so worthless it's unbelievable."

I was nervous. I agreed with whatever she told me.

"Fuck the police," I said.

"Ugh," she huffed. "I hate that song. Why do you listen to that shit?"

"I don't," I told her. "I was just kidding."

"Hilarious," she said. "Really funny. But, seriously, did you know that Dahmer had already been caught molesting some kid however many years ago and the parole officer never even checked up on his apartment? The place was a fucking morgue and he was just too lazy to stop by. Isn't that unbelievable?"

I did know that. Since the story had broken, I'd learned all I could about the case by watching the news and reading the papers. I'd even bought a copy of *Time* magazine at the grocery store while shopping with my mom. She looked worried about my interest in this but didn't press me on the subject. In those days, she didn't press me on anything.

"No," I told Lindy. "I didn't know that."

"It's true," she said. "And what about that foreign kid who escaped from Dahmer's apartment and ran to a neighbor for help, all naked and drugged and bleeding from his ass? The cops just gave the kid back to him because they didn't want to get involved with a couple of gay guys. Seriously, could they be any worse at their jobs? Somebody should eat them."

I thought I understood Lindy's outrage.

After all, it had been two full years and no arrest had been made in her rape, a tragedy likely as large to her as Dahmer was to each of these individual victims. As far as I knew, the cops never did anything more than conduct those initial visits, anything more than question the neighbors as if somebody's lawn mower had gone missing. I'm sure there was more to it than that, at least I'd hope so, but I didn't see it. And like I'd overheard Mrs. Peggy tell my mother, the police had stopped calling. The case itself had gone cold. It therefore wasn't hard for me to imagine Lindy viewing all cops as

slothful and uncaring, to see every policeman as off duty and overpaid. She could
say whatever she wanted about them that
night. I wouldn't stop her.

More important to me, at the time, was
what Lindy may have *looked* like as she was
talking. The fight on the lawn was the last
time I'd seen her, and that had been from a
distance, a light-year. Before that, it was the
dance where she wore makeup and gunmetal blue. Who was she now? I wondered.
What color hair? What socks? What shoes?
How many scars?

"You have to admit, though," she said, "it
is kind of badass. I mean, this Dahmer guy
just not giving a fuck."

"Where are you?" I said. "Do your parents
let you cuss like that?"

"No one *lets* me do anything," she said.
"But, yeah, I'm in my room."

I walked to my window. Her light was off
and her shades were drawn. I looked over at
my clock and realized that it was one a.m.
and we'd been talking for hours. It is possible that I had never been happier.

Still, I should have understood even then
that when Lindy and I spoke in those days,
we were often talking about different things.
My version of the Jeffrey Dahmer story, for
example, was something out of a nightmare

266

while hers seemed like an interesting dream. There was awe in her voice, a peculiar respect for the murderer. And as confusing as that sounds, I've since come to learn that this is not uncommon with victims of sexual violence. It is called rape trauma syndrome, in the clinical journals, and often manifests itself as vivid fantasies in which the victim of the violence becomes the aggressor. Female victims especially, it is said, still many years later, may often fantasize about killing their husbands, their sons, their brothers. They say they can't help it. They say they feel terrible about it. They say they feel guilty. They say the most frequent method of murder, in a landslide, is by stabbing.

"Why is your light off?" I asked her. "I mean, if you're in your room."

"Here's another question," she said. "Why are you always watching me?"

My stomach sank.

I remembered what Lindy had accused me of at the party, the way she'd told everyone how I watched her. I'd gone over it in my mind every day those past months. Was it possible, I wondered, that she had seen me in the water oak those nights, squatting like a thief outside her window? If she had, why didn't she say something? If

267

she hadn't, why make it up? Why try to hurt me? How much about me did she know?

"I don't watch you," I said. "Why do you keep saying that?"

"What are you talking about?"

"At Melinda's," I said. "Don't you remember?"

"Look," Lindy said. "I have zero interest in talking about that night. And my light's off because I'm lying in bed. That's what people do when they go to sleep. It's not a big mystery."

"You're in bed?" I asked.

Lindy laughed. "Jesus," she said. "Do you want to know what I'm wearing, too?"

"No," I said.

"Good. Because maybe I don't want to tell you."

But here's the thing. I thought I'd heard something sly in Lindy's voice when she said that. I swore I heard something crafty. Despite her new cynicism, her hard outer shell, Lindy still had the ability to place herself directly between what I imagined I both could and could not have, both could and could not understand. Therefore, part of me thought she was being flirtatious while the other part became a paranoid wreck. I thought she was teasing me. I thought the few friends she still had might

268

be listening in the background, hoping I'd say something they could bury me with. The telephone connection seemed suddenly sharp and crystal clear and I had no idea how to react.

I tried to be funny.

"Why don't you want to tell me?" I asked. "Are you wearing fuzzy bunny slippers?"

"Ooh," she said. "So close."

"An evening gown?"

"Nope."

"A gorilla suit? A garbage bag?"

"Silly boy," she said. "Who said I was wearing anything at all?"

I had no retort.

In our silence, ocean liners moved across the sea.

In the world, mountains grew.

"Wow," Lindy said. "You need to get laid."

"No, I don't," I said.

"Right," she said, and I thought I heard her sit up in her bed after this, maybe move around and adjust some pillows. She also made a noise to sound as if she was leaning over, reaching for something, and I imagined her bare breasts against her sheets. I imagined her clicking off her night-light to get comfortable. Her white bed. Her pink comforter. Her soft skin. Her legs. The way she used to wear her hair when we were only slightly younger than we were then. The way she used to run. A small brown freckle that I saw, once, on her neck. Her tan fingers.

Maybe she was right about me.

"Anyway," Lindy said. "I'll talk to you later, okay?"

And that was it. She hung up.

Across the street and two doors down from me I watched a faint blue light click on in her room. I imagined her turning on a television before bed, falling asleep to the drone of an anchorman's voice, and I wanted to watch whatever she was watching. I wanted to be with her even if I couldn't. It was like I already missed her.

So I left my room and walked toward the den, where our TV was also on. In those days, it was not a strange sight to see my mother up late. Whenever I would venture through our dark home to raid the pantry, thinking everyone asleep, I'd often find her standing alone in her nightgown, milling around in different rooms, quiet as a ghost. And if the glow from the open refrigerator lit her up, or if I'd ask her what she was doing, she would just tell me that she had forgotten to lock some door or turn something off and would kiss me on the forehead and go back to her bedroom. "Good night, Mom," I would say. "Good night, son," she would say. And we wouldn't mention it again.

That night, she sat on the couch with a blanket on her lap. The room smelled sour. In the soft light of our television her eyes appeared dark and expressionless, and I couldn't tell if she was looking at me. The TV was tuned to CNN and, as had become common, a mug shot of Jeffrey Dahmer took up most of the screen. It surprised me that she would be watching this.

"Mom?" I said, and sat next to her on the couch.

I saw a wastebasket on the floor, a wet towel on her wrist.

"What are you doing up?" I asked her, although I knew.

In the months since Hannah's death, Rachel told me that she had often heard our mother, late at night, throwing up by herself in the bathroom. This image of grief was so devastating to me that I didn't believe her. I made up excuses to explain it. I told her that Mom had mentioned to me she was feeling sick, maybe coming down with something. I said that Mom was fine, and she was probably just hearing things. Rachel told me that I wasn't hearing anything at all.

Sitting beside me on the couch, my

mother closed her eyes.

"Do you think it's better?" she asked me. "Do you really think it's better that they caught this guy?"

I looked at Dahmer's picture on the TV.

People often remark, after their initial arrest and scandal, about how much serial killers look to them like "regular people," like any random guy you could meet at a bar one night, anyone working a cash register. This was never the case with Jeffrey Dahmer. The more we stared at his mug shot that late summer — on our television screens, in our newspapers and magazines — the more obvious his guilt became. His eyes were, to everyone who saw them, a stranger's eyes. His mouth was, to everyone who heard it, a dirty one. Even his mustache looked crooked and pasted on, like part of some devilish disguise, and simply by staring at him for a while we knew it was true, what he had done to those men. We could see it. This person was not like the rest of us. His lips were made to kiss people, yes. But his tongue was made to lick their dead skin.

So, I didn't understand my mom's question.

"What do you mean?" I asked her. "Of course it's better that they caught him."

272

"I meant for the families," she said. "Do you think it's better that they know what happened to their kids? All these details on the news? Is it better they found out?"

"I don't know," I said. "I think it's probably hard either way."

My mother looked over at me and seemed to suddenly surface from whatever hole she'd been in. She held up the remote control and turned off the television and touched my face and neck with her hands as if she had just found me, as if I had been missing.

We then sat quietly in the moonlit room and looked at each other a long time, and I began to feel as if we hadn't spoken in months, although we saw each other every day. I also recognized, perhaps for the first time in my life, that there were many fundamental ways in which I looked like her, in which I was a part of her, ways in which people could have deduced that we were related. It was something about our noses, the set of our eyes. We looked so obviously kindred in that moment.

After a while, she palmed my forehead as if checking my temperature. She moved my hair away from my eyes. "Are you doing okay?" she asked me. "Are you doing okay about Hannah?"

I felt my throat tighten up.

I didn't know what to say about Hannah. I never did.

So instead I leaned over and put my head in my mother's lap. She placed her hand on my shoulder and then, for a long time, she rubbed it.

"You know I'm here, don't you?" she asked me.

"I know, Mom," I said. "Me, too."

I meant this when I said it. But I wonder now if she believed me. If so, why? What had I done for her in those years? And, if not, how? What more could I have said to let her know?

Is there ever a love, any love, made of answers?

26.

After this, July became August in 1991.

School was still two weeks away, and rumors of a new whitefly infestation had people tooling around in their yards. All this activity was made bearable by an unusual wave of cool air that came down the Mississippi River from the Ozarks of Arkansas, as if to blow directly onto the people of Woodland Hills. Temperatures dropped into the low eighties and neighbors felt friendly. I saw Mr. Kern and Mr. Simpson, for example, chatting casually across their driveway, as if their fight on the lawn that previous month was already forgotten. I saw my old buddy Randy, now a starter on the high school football team, helping his mom spray down her azaleas with Safer soap. I saw Artsy Julie walking her family dog, a standard poodle named Guinevere, up and down the sidewalk in front of our house. I saw Jason Landry burning anthills with a magnifying glass. I also saw his father, the enormous Mr. Landry, still stalking the woods for that stray. More important than all of this, though, I noticed that when people saw my mother out on the front porch, watering the potted ferns she hung from hooks, they would stop to ask her how she was doing, and she could answer them without breaking into tears. So time was moving on. Things were looking better. The hot grip of summer pretended to loosen and, everywhere you looked, people were talking again.

None talked more than Lindy and me.

Our chats about Dahmer became nightly and, once established, quickly diversified and spilled into the day. Still, we never saw each other face-to-face. We never hung out. We instead holed up in our separate bedrooms, gabbing on the phone like retirees, and went to a great amount of trouble to act as if these conversations were totally unimportant, nearly meaningless, only one step above our excruciating teenage boredom.

I, of course, never believed this.

In the week she began calling me, when I first understood that the ringing phone in my house might actually be Lindy, my world became new. Nothing could bother me. In the stretches of time between our conversations, I felt good and beneficent. I stopped sneaking into the woods behind our house to smoke dope, stopped locking myself in my room, and instead began helping my mother around the house. We hung new curtains in the living room. We pulled up weeds from our backyard patio. I changed floodlights that had been out since my dad left. I was wired with energy. I felt so eager to please that I even helped Rachel do the dishes after supper. I watched *Full House* episodes in her bedroom and didn't change the channel when she left. I didn't give her a hard time at all. It was as if I hovered over ground in those days, grinning like an idiot while Rachel taught me to drive her old Honda, a stick shift, up and down Piney Creek Road. *Turn left,* she'd tell me. *Left! What are you doing?*

I had no clue.

I was entirely lost in romantic fantasies, the kind only teenagers without experience can have. While sitting in the car with Rachel, for instance, I'd think about picking Lindy up on a date: a dozen roses on the passenger seat, the wild night ahead, maybe a kiss at full speed. "Remember," Rachel would tell me as we drove, "God says everything happens for a reason. We have to trust that. Accepting Hannah's *death* means having *faith.*"

"Yep," I'd say, and grind the clutch. "I believe it."

Or, while helping my mom in the kitchen, I'd think of Lindy and I in a domestic setting; already married by now and sweet to each other. Maybe her with a baseball cap on, a lazy ponytail tucked underneath. I could rest my hand on the small of her back and maybe help her stir something hot, and we would never be the mess that our parents were. Our lives would be easy, our home warm and spacious. All this as my mom would say, "I talked to your father yesterday. Did you know he's moved in with that *Laura*?"

"Everything happens for a reason, Mom," I'd tell her. "We have to believe that."

"Oh, I do," she'd say. "What on earth would I do if I didn't?"

Then our telephone would ring and I'd be gone.

I'd drop the clothes I was folding. I wouldn't even turn off the sink.

"Sure," I'd say to Lindy. "I can talk."

"No," I'd tell her. "I'm not busy at all."

On the average, our talks were uneventful. Lindy liked Camel cigarettes. Lindy hated group therapy. Lindy liked *A Nightmare on*

278

Elm Street. Lindy hated Whitney Houston. Still, I always imagined that our next conversation might establish a real bond between us, might break down the walls. Perhaps we'd finally stop acting like superficial high school kids and talk instead about our deeper connections to each other, our youth together, our future. Perhaps I'd be brave and just say, *Enough about Dahmer. Enough about music. Check this out, Lindy: I draw pictures of you when I'm bored. I've thought of several smart names for our children. I love you is all that I'm saying. Don't you understand that? Don't you know that we are meant for each other?*

If Lindy only knew this basic fact that I lived with, then perhaps I could play all the songs for her that I'd written. I could ask her to a movie and she could say *yes.* I could open my palm and, without speaking, she could take it. I could tackle her, jokingly, and it could turn into a hug in the yard. I could finally tell her how sorry I was for that summer, for what happened to her, for my role in it, for how it changed her, and that as far as I was concerned we could forget it. We could move someplace else and build a life there.

I could say, *What do you think about that, Lindy?*

She could say, *My bags are already packed.*

None of this seemed impossible, but then a weird thing happened.

Near the end of that summer, I'd foolishly turned down a party invitation that Lindy had accepted. The party was thrown by a guy named Hanes Burke, a rich kid from Perkins who is probably doing well for himself now. He is one of those people who were born popular — the great-nephew of some long dead Louisiana senator — and, even at seventeen, he'd already established a reputation of being a good host, likely a Southern Democrat one day. There would undoubtedly be kegs at this party. Probably some light drugs if you wanted them. No cops to worry about. It was all a teenager could ask for.

Burke's party itself, however, was not the strange thing. This type of A-list invitation had actually become more common for me since Hannah's death, since I'd gotten wasted and played "Sweet Child O' Mine" at Melinda's. Still, my decision not to attend this particular event was a no-brainer, since I was expecting Lindy to call me after dinner, as had become her habit. She would tell me about the predictable meal she'd eaten, the intolerable conversation her parents had made her endure, and we'd sit around listening to music until she got bored or took another call. There was nothing else to do.

This was 1991, remember. We didn't have the Internet. So, as teenagers, we lived on the phone. There was no webcamming, no social networking. We dreamt simply of having our own personal phone lines one day, along with uninterrupted hours to talk, and we rarely got that. No matter who we were talking to, no matter how private the conversation, parents picked up the phone accidentally, siblings demanded their time. The introduction of call waiting made all of this even worse, as it allowed aunts and uncles and people you didn't even know to butt in. This is part of why we talked so late in the night, Lindy and I, all of us teens. This is why we looked so pale in our grunge clothes. These night hours were the only times we felt we could tell the truth without danger, the only times we could live separately from our parents while still inside of their homes. There were no cell phones. No private text messages. It was simple one on one conversation and, if it was any good at all, you had to whisper.

But since the bulk of our conversations that late summer revolved around how much Lindy despised everyone at our school, including Hanes Burke, it never occurred to me that she would go to his party. More important, it never occurred to me that she would go without telling me. So when Letterman came and went and the phone still hadn't rung, I realized what had happened and grew furious. I pictured Lindy standing around at the party with a drink in her hand, laughing with people, and I felt like I had been made a fool of, like I had been lied to.

I took up a lonely post at my bedroom window and strummed heavy ballads on my guitar. I eyed the empty street like a parent. Finally, at around two a.m., I saw a car pull up to Lindy's house and I panicked as it idled, wondering who she was with, who she may have been kissing, who she may have been allowing to touch her, and then I recognized the car.

This was good news.

The car belonged to Meagan Doucet, a large and unpopular girl who'd come to worship Lindy after her rape. Meagan was chameleon-like in her personality, almost fanatical in her pursuit of a social niche, and it was easy to despise her. She constantly smelled of patchouli oil, for example, but she was not a hippie. She did poorly in school, like many others, but Meagan did it without irony. She simply was not smart. As a by-product of this, she was perpetually cast in the smallest roles of our school plays — maybe some extra selling newspapers in a crowd scene, some secretary pretending to talk on a phone in the background — and yet she often bragged about being an actress. She talked about boyfriends in other towns that nobody knew and had twice faked suicide attempts for attention. I'd spoken maybe ten words to her in my life.

Still, I knew her story because she was Lindy's best friend in those days, one of the few remaining at Perkins. The two of them drove around in Meagan's blue Toyota and smoked Camel Wides. They bought glow-in-the-dark skulls and ironic bumper stickers with curse words on them at a place called Spencer's Gifts in the mall. They looked, at all times, like they were conspiring. Yet, like so many other students, Lindy often ridiculed Meagan Doucet behind her back. She complained about her desperate personality, her stringy hair, her rich parents who gave her anything she wanted. She said that Meagan had "hellacious halitosis." She said that she was only friends with her for her car. In other words, she said a lot of stuff that high-schoolers say. Sometimes, though, Lindy took it further.

Whenever it got late and Lindy seemed bored, she would tell me personal and embarrassing details about Meagan that I'm sure she'd been trusted with: sexual experiences she'd had with guys that were then mean to her, private concerns Meagan had about her body, her weight, her feminine odor, her dark nipples.

"She has dark nipples?" I asked.

"Ugh," Lindy said. "They're disgusting."

I knew these things must have been blood oaths between Meagan and Lindy, pinkie swears, and yet Lindy's betrayals didn't bother me then. I was happy to talk about anything she brought up. I thought she was confiding in me. I figured we were getting close.

On the night Meagan dropped her off, Lindy was staggering drunk. She stumbled up the sidewalk and through her front door in an obvious way that I would never attempt at my house. I always thought it would crush my mother to see me drunk, to see me stoned, or even to see me smoking a cigarette, although I'm sure she knew I did all of these things. She was no idiot. She had seen the contents of my hidden box, after all. She'd heard my music, read my strange poetry, smelled my dank clothing. She'd also, I knew, considered deeply the

284

idea of me being a violent criminal. She'd thought of me unbuckling my pants, hurriedly, in the heat of a Louisiana night. She'd imagined me forcibly taking sex from an innocent girl, shoving her face into the grass and knocking her out, right outside the home she had made for me, the one I was raised in. I wonder now how often she thought of these things, how realistically she entertained them, and how much this aged her. These thoughts could be no small deal for a parent.

My awareness of this, even then, may be why I continued to hide relatively insignificant things from my mother, well into my late teens, in order to spare her feelings: half-empty cigarette packs in the molding above my closet door, mediocre grades on algebra exams. I was careful about everything. I stashed joints in old cassette cases. I never once brought a roach inside our house. It all felt very natural to me, squirreling things away from her, protecting her from her own child.

Lindy felt differently.

I watched her ramble through her house, clicking on the overhead lights in each room. I could see it all from my window, her home like a waking yacht at sea. The foyer lights first, then the den. After a while, a dull hue from the refrigerator, maybe, an open microwave. Another long pause and then the bathroom light upstairs. A lamp, I imagined, in the hall. Eventually, her bedroom. A television set. Finally, the glow from her telephone keypad and then some darkness, to my delight, as Lindy pressed the seven numbers to call me.

I didn't even let it ring once.

I picked up the phone and watched through my binoculars as Lindy opened her second-story window. She pulled up a chair and lit a cigarette.

If I was up in the water oak that night, you understand, in the full bloom of summer, Lindy still would not have been able to see me. That's how good a spot it was.

"My God," Lindy said. "Te-quila."

I wanted to slam down the phone. I wanted to break something.

The joy I'd felt upon seeing her with Meagan was gone. I was instead enormously jealous that she was drunk without me, jealous she had gone to that party, jealous that other people had spoken to her, that other people had seen her. This was an emotion I had no handle on then. If Lindy talked about smoking pot I got jealous, although I smoked pot all the time. If she talked about going to the mall I felt jealous, although I had no desire to go to the mall whatsoever. If she talked about other schools where she knew people that I didn't know, other towns where she vacationed as a child, other streets besides the one we lived on.

Worst of all, if she talked about boys.

I couldn't stand it.

The slew of jerks she'd dated, the cute guys that bored her, the bozos she'd "only made out with." Information like this turned me inside out. Yet for some reason, I couldn't get enough of it. I was like a masochist in his becoming and constantly mined Lindy for sexual anecdotes even though they all inevitably left me feeling miserable — the torturous details about how Jimmy Cants kissed too softly, about how Alex Boudreaux had what Lindy called a treasure trail. It killed me. The idea that she could so casually give to these people what I would cherish. It was outrageous.

I became overwhelmed, I suppose, by the simple fact that the past is unchangeable and that Lindy had a past I couldn't tidy, that the two of us had a past that I'd perhaps ruined. It frustrated me to the point of devastation, and yet I still believed that if I could only create another situation like the one I had blown at Melinda's, one that would allow *me* to kiss her, allow *me* to touch her, then Lindy would understand where I was coming from. If only she knew that I was honorable, that I was genuine, that I was there for her. If only everybody else would get out of the way, I figured, things could be good for us.

So I became a petty and manipulative person. Whenever Lindy would mention a guy's name, *any* guy, I did what I could to vilify them. Some of these people were my friends. Some of the things I said were patently not true. I became a liar, a backstabber, a sellout.

I just wanted the girl, so badly, to like me.

"Why didn't you tell me you were going out?" I said.

Lindy laughed. It was a low and boozy sound.

"Why would I tell you that?" she asked.

"I don't know," I said. "I just sat here all night. I thought you might call."

"Wow," Lindy said. "That's really pathetic."

My heart felt like a fist.

"You didn't miss much, anyway," she said. "Assholing Jenny Linscomb was there. I swear, one day I'm going to punch that bitch in the tit."

I'd heard this story before.

Ever since I'd let the word slip out about

her rape, Lindy had cultivated an impressive number of enemies at school. As such, I spent much of that late summer listening to her skewer them. There was the aforementioned Jenny Linscomb, for instance, who had written "Whorebag" on Lindy's gym locker. There was Amy Broad, who told the principal that "girls like Lindy Simpson" snort coke in the school parking lot. And on the guys' side, there was Russell Kincaid, who called Lindy by the nickname of Lindy Simplex instead of herpes simplex, which we'd learned about in biology class sophomore year.

"Who cares what those idiots say?" I'd always tell her. "They don't really know you."

"Nobody knows me," she'd say.

"I do," I'd tell her.

"You *think* you do," she'd say.

She was right. I thought I did.

But my knowledge had a certain disorder.

I knew, for example, that at that *exact* moment, Lindy was sitting Indian-style on a white wooden chair with her hand outside her bedroom window. I could see the cherry of her lit cigarette through my binoculars, a silhouette of its smoke. I knew that her bicycle, the banana-seated Schwinn, now had weeds growing up through the spokes. I knew that she would likely sleep late into the afternoon the next day, opening her window to sneak a cigarette while her mom tidied up the front porch. I knew, also, that I wanted to be with her.

"Anyway," I said. "I just wish you would have told me you were going."

"Poor little kitten," Lindy said. "You should have come. Artsy Julie was there. Aren't the two of you, like, lovers or something? She's always walking that big-ass dog in front of your house. I saw you watching her at the dance. I figured y'all must have weird Dungeons and Dragons sex all the time. Are you her dungeon master?" She laughed. "Do you put your magic wand into her boiling cauldron?"

"What are you talking about?" I said. "We got set up for that dance. My mom made me take her. I had nothing to do with it."

"Relax," Lindy said. "I'm kidding. Plus, I know all about that."

"You know all about what?"

"The dance, idiot," Lindy said. "Your mom asked me to take you, too."

I watched Lindy put her cigarette out in a cup on the windowsill and suddenly believed myself at more of a disadvantage with her than I had ever been before. I suppose now that I could have interpreted this news as a positive, perhaps the final piece of evidence that my mother did trust me with Lindy, after all, that she always thought I was innocent. However, I didn't even think of it then. The simple idea that the two of them had shared information about me, that they had corroborated, was humiliating. I imagined a touching scene between my mother and the Simpson women, all sitting around a table drinking tea as if embarking on some philanthropic enterprise, and I grew furious.

"Are you fucking serious?" I asked.

"Yeah," she said. "It was right after your sister died."

"I know *when* it was," I said. "I can't believe she did that. What did she tell you? What did she say?"

"Why are you freaking out?" Lindy said. "It was kind of sweet. She was all worried about you. She thought you were depressed or some shit. But, you know, Matt Hawk had already asked me."

"Awesome," I said. "Isn't that great. Congratulations. Lucky you."

"Don't be a shit," Lindy said. "I probably would have gone with you otherwise. I felt bad."

"For who? Me or my mom?"

"Both, I guess," Lindy said, and her tone

softened up a little. She sounded genuine for a moment, even a bit wistful. "I always thought your sister was so cool, you know? I totally worshipped her when we were growing up. She had those big sunglasses. She had those big boobs. She made me want a sister so bad. I couldn't believe it when she died. But then, on the other hand, I totally could. She was cool. She seemed nice. It made sense. Nobody gets what they deserve."

It is funny to think back about your life.

Whenever I do it, scenes like this baffle me now, the way I was always listening to the wrong thing. Maybe that's all a childhood is? When Lindy was telling me Meagan's secrets, for instance, or when she was idolizing Jeffrey Dahmer, I wasn't really listening to her at all. All I was thinking was, Okay, so how does this affect me?

As another example, I can remember a short time after my parents' initial separation, when they attempted to get back together. This was the fall of 1985 and I was ten years old and, earlier that day, Randy and I had made a bet about who could score the highest on a computer game we both owned called Bruce Lee, played on the Commodore 64. We would call each other after each round, two kids in heaven, and compare our performances. That evening, my father came over to the house unexpectedly and he and my mother gathered us all into the kitchen. They sat us down at the large oaken table and they looked uncomfortable, almost shy, standing there before us. My father said, *It's not going to be easy, kids. But we're going to give it another shot.*

Hannah said, *Mom. Is this really what you want?*

My mom said, *Of course, honey. We love you kids so much. You know that, don't you?*

I said, *Can I go now?*

Or another time, much later in life, when my mother told me she had been feeling a little confused lately, and that she had almost gotten lost in her own neighborhood. She was living alone, then, and I had briefly moved out of town for work. I was in my late twenties and, like most, considered myself busy. My mother and I still spoke often and visited on the holidays, and yet I secretly believed that she was so devastated by my departure from Baton Rouge that she was conjuring up ways to get me to return to her. Small guilt trips about some downed limb in her yard. Strange symptoms that matched vague illnesses she'd heard about on TV. She was not yet sixty years old, often had lunch with friends, and looked great, so I thought she was making it up to reclaim me. Every child, I hope, thinks this highly of themselves.

And so I would say things like, "I don't know, Mom. You seem pretty sharp to me."

"Thank you, honey," she'd say. "That's sweet."

She was right. That's all it was.

I did a similar thing on the phone with Lindy that night. Drunk or not, there she was, talking to me about my dead sister, recalling her in specific ways that become so much rarer with time. Yet I barely even listened. "Do you remember all those gold bracelets she used to wear?" Lindy asked me. "Those big pink hoop earrings? I used to beg my mom to buy me that shit."

"Is that why you would have gone with me to the dance?" I asked her. "Because you liked Hannah?"

"I don't really know if I liked her," Lindy said. "It's not like we hung out. I just saw her. I just worshipped her. You know how it is. And your mom, my God, she looked so fucking sad."

"So, is that what Melinda's was about, too?" I said. "You felt sorry for me?"

Lindy groaned.

"I don't know," she said. "Maybe. Why do

you have to analyze everything?"

"I don't," I said. "I just think about it sometimes, about that night."

"Well, you should stop," she said, "because all that night was really about was drinking way too much vodka and about how much people fucking suck. My date made out with some skank in the laundry room. I passed out in the goddamned grass. It was horrible. I had to walk home. I fell asleep on the stairs. When I woke up, my dad was crying. I didn't know that shit was written on my face."

"You should have gone with me," I said. "Matt Hawk is such a dick."

"No," Lindy said. "Matt Hawk has a dick. A great dick. That's his problem."

I wanted to vomit. I wanted to jump off a cliff.

"Why do you say stuff like that?"

"What?" Lindy said. "I can't talk about dicks? Guys talk about tits all the time."

"I don't."

"That's right," she said. "I forgot that you're a saint. I probably should have gone with you to that dance, now that I think about it. I probably should have been dating you forever. That way I wouldn't have any problems. That way I'd just be this happy person with an assload of brownie points."

"I'm no saint," I said.

"Right," Lindy said.

"I'm serious," I told her. "You have no idea what I'm capable of."

"Okay," Lindy said. "Prove it."

27.

The game that Lindy chose was Truth or Dare.

How many fates, I wonder, have unraveled this way?

"All right," Lindy said. She was still drunk. "Let's test your sainthood. Which will it be?"

My answer, of course, was Truth. It was all I'd ever wanted between us.

"Okay, Truth," she said. "Are you watching me right now?"

I picked up my binoculars and looked across the street. I knew that Lindy couldn't see me, even if she was trying. I had studied my own house from her oak tree so often that I understood the look of it with my bedroom lights on, my bedroom lights off, the porch lights on, the porch lights off. I knew the orange glow from the lamp on top of our piano when Rachel had forgotten to turn it off before bed. I knew the look of the vent lights above our kitchen stove, the shadows cast by our rooftop dormers in both the waning and waxing moons. So I also knew that my bedroom window, the place where I was watching her, was just a dark square from her vantage point, barely even visible due to the fortunate angle at which our homes had been constructed before Lindy or I were even born. I adjusted the binoculars to get a clearer look. When the lenses focused, I saw that she was sitting at her open window and flipping me the bird.

"No," I told her. "I'm not watching you."

"I thought this was Truth or Dare," Lindy said, "not bullshit time for little boys. I know when somebody's looking at me."

"I just told you I wasn't a saint," I said. "That doesn't mean I'm a freak. There's room between being an angel and being, like, a pervert."

"You think so?" Lindy said.

"I do."

"You know what I think?" she asked, and set down the phone.

Lindy then stood up from her chair and looked directly at my house, directly at the place she knew my room was, and lifted off her shirt. She tossed it out of sight and stood there. She put the phone back to her ear. She lit another cigarette.

"I think you're full of shit," she said.

Of course I was.

From that great distance I could see only her forward-most features, lit up by floodlights the Kerns had installed outside their garage those two summers prior, and I stared at her unadorned outline. Her skin appeared yellow and smooth in this light. Her bra was dappled by leaf shadows, and her stomach looked taut as a board. She still had the form of a distance runner, Lindy did, although she hadn't competed in nearly two years. She had the waist of an athlete, of a sportswear model, of every fit seventeen-year-old girl that even upstanding men of middle age — through some pull of nostalgia, perhaps — remain drawn to. I watched her stand shirtless in the dim light. I had little to say.

And the strange thing is, I had actually seen Lindy in this manner of dress before: in bikinis out in the yard, in sports bras as she cruised the track at Perkins, in nothing but underwear as I sat in the water oak. I'd seen even more intimate angles as well, the back of her bare neck as I stood behind her in the lunch line at school, the curve of her knees as the gang of us ran through lawn sprinklers in what seemed so long ago. And

I'd come close enough to touch her body as well, tackling her in the hot grasses of our neighborhood and running my finger over her scars at Melinda's party. But this was something else entirely. This time she was looking at me. She was presenting herself to me. It was more than I could stand.

"Hmm," she said. "I wonder why you're being so quiet."

Then, as if to torture me, Lindy held the phone between her neck and bare shoulder and placed her cigarette in the cup on the windowsill. She then reached down to unbutton the top of her jeans. She casually unsnapped the fly and flared it open, and I could see only the highest seam of her underwear, panties of a dark color that did not match her bra. I couldn't remember the last time I'd spoken.

What on earth could it have been about?

"I mean, if you're just sitting there and not looking at anything," she said, "I wonder why you're not talking?"

Lindy bent to remove her jeans, and when she stood back up her face was a rounded shadow that I could not see the expression of. With her right hand, she reached behind her back and unsnapped her bra, and I watched it fall down her arms like a dream. I could now see the sides of her small breasts in the low and yellow light, and this vision became a touchstone of my permanent memory, despite what happened next between us.

Lindy walked away.

Without a word, she turned and disappeared into the dark of her room and all I could see through my binoculars was the smoke from her forgotten cigarette, left to burn in a cup on her windowsill. Yet I could still hear Lindy there, her breathing close to the receiver, and so I put all of my energy that way. She was crawling into bed. I knew that sound from our previous talks, when she'd flopped down to tell me some awful thing about group therapy or serial killers or her parents. I heard the mattress creaking beneath her slight weight. I heard the tick of the ceiling fan spinning above her. Then, once she got settled, I heard Lindy herself make a noise. It was a mature and pleasurable sound, a deep and satisfying sigh, and it was a thing I'd not heard from anyone before.

"Okay," Lindy said. "Now it's my turn. But no more Truth. I want a Dare."

Every idea I had was weak-minded.

I had played Truth or Dare only sparingly in life and, previous to this occasion, it had always been for low stakes. Once, for instance, back in the neighborhood days, when Arsty Julie dared me to kiss her dog. "How are we supposed to know what animals are princes," she asked, "unless we kiss all of them?" Another time at a high school party when, out of boredom, I halfheartedly dared a guy named Judson Vidrine to stick a sewing needle through his forearm (he did it) and then only once more, when Jason Landry dared the circle of us on Piney Creek Road to drink a whole jar of pickle juice. When we balked at this idea, and the Kern boys told him to go away, Jason said, "Okay, *truth,* then. Have your parents ever made you drink a jar of pickle juice?"

Some unfortunate things are so clear to me now.

Yet I'd always considered Truth or Dare a juvenile game. It was not at all sexual to me until Lindy undressed in front of her window and said the word "dare," and from that moment on I could think only of the way that her tongue touched the roof of her mouth as she reclined in her soft and cold bed to say it. I suddenly saw no other way for this game to operate. It was all about sex. There was nothing else, nor had there ever been.

But I was inexperienced.

How could I offer Lindy a dare bold

enough, I wondered, to erase the errors I'd made with her since the *Challenger* fell into the ocean? How could it be powerful enough to erase my guilt over letting her secret slip out? How, too, might it be provocative enough to get her to do the favors I wanted? How could it be honest enough to let her know that behind our strange friendship, I believed that there were important things like true love and perhaps, one day, the physical making of that true love? In other words, how could I craft a dare so powerful that it might rip the siding off Lindy's house, turn Piney Creek Road into an escalator, and deliver her body to me?

I didn't know.

Before I could even try, though, I heard Lindy on the other end of the line, grunting softly with her throat. The air came to her in irregular bursts as if she were involved in some small task. It reminded me of the way people breathe when tying their shoes or threading a needle, when struggling to remember a thing that should be obvious, and I immediately knew what she was doing.

After watching her undress, I'd begun doing the same.

"Lindy," I whispered, "I dare you to tell me what you're thinking."

303

She let out another long sigh. She said, "I'm thinking that you're not very good at this."

"Why?" I said. "It's a good question."

"It's also a Truth, idiot. Not a Dare."

"Okay," I said. "You tell me, then. What would be a good dare?"

She didn't even have to think about it.

"A good dare," Lindy said, "would be, like, I dare you to come over here and fuck me."

I sat quietly on the phone and, to this day, there has only been one other time in my life that I felt so worked up. It was a memorable night in the early years of my marriage, more than a decade after I had this talk with Lindy, when my wife and I discovered that she was pregnant. We'd been lying in bed for an hour and crying sporadically because our deepest-held anxieties had become so obvious to us. The feelings we shared that night were enormous and strange and, as this panic turned to excitement, we moved closer to each other beneath the covers. We said silly and honest things like, "I hope it doesn't look like your aunt," and, "You know I'm totally going to screw this up, right?" all while my wife allowed me to touch the back of her thighs in a gentle way I had done thousands of times before. There were patches of dry skin there, some wrinkles I'd grown so accustomed to, and yet when there was a long, quiet moment between our laughter, when I thought she may have fallen asleep, my wife parted her legs and exhaled in a manner so deeply satisfying that I went crazy. She reached down and placed her hand on top of mine and, as she moved her hips against me, I knew more clearly than ever before that I was doing a thing that another person wanted. I also knew that my touch alone would be the one to give her pleasure and that her physical offering to me was one of tremendous love to be born out of her body in the months to come. And I understood that everything that had happened in my life before this event had been in preparation for it.

But with Lindy, I wasn't prepared at all.

"Are you serious?" I said. "Is that your dare?"

"It doesn't matter if I'm serious or not," she said. "It's not my turn."

"But were you serious?" I asked. "Is that what you're thinking about?"

"Jesus," she said. "Is all you ever do ask questions?"

"No," I said.

"You really want to know what I'm thinking about?" she asked. "Are you sure?"

"Yes," I told her. "Yes, I'm sure."

"Okay," she said. "Do you know Chris Garrett?"

I did know him.

He was a tall guy, a runner on the cross-country team. He was my age. We used to play soccer together. What else was there to know?

"Of course I do," I said. "He's in my class."

Lindy took her time.

"Yummy," she said.

I didn't get it. Chris Garrett was neither popular nor interesting by any means of calculation that I had access to. He had short brown hair that was often neatly combed. He was in a number of honors classes, held ludicrous posts like treasurer in our student government, and was a member of something called the Fellowship of Christian Athletes. Whenever the Perkins School hosted inspirational speakers during our common hour, some ex-athlete or recovered drug addict who asked us to close our eyes and pray to the Lord if we felt comfortable doing so, Chris Garrett closed his eyes and prayed to the Lord and looked comfortable. He was so pure, so harmless, that I'd never before thought to hate him.

Now, of course, I would have to.

"Why are you thinking about him?" I asked.

"I know," Lindy said. "It's weird, isn't it? Something about him just makes me so . . . ugh. I can barely stand to look at him."

"What do you mean?" I asked. "Makes you so what?"

"You know," she whispered. "Wet."

The thought of this was too much for me. My stomach moved in strange knots, my chest tightened.

I must have made a noise, I'm not sure what, but Lindy knew my secret.

"Are you doing it, too?" she said.

I couldn't answer. I didn't need to.

"I do it at school sometimes," Lindy said. "I can't stop thinking about him. I did it under my sweatshirt in Spanish class when he was giving a presentation on bullfighting or some shit. He was like, 'Does anybody have any questions?' and I was like, 'I do. Will you *please* fuck me right now?' "

"Lindy," I said.

"God, his fucking body," she moaned. "I just want to lick him all over. He probably thinks I'm some slut, though, doesn't he? Do you think he's a virgin? I bet he is. I bet he's a fucking virgin." And then Lindy was off on her own, revisiting some fantasy she'd apparently had hundreds of times before about Chris Garrett, perhaps, or about boys in general, about virgins. But this time, I also just happened to be there. She mumbled and whispered things I couldn't understand and the noises became muffled as the receiver brushed roughly against her cheek. "Tell me," I thought I heard her say. "Tell me you like me."

"Lindy," I said. "Of course I do."

"Touch me," she said. "I want to feel you."

"Okay," I said. "I want that, too."

"Kiss me," she said, "tell me," and then Lindy began to gasp in tight bursts. The simple sound of this took me over the edge and I listened quietly as Lindy continued to buck hard against something invisible. "Tell me you want me," she said again. "Tell me you like me."

"Lindy," I said.

"Chris," she said.

And before I could say anything more, before I could correct her, I saw my reflection in the window. The sides of my head were shaved and the thin strands of hair on top stood around my face like I'd been shocked and it appeared to me, for the first time, as if I was wearing a wig. All the jabs my sister had made about my ill-fit appearance came bounding back to me as if obviously true and this unfortunate feeling multiplied. I reached around for something to clean myself off with and when I saw my own pale and skinny arms in the moonlight I clearly recognized that I was no athlete, no Chris Garrett, although there was a time in my life when I probably could have been. I wasn't a good Christian, either, and ever since the death of my sister would not feel comfortable closing my eyes to pray around anyone. I was instead merely a manipulative boy who had somehow finagled his way into sharing an intimate moment with the girl he adored and I was not proud of this, even in those first moments. Yet as I listened to Lindy find pleasure, I still held out hope that we may have finally crossed whatever threshold it was that we needed to cross. A flickering part of me felt this may be the very thing to bring us closer.

On the other end of the line, Lindy's breathing eventually became slow and exhausted. She was quiet and, I thought, content. I wondered if her thoughts were circling back to me, or if she now felt curious about my body, my sexuality, or my imagination, and I said nothing to interrupt this moment. I didn't feel the need to. We had shared something private and atypical and tremendous that night and the real question for me became whether or not this would be a thing we did regularly in the years to come, at the end of a long day, perhaps, before drifting off to sleep. And so I listened for Lindy's parting words to me on this occasion. A *good night,* perhaps. Maybe an *I Love You.*

After a while, she finally spoke.

"Sometimes," she said, "I swear. I just want to blow my fucking brains out."

28.

How can I explain it, now some twenty years later, the real difference between me and Lindy? The way her voice on the phone that night still haunts me, at times, and the way it has shaped who I am? The way I've had to find peace with my role in this?

Perhaps I could start by telling you:

Baton Rouge is not New Orleans.

They get all the press, yet we are the capital city of Louisiana. Our downtown is flanked by gray government buildings, a courthouse, and two governor's mansions — one retired and turned into a museum. Our state capitol building, once the tallest structure in the South, still bears the bullet holes from Huey Long's assassination in 1935. This makes it unique, and so a few people visit this place.

Downtown New Orleans is called the French Quarter.

Maybe you've heard of it.

It is a mash-up of whites, blacks, immigrants, Cajuns, and Creoles: New Orleans. It is a city of great poverty and also of great wealth, often located on the same street, and so all the best minds have studied it. Baton Rouge is a city whose problems, on a statistical level, are largely predictable. We have traffic at peak hours. We have violence in the roughest parts of town. Our public schools, when filled with poor children and ill funded, are likely to crumble and die. Our officials, if elected by wide margins, usually fall short of their goals. When compared to the national averages, Baton Rouge normally ranks around thirty-seventh in the top one hundred metropolitan areas of America, no matter what you are measuring.

However, we always score well in odd polls. When demographers and social scientists get past the numbers, when they ask more qualitative questions, Baton Rouge inevitably ranks high. We're off the charts in mysterious categories like "enjoys their neighbors," "had a good weekend," and "hopes their children will stay close." There are several reasons for this. Flowering plants do well here. Things grow like crazy. When it's hot it's really hot and when it rains it really rains. Our weather is not enigmatic.

The food in Baton Rouge is also good and cheap, which is important. There is no place to get a bad sandwich. Open a mediocre restaurant and go under. Open up a new place where there used to be a bad one and pray that we forgive you. We don't draw enough tourists to float a halfhearted kitchen. Thank God.

Baton Rouge is also, in large part, a college town, and this makes people feel young. On fall Saturdays, the LSU football team draws crowds of ninety-two thousand people to watch them play. On these days, Tiger Stadium itself becomes the sixth-largest city in Louisiana and you will struggle to find a person in town, interested or not, who doesn't know the score. During the game, the LSU campus — dotted with oak trees, Spanish tile rooftops, and two Indian burial mounds — holds another one hundred thousand people who couldn't get a ticket but decided to come anyway. They sit around in fold-out chairs and talk to one another. They share cold beer and hot food. They all have the same thing to root for. This helps.

It is also helpful that Baton Rouge is built on a bluff to the east side of the Mississippi River, which often protects us from major hurricanes. This is not to say we haven't had our asses kicked. In 1992, when Hurricane Andrew barreled through South Louisiana, my mother and I watched the winds of it rip a forty-foot oak tree out of our yard. In the seconds before it fell, the thick roots snapping beneath the slab of our house sounded like popcorn popping. By the time the eye of Andrew hovered above us and we could step outside on the leaves and limbs and thrown shingles, the crater the oak tree left was already full of debris and rainwater, never to be even again. This type of damage was common in our neighborhood. At Lindy's house, for instance, the water oak I'd spent so many nights in toppled and crashed through her bedroom wall. It smashed the roof, shattered her window, and also broke a support beam in the second-story floor that allowed rainwater to pour through the entire house. At this point in time, however, in the fall of 1992, nobody lived there anymore.

Still, we have often been spared major disasters.

In 1973, for example, Baton Rouge was able to avoid historic flooding along the Mississippi River by opening man-made spillways and floodgates. Although it seemed like a simple decision to save our city, the cradle of the state's government, this action flooded dozens of less populous towns and bayous along a waterway called the Atcha-falaya Basin. River silt clogged people's tailpipes. Homes floated away as if children were steering them. Wildlife disappeared. New species invaded. Entire ecosystems changed. Baton Rouge stayed dry.

Even worse, though, is that we were spared the floods of Katrina.

You have to understand. When people think of Louisiana, they think exclusively of New Orleans. We are okay with that. New Orleans has the culture, the allure. They are The Big Easy. The Crescent City. The Birthplace of Jazz. The people of Baton Rouge don't even have accents. Our pa-rades, when compared to New Orleans, are amateur hour. Even our most raucous bars close at two o'clock in the morning. Theirs don't close down at all. So, whenever people in Baton Rouge feel wild, we drive the sixty miles to New Orleans. We stay in upscale hotels and spend gobs of money. We drink beer on the street and make bad decisions. We take wrong turns at intersections and feel perpetually lost, and when we wake up in the morning, regretful and satisfied, we go back home saying, "It's a fun place to visit, but I wouldn't want to live there."

In other words, we make a lot of sense.

New Orleans doesn't.

For instance, New Orleans is the only American city below sea level that is actually located by the sea. Sunny settlements in the valleys of California mountain ranges don't count. The Gulf of Mexico, Lake Pontchartrain, the Mississippi River, they surround this storied city and push on it, they press on it, they ingest it. New Orleans is so low, in fact, so waterlogged, that they must often bury their dead above ground.

The city of New Orleans is also ironic. On a national scale, it consistently ranks first in both violent crime and in the number of city permits granted for public celebrations. It is a place that has known both slavery and brutal prejudice, and yet is vibrant with gays and transsexuals. It has been decimated, repeatedly, by plagues and battles and record-breaking storms and, rather than leave this place, the people of New Orleans instead take pride in the fact that the circumstances beset upon them are extraordinary and tragic. So, for anyone to act as if New Orleans is not the most interesting place in the world is, to a New Orleanian, uninteresting. For people to act as if New Orleans is anything other than its own planet, its own universe, is naïve. As such, the people of New Orleans have been known to wonder what a generic place like Baton Rouge, at its core, has to offer.

For a long time, we had a hard time coming up with an answer.

But now I can tell you.

We have guilt.

When Hurricane Katrina entered the Gulf and turned north in 2005, the wealthy made their way from New Orleans to Baton Rouge. They heard on their digital televisions and satellite radios the order of mandatory evacuation and had crammed our hotels and empty parking lots by dusk. Traffic was heavy with cars and RVs as the state employed what is called contra-flow to reverse all westbound and northbound lanes on Interstates 10, 55, and 59. Baton Rouge was happy to help. We were neighbors, after all. We'd always been polite.

So, when we went to stock up on our own supplies that day — batteries, bottles of water, propane for grilling — we were fine with the fact that New Orleanians were strangely there, too, buying toiletries and bags of chips for their hotel rooms. Lines were long and things were inefficient, and they did their comedic best to make this known to us. They were loud and gregarious and immediately skeptical of things like our bread selection. It was funny, how strange they found our city, as if they'd been set down on Mars. They didn't know where the juice aisle was. They couldn't find Jax beer. They weren't sure exactly which lane of the road was the turning lane and they honked their horns a lot quicker than we did, even when they were in the wrong. This was not a big deal. *After you,* we said. *We hope you enjoy your brief stay.* And then, on that last night before the storm, we packed our local restaurants and drank heartily, the people from Baton Rouge and New Orleans together. We joked about how crazy it was, living down here.

This was August 28. On the next day, it began to rain.

Then the wind came and the power went out.

After this, the inconceivable news trickled in.

By August 31, nearly fifty sections of the New Orleans levee system had failed.

Most areas of the city, eighty percent in some estimates, were underneath ten feet of water. Cell phone service became spotty for everyone, and there was suddenly an issue of missing people. Nobody knew where their neighbors were, their cousins, a grandma. I got word that two friends of mine who lived in uptown New Orleans, an old college pal and his wife, had spent the last two nights in their Subaru Outback, parked at a strip mall in a nearby town called Denham Springs. They didn't know what else to do. The woman, whose name was Jennifer, was enormously pregnant, and my buddy wondered if I knew of any hotel rooms, anyplace she could get a shower. Like every Baton Rougean worth their salt, I opened up my home to them. I held Jennifer's hand as she walked up the few stairs to my front door and apologized for the heat, which, without power and air-conditioning, was inescapable. She put on a two-piece bathing suit and stood outside, washing herself in the garden hose, and she was a sight. When the power came back on that next day, we stood around like imbeciles and watched the television.

The devastation to New Orleans was total. It was obvious. It was tragic.

And although I feel close to that disaster, although I was forever affected by it, and although I truly do love and care about that great city, her story is ultimately not mine to tell. I understand that.

Baton Rouge's, however, is.

We had some trouble of our own.

After the levees broke and their streets filled with water, the stranded poor of New

Orleans, of which there were many thousand, began to make their way west on Interstate 10. Some were transported in school buses, commandeered by Governor Kathleen Blanco's executive order, and sent to generous places like Houston, Jackson, and Shreveport. Others simply walked. It was ninety-six degrees and their shoes were still wet. Men went shirtless and the women wore dripping tank tops and bandanas on their heads. Minor injuries had gone unattended: a deep red gash from a fallen tree branch, a strawberried bruise from a slip on slick asphalt, swollen sets of fingers on swollen pairs of hands that were all perhaps broken. Those in wheelchairs got help from strangers and kin and either slept or read Bibles, and the lot of them looked like Third World migrants moving up the American causeway, toting heirlooms in plastic Walmart bags.

Helicopters sent footage of this to network affiliates, and army trucks rattled by, tossing out cases of bottled water. On a national level, people were outraged. Locally, many of the stranded poor, when they reached the first small town they came upon, were turned away at gunpoint. Baton Rouge, however, opened its doors.

And the people kept coming.

Nearly overnight, our population doubled. In the weeks that followed Katrina, some studies estimated that two hundred thousand additional people were still living in East Baton Rouge Parish alone. Schools overflowed, property values skyrocketed, and restaurants opened like flowers. Many saw this as an opportunity, a chance for Baton Rouge to show the world what it was made of. Our mayor, for example, called the situation unprecedented, and so we felt obliged to be hospitable. We hired refugees to work our cash registers. We increased our bus routes. We changed the cycles on our stoplights. When the relocated asked us where to get a good sandwich, a good cup of gumbo, we gave them a list of places. We wanted so desperately to impress them, to please them, and we felt close for a time.

But what eventually happened is this:

Reality set in.

Baton Rouge is not New Orleans. Our po'-boys, they let us know, were not as good as theirs. Our traffic, to these people who were causing it, was intolerable. There was no place to get a decent omelet, we were told, though we'd been breakfasting happily for years. There was nothing fun at all to do in Baton Rouge, they explained, and we agreed, because our best theaters and malls

and bars and bowling alleys were now overrun from all the new people in town.

That's not what I mean, they'd say.

We knew what they meant.

And, truth be told, we took it hard for a
while, our wealthy and poor alike.

Our mansions, apparently, lacked character. Our garden district was some cheap
knockoff of their garden district. Our finest
eateries were no Antoine's, no Commander's Palace, nothing like the luxury you
could find in the French Quarter. Our
casinos, our amusement parks, our zoo,
well, they were depressing. And on the dark
streets of old Baton Rouge the poor had
their differences, too. New graffiti sprang
up that our kids hadn't seen before. Our
area code was 225, yet someone had carved
504 into the hood of a local gangster's
Cadillac. This was the beginning of gunplay,
turf wars. Three men — just boys, really —
were murdered on the stoop outside of their
grandmother's house in broad daylight.
Several different gangs claimed responsibility and so nobody was sure of the meaning.
As months passed, alarming reports came
out of our high schools: increased improprieties in the bathrooms, more confiscated
weapons, threats against teachers. We were
told that this was a form of post-traumatic

stress disorder, what these children were going through. We were told not to be alarmed, not to rush to judgment. We were told that it was impossible to blame people who were so distressed, so displaced, so confused, and we understood this.

We thought they were talking about us.

As these weeks turned into months, even more advice poured in.

If we really wanted this to work, the pundits said, it was time for Baton Rouge to make some big decisions. It was time to grow up. The city would need to be reorganized: all two-lane roads turned into four, entire intersections scrapped and reengineered, trees cut down to widen a boulevard. We were told to lock our car doors, roll up our windows, and that we probably should have been doing this anyway. The world, after all, is not as simple as football games on fall Saturdays, a bunch of friendly people being friendly. Everybody knows that. Life in a real city is difficult and complicated and terrible things happen to wonderful people. Like they say, if you want to mature, if you want to expand, you have to be prepared to invest. And, of course, you have to be prepared to lose that investment.

So, we did.

We put shovels in the ground. We opened old office buildings that had been condemned for years. We built new strip malls that didn't really suit us, because we felt the demand was high and immediate. We took giant leaps of faith and opened niche grocery stores that sold things we thought would appeal to our new residents. We then threw open the doors of these places and stood there, breathing heavy, still trying, after all this time, to impress them.

And then they left.

Those with the means either went back to New Orleans to rebuild or retired in sleepy towns like Natchez, Mississippi. Young professionals took off to Dallas. Many of the displaced restaurateurs found footing in places like Gulf Shores and Destin.

The street gangs, however, decided to stay put.

And the woman named Jennifer, I should mention, had her child in Baton Rouge as well. The contractions hit her in the middle of the night while she and my friend were sleeping in my bedroom, which I'd let them use so they could have privacy. I was living alone then, and didn't mind sleeping on the couch or staying at my mother's house. I was entering my thirties, and my mom, although she had begun to age in obvious ways, remained independent and proud and now lived in the same neighborhood as Rachel and her family (a Christian man and two toddling girls, all of whom I love), and I visited her often.

I was at my mother's house, in fact, when I got the call. My buddy was a mess and I could hear Jennifer yelping in the background. They didn't know any doctors in Baton Rouge, he told me. There was some confusion about insurance. He thought maybe the contractions might pass. He admitted that nothing, nothing at all, was going as planned. This was after midnight, and I drove back to my place, where her water had broken by the time that I got there. I rushed them both to the emergency room, my buddy in the backseat of the car with his wife. I did her small favors on the way, like adjusting the AC blowers and running through red lights, and I felt for some reason as if I myself was having this child. Who knows why? The emergency room was packed with Katrina victims when we arrived, although we were already weeks removed from that tragedy, and these people were belligerent with us as we carted Jennifer to the front of the line. After only a few minutes, the two of them were ushered away and I used my buddy's cell phone to call his and Jennifer's relatives, who were scattered all over the country.

They were all happy to hear of the contractions, the impending birth, but wondered if it was even possible to travel to Louisiana at that moment. They wondered if we were still underwater, if the National Guard was still there, if people were still looting and murdering one another, and I told them no, we're okay. I told them that although it is a common misconception, Baton Rouge is actually not New Orleans. By mid-morning, my mother and sister and the woman who would soon become my wife had shown up at the hospital. They wanted to make Jennifer feel special, although they barely knew her, because she was special, the moment was special. They brought her flowers and a soft blanket, and we gathered around her like an oracle after she had birthed the child. It was a girl that they would name Marigny, she told us, after one of the most fabulous areas of New Orleans, which they believed was the most fabulous city in the world.

"It's a beautiful name," we told her, and I know that I for one secretly wondered how long I would be expected to help raise this child. I wondered how attached I should get. It sent a panic through me, the reality of it. I was not ready for a baby, I thought, and suddenly worried that I might never be.

And it is not until times like these, when there are years between myself and the events, that I feel even close to understanding my memories and how the people I've known have affected me. And I am often impressed and overwhelmed by the beautiful ways the heart and mind work without cease to create this feeling of connection. It is like the way Lindy always reminds me of New Orleans, when I think of her now, although together the two of us never stepped foot there.

29.

The final suspect in the rape of Lindy Simpson was the psychiatrist Jacques P. Landry. He had a private practice out on Harrell's Ferry Road, a little house with his name on the sign that my mom would mention to me whenever we passed it, if only to question whether or not any cars were parked there. He also had the large home in Woodland Hills, the walking stick that he stalked our back woods with, the mop of black hair, the thick eyeglasses, and, along with his wife, Louise, he had fostered approximately twelve children in the time that I knew him on Piney Creek Road. And although his family was always regarded as an unpleasant force in our pleasant neighborhood, Jacques Landry came under increased suspicion in regard to Lindy Simpson only when one of these children, the adopted son, Jason, disappeared.

A little more about Mr. Landry, who I've

tried to sequester in my memory:

His size was outlandish. At six-foot-five and three hundred pounds, the man was a giant, an ogre. Yet there is something awesome to me about the truly enormous. I can't help but stare at them, the size of their fingers, their thighs. Even those mountainous men that I am afraid of, that I find despicable, I can't help but pity in some ways. I wonder how difficult the most ordinary tasks must be to accomplish in a world that was not built for them. Getting into a compact car, for instance. Touching the push buttons on an outdoor stereo. Finding clothes that fit. Listening to any other viewpoint. Not simply taking for their own, perhaps, what could so easily be taken. It has to be hard for them. Any denial, to a man that size, has to be confusing.

As was he.

Although his name is French and common in South Louisiana, there was something of the Eskimo in Jacques Landry as well. Something of the Huns. He had a broad and tan face with high cheekbones. His thick black hair adhered to no particular style. I imagine now that his wife Louise must have cut it, using a bowl that she had just rinsed free of some spare ingredient her kin alone still used in those days: unrefined cornmeal, maybe, the dust of some country root. Perhaps on Sunday mornings, by way of truce, after Mr. Landry had been so mean to her the night before, she would place the bowl on his head and scissor his hair and, when done, gently smooth those thick eyebrows that always looked cross when he spoke, unless lifted by a wide smile that no one else knew the meaning of. Perhaps she would then clip his toenails and brush his teeth, perhaps hold his hands that were like bear paws and say, *It's okay, my giant. I know you don't mean to hurt anyone.* How else could she have lived with that man? I do not know.

Jacques P. Landry also had trouble with the law.

In additional knowledge that came to me later in life, in random and separate conversations with my mother and father about our pasts, our years spent on Piney Creek Road, I learned that Mr. Landry had on more than one occasion had his license to legally practice psychiatry suspended due to what my mother vaguely called improprieties and my father called prescription issues. This didn't surprise me. After all, I'd seen him lean a little too close to the girls in the neighborhood when they still had soft hair on their legs and jelly jewelry on their

330

wrists. I'd seen the way his own adopted son hated him. I had also seen a case of syringes and box full of vials in the darkest room of his house, in a time that I've not told you of yet.

This came about in a peculiar way.

It was two weeks before the fall semester of 1991, my junior year of high school, and Lindy and I had not spoken since that night of Truth or Dare on the phone. She'd hung up on me after her mention of suicide, and I'd sat at my window for another hour, spiraling through a series of thoughts about our relationship that left me lower than I had ever felt. I thought about calling her back, of course, I thought about our erotic conversation, but what was really taking place inside me was the belated realization that nothing romantic was ever going to spring up between us. I also understood, perhaps for the first time, that I was not the only person on Piney Creek Road who was unhappy in life, and that my particular level of unhappiness, in comparison to Lindy's, was more like joy.

Not that my life was uncomplicated.

To be fair, I'd had a statistically difficult childhood. In fact, research suggests that adolescents who lose a sibling experience a wide range of long-lasting effects: survivor's guilt, shame over their own immaturity at the time of death, remorse over their selfishness during the grieving process, and so on. But the interesting thing is, there is also data suggesting that positive outcomes arise from these family tragedies. New studies note increased creativity, productivity, and innovation in the surviving siblings, as if they are motivated to prove something beyond what their peer group feels the need to prove. Such as, I would imagine, their basic value on Earth. These surviving siblings often grow to cultivate other positive traits as well, mature things quantified in categories like "involved parenting" and "increased empathy." The same can actually be said, in some cases, for the children of divorce.

Yet in all the research I have done to try and wrap my head around both the Lindy I thought I knew and the Lindy that may have actually been living across the street and two doors down from me in my youth, the outlook is less hopeful. There is little talk of positive outcomes while the negative symptoms for victims of sexual violence are abundant and diverse. You name it and a group of women have suffered through it. Yet there is one phrase that reappears in nearly every study I've come across, a description that breaks my heart when I see it and think of Lindy, when I think of anybody. It is a catch-all category that scores off the charts and, as the data suggests, often does not lessen with time. The symptom is called "the decreased capacity to enjoy life," and, for some women, it is a killer.

I didn't understand it all then, of course, but after Lindy's mention of suicide I was beginning to feel it. This feeling is commonly known as "having perspective," and it is no small deal for a teenager. It changed me completely. So, on the day we had our annual pre-semester orientation at school, a three-hour meeting to get ourselves acquainted with our new responsibilities and classrooms, to meet our new teachers, to roll our eyes, I found myself acting out of body.

Standing in a line outside the Perkins gymnasium, waiting for my turn at one of the intolerable community-building games that had been set up for us (things with names like the Trust Fall and the Family Circle), I noticed Chris Garrett a few places behind me and I casually let some people skip ahead so that I could be next to him. He had a spot of acne on his cheek and smelled like Ivory soap. He had brought with him from home a milk jug full of water to stay hydrated before anyone had ever thought to bottle water for profit and, around his tan neck, he wore a wooden crucifix likely earned on some mission trip. He was, I could see now, so obviously handsome. And after a little small talk about our summers and homerooms, our boredom, I found myself asking him what he would think if, let's just say hypothetically, I may or may not have heard that Lindy Simpson liked him.

He looked confused.

"Lindy?" he said. "I don't know."

"What do you mean?" I asked.

He squinted his eyes and stroked at his chin. He made a face as simple and innocent as that of a person choosing between french fries and onion rings. "Well, for one thing," he said, "she's not very good at Spanish."

"What?" I said. "Who cares about Spanish?"

"In twenty years," he told me, "we're all going to be speaking Spanish."

Chris Garrett lifted and grabbed his foot in a way that allowed him to stretch out his quad. He then did this with his other leg and I must admit that it was difficult for me not to assault him. But I was just jealous. I knew it even then. He was tall and fit, and

334

by all normative measures likely a much better person than me. I also knew that without even trying, he could probably have all that I'd ever wanted. This injustice, however, did not enrage me in the way it did with Matt Hawk or any of the other unworthy thugs I had seen Lindy with. With Chris, I found myself dwelling on benign thoughts such as, *Will Lindy go to his track meets?* and, *What will his parents think of her?* I was suddenly experiencing an idle curiosity without pain and I was unsure of what to do with it.

"She is pretty, though," Chris said.

I looked up to see that Chris had spotted Lindy across the quadrangle, where she was standing in line for the bookstore. Her hair was dyed jet black, and it kept slipping from behind her ear. We stood and watched her as if she was a foreign exchange student just come to campus. She was dressed casually in a rock-and-roll T-shirt and shorts, and was apparently listening to the conversation going on in front of her, although she was pretending not to. It was a couple of jocks, Brett Manner and Curren Boyle, energetically telling a story that required the both of them to be put into headlocks. As their excitement escalated, Lindy scrunched up her face and chewed her thumbnail and was trying very hard, I think, not to smile.

"Coach still talks about her all the time," Chris said. "He calls her the best that never was. Why'd she quit running, do you know? I never understood that."

I watched Lindy crack a smile as the jocks in front of her began to wrestle with each other on the ground and I felt close to her in new ways. I was not, for perhaps the first time in my life, thinking up schemes to attract her and yet I still felt totally energized by her appearance. I still felt alive and involved. That had not changed. And although it angered me to hear people talk as if Lindy had made some sort of mistake in life, as if she had done something wrong, I was more interested in the idea that Chris might not actually know why she quit. I liked this idea, that Lindy might be the one to tell him, if and when she decided to, and that he might see her in a way that I had become unable to.

I also enjoyed the possibility, of course, that, in this new dream world of mine, I hadn't ruined her chances at everything.

So I told him, "I'm not sure why she quit."

Chris looked at me and smiled. "She's never spoken a word to me before," he said. "You really think she'd talk to me?"

"I know she would," I said. "But you

336

didn't hear it from me."

"That's crazy," he said.

"Yep," I said. "It is crazy."

Chris hopped up and down on his toes as if working out his calves. He rolled his neck around on his shoulders. "Speaking of quitting," he said. "Why'd you quit soccer, man? We suck now."

"I don't know," I told him. "I sometimes wonder the same thing."

After this, a teacher named Mrs. Kornegay came up to our line and blew a whistle and so we all shuffled forward into the gymnasium, where the pep squad was singing our fight song. I didn't speak to Chris Garrett for the rest of that day and, when orientation was over, I walked home alone.

When I got there, my mom was a wreck.

I found her sitting in my bedroom, holding the confiscated black-and-white photo of Lindy that caused me trouble so long ago. Her hands were shaking and she had been crying, I could tell, but as this was a common occurrence since my sister's death, I had no idea its source. She could have been crying about Hannah, of course. She could have been crying about Mrs. Simpson or Lindy, and it was also possible that she could still be crying, even all these years later, about my father. Or it could have been me.

"Mom," I asked her, "what's going on?"

She didn't even look up.

"I need you to tell me," she said. "I need you to tell me about this photo."

So, I finally did.

I told her in greater detail what I had only mentioned when she was first overwhelmed by the collected perversions of my lockbox. I told her about what had happened at Jason's house that day, about how he had a stack of these photos tucked away in his closet. I told her how I saw pictures of other people from the neighborhood in there, as well, including her. People driving cars and playing in the yard. People watering their gardens and spraying for whiteflies. I said that most of the photos that I saw were of Lindy, though, and as I recalled this scene to my mother, it took on an entirely new meaning for me. Now that I was removed from that moment, now that I wasn't maniacally focused on making sure Lindy didn't find out about my secret, I began to understand how strange it all looked from the outside, this black-and-white photo of Lindy singing to herself as she walked, taken from the closet of a troubled household. It was not celebratory, this picture. It was not a snapshot to be shared among friends. It was not even, on the surface of it, lewd. There was by all conceivable measure no good reason for the photo to exist. I understood then that it was not for my eyes to have seen, nor any child's, as it was not to have been taken in the first place. So the horror of it all simplified for me in the way it must have for my mother so long ago, and I felt sick with guilt.

After I finished explaining, my mom asked me, "Did Jason take these pictures?"

"I don't think so," I said.

"I don't think so, either," she said.

My mom then placed the photo on the bed and took me by the shoulders. "Listen," she told me. "I don't want you to ever go to that house again. Do you understand me? I don't want you to talk to Jason or to his father. Just stay away from them." She looked serious and afraid as she said this, and I felt embarrassed, like I was being counseled by a stranger.

"Mom," I said, "what's going on?"

"Shh," she said. "Did you hear that?"

I did.

Someone was on our front porch. We could hear their footsteps.

A large shadow passed my bedroom window. My mom looked at me.

"Did you lock the door when you came in?" she asked.

"I don't know," I said.

She sprang off the bed and I followed her. We ran to the front of the house, where we stopped and stood like statues in the foyer. I had no idea what was happening. The dead bolt and chain were both fastened, so we kept our distance, watching a shadow so big that it could only be Mr. Landry's behind the frosted glass that surrounded our door frame. After a minute of standing there, oddly quiet, Mr. Landry rang the doorbell.

My mom squeezed my hand.

"Don't open it," she whispered.

He rang the bell again.

"Kathryn," he said through the door. "I think there's been a misunderstanding."

I looked up at my mother. She stared at the door as if it required her attention to remain shut, and her hand was hot over mine. She motioned for me to watch the door as well, and when I did, I saw Mr. Landry trying the knob, turning it gently from side to side. When this didn't work, he reached to the top of the door frame to check for a key. We heard him bend and look under the mat. Woodland Hills was a generally safe place, remember, and so the key was indeed out there. We kept it in a fake birdhouse, a small replica of our own home that hung maybe ten feet from where Mr. Landry was standing. What luck, I think now, that he didn't think to check there. What blessing prevented him from seeing it? How much of our lives, when we think back upon them, are owed to these minor miracles?

Are any miracles minor?

My mom leaned over to me. "Lock the back door," she whispered. "I'm going to call your father." She then turned and ran to her bedroom as I watched the large shadow move past our door and across the porch. I followed it to the side of the house, where I could eventually see Mr. Landry from around a corner, shading his eyes to look in through our kitchen window. He had a bandage on his hand and stood there for a long time. He did not appear angry or passionate or vengeful, and so I had no idea the source of our panic, yet I also did not doubt it. My legs were shaking. I could smell myself sweating. As soon as he left my sight, I ran to the back door and flipped the bolt and laced the chain.

I hurried to my bedroom after this and grabbed a baseball bat that I had not touched since Little League. I crouched next to my window and raised one of the blinds to see Mr. Landry, dressed in slacks and a short-sleeved dress shirt, plodding back across our lawn. He walked past the Stillers' and to his house, where he climbed into his old Jeep Scout and drove away. When I got to my mom's bedroom to tell her that he was gone, she was on the telephone and nearly hysterical.

"What do you want me to do, Glen?" she said. "I know what I saw."

We then heard the gate to our back patio swing open, and my mom looked at me as if her life had drained away. I readied the bat and peeked through her bedroom window to see Rachel walking in from the carport, fumbling with her keys.

"It's just Rachel," I said, and my mother began crying.

"Hurry," my mom said. "Go let her in."

For reasons that make sense to me now, I was kept out of the loop that night.

Rachel had run to my mother when I explained to her what was going on, and they had a conversation I was not privy to. Although it may seem odd that I would have been all right with this seclusion — that I wouldn't have demanded to know what was happening — it only seems that way because I am an adult now and then I was a kid.

And as a kid in my house, even as a teenager, whenever I approached my mother's bedroom and saw the door closed like it had been so many dozens of times since Hannah's death, when she and Rachel wept themselves to exhaustion, I did what all children do and fell into the pattern of grieving that we had already established. None of this was my mother's fault. It wasn't anybody's fault. It was merely the path of least resistance, and that is the nature of grief. I was being protected from something my mother felt that I was not ready for and the fact that I didn't bust down her door and demand to know is evidence, I think, that she was probably right.

So, I sat on the couch and waited. And, in this time, I thought of Lindy.

I felt deeply upset about the violence inflicted upon her in her very own neighborhood those years back and now, when I was still fresh off the first legitimate feeling of panic I had ever experienced, it suddenly crushed me to think of her crushed. I thought, too, of the way it had hurt me to see my mother look so vulnerable when that shadow appeared, so scared when she heard those footsteps, and then of what Lindy must see every time she looks in her parents' eyes. It made sense to me that this would destroy her, and that it would destroy her family.

Then I felt a sharp click inside of me, as if my heart and mind had come together.

It was simple, I figured. Lindy needed to know who did this to her.

And since I was the one who'd made it all worse, I needed to be the one to tell her.

That this was the first time the idea had dawned on me, nearly two years after her rape, is one of the greatest shames of my life.

After I'd gone through half an hour of soul searching, of planning, of nearly forgetting what planet I was on, our doorbell rang. My adrenaline cranked up again, and yet I sat still as a stone as my mother and sister walked into the living room. They held hands like a unified front and my mother motioned for me to join them.

We heard a soft knock.

"Kathryn?" she said. It was Louise Landry.

She sounded tired and worried, and spoke weakly through the door.

"Have y'all seen Jason?" she asked us. "He hasn't been home in a week."

My mom looked over at me and I shook my head no, that I hadn't seen him.

"Please," Louise said. "I'm worried about him. I'm worried about what he might have done. I'm worried about what he could do."

I assumed that my mom would keep her distance from Louise the way she did with Mr. Landry. I imagined her lumping them both together, but she didn't. Something sad was happening between a mother and son in our neighborhood, and my mother felt it. And so the real sound of parenting, for me, has always been that of my mother unlocking our deadbolt and clearing her throat, of opening the door to look at this woman and say, earnestly, "I'm so sorry, Louise. We'll keep our eyes open, okay? I promise you. We'll keep you both in our prayers."

30.

It did not take long to find Jason Landry. As if a figure from some urban legend, aware that we had spoken his name, Jason appeared at my bedroom window that same night. He drummed the glass and whispered, "Hey, Fuckhead," until I opened the blinds. It was near midnight by then and I'd already had a strange evening of sleep. After Louise left, my mother and Rachel and I sat on the couch of our living room and stared out of the back windows like catatonics. My mom told us that our dad would come by the house soon to check up on things, that in her panic she hadn't known who else to call. Her voice was monotone and lifeless, and she apologized for frightening us. She encouraged us both not to worry too much, said that she may have overreacted, and the next thing I knew we were all knocked out. I awoke with my neck craned to the side and Rachel's legs slung over my lap. My mother lay stiffly toward the armrest next to me, as if she had been frozen in the sitting position and tipped over by some prankster. It looked like we were staging an accident. Rachel and I woke up at the same time, around nine o'clock, and nudged our mother awake as well. We then shuffled off to our own private bedrooms without supper.

I couldn't fall back to sleep. The fact that it had gotten dark while I was unconscious bothered me. I felt that I had lost an important stretch of time in my life and I tossed around in bed feeling restless and guilty. I worried that Mr. Landry could have returned while I was passed out, of course, but I was actually more disappointed in my inability to stay focused on Lindy. I was supposed to be thinking up ways to explain the crime against her now, piecing together some closure for her family, and I had already fallen asleep on the job. I was torturing myself about this when Jason arrived at my window and, as such, I first mistook the sound of his voice for my own conscience. *What are you doing?* it asked me. *Why are you just lying there?* These were good questions. Then Jason said, "Stop yanking it and come to the window, you perv. I want to show you something." So I did.

347

When I lifted the blinds, Jason Landry turned up his palms like he had been waiting for hours. He may have been. I didn't know. He was dressed in camouflage from head to toe, baggy pants and a T-shirt, and had a look of strange glee in his eye. "Christ, you hornball," he said. "I thought I was going to have to come down the chimney."

"What are you doing out there?" I said. "People are looking for you."

Across the street, an automatic porch light clicked on. Jason ducked his head. "Open the fucking window, you stroker," he said. "I'm trying to do you a favor."

I unlocked and opened the window but kept my body in the frame so he couldn't climb in. He looked around my room to be sure we were alone and I realized that, through all the years we'd known each other, he'd never been inside of my house. I wondered how he even knew which window was mine, and then thought of the horrible likelihood that he had looked through all of them to find it. His face was dirty and streaked with mud, and he was sweating. His hair, white and thin, was longer than I had ever seen it.

"Either come with me or let me in," he said. "I'm like a sitting duck out here."

"Hold on," I said. "Don't move."

I backed away from the window to pull on a pair of jeans, and by the time I turned around Jason was standing in my room. He was leaning over my desk, looking at my old Little League trophies and riffling through random scraps of paper. I could smell him. He smelled older than me, and he was. Nearly eighteen by then; the damp odor of Jason's clothing, the rank sweat of an unwashed man filled my room as quickly as smoke might. He studied the posters I had on my wall: a couple of the bands Lindy liked, an advertisement for Rumple Minze liquor with a scantily clad barbarian woman on it, and a few miscellaneous sketches I'd done in art class that my mom had tacked up. He seemed quietly amused by it all. I watched him lean close to a framed photo of my seventh-grade soccer team and look for me in the group of us huddled together on one knee. He put his finger on the glass when he found me, clean cut and smiling in my pre-Lindy days. He then scanned the rest of the place, looking up at my ceiling fan, at my closet, at all the structural things I knew he had in his own room as well, and I could smell the mud of our local swamps on his shoes.

"Do you have any food?" he asked me.

I pointed to a half-empty box of Oatmeal

Creme Pies sitting on my amplifier.

"Of course you do," he said, and put the box beneath his arm. "You live in paradise."

"Jason," I said, "it's the middle of the night. What's going on?"

"Just a little war, a little vengeance, a little mayhem," he smiled. "You know, the usual stuff." I didn't understand. "Okay," he said. "Let me put it this way. Do you still like that Simpson chick?"

I wasn't sure what to tell him. The question seemed inappropriate. The answer was complicated. Jason then motioned at my bed, where my mom had left the black-and-white photo of Lindy earlier that afternoon, and I guess that told the tale.

"What I'm saying," Jason whispered, "is that old picture is nothing. Nothing. That's just scratching the surface."

"What are you talking about?" I said.

"We're friends, right?" Jason said. "I mean, we're on the same side in this. It's us against him." He searched my face for some sort of agreement. "Shit, man," he said. "You know how much trouble I could have gotten into for showing you those pictures? You know what that asshole would have done to me? Do you know what he's already done?"

"Take it back if you want," I said. "I never

even look at it."

"I don't want that stupid picture," he said. "What I'm looking for is justice, maybe a little revenge. I thought you might want some, too." He nodded again at the picture on my bed. "You know," he said. "For her."

"Jason," I said, "do you know something about what happened to Lindy?"

He looked at me and raised his eyebrows and, with that small gesture, I knew that my life was going to change.

"What do you know?" I asked him.

"I know that we're wasting our time jacking off in this room," he said. "Put on some shoes and come with me. You'll see what I'm talking about."

"Okay," I said.

Once outside, we traced the dark fences of my enormous backyard like burglars in the shadows. I was familiar with this area, as it is where much of my life had taken place: romps with the neighborhood kids, football with Randy, the first time I ever saw Tyler Bannister smoke a joint, and the first time I walked from this place to Lindy's water oak. I knew all the frog sounds, the occasional rustling of branches by squirrels or birds of prey, and had seen the random opossum or coon scuttling toward our garbage cans for dinner. But as soon as we ventured past the reach of my backyard floodlights, I felt transported. I no longer recognized anything I saw, and I panicked. Everything my mom had said about the Landrys came roaring back, and I worried where he was taking me. Part of me wondered if I would arrive at some pagan circle to find Lindy bound and gagged, all of the neighbors chanting around her — Randy and Artsy Julie, the Kern boys — each a part of some sinister reality I had been sheltered from. Bonfires, nooses, rituals: all of human life from any era of history, I imagined, is possible in the dark Louisiana woods.

We picked up the pace as we sloped down a hill and were jogging by the time we left my property. We crashed through a screen of weed trees and flimsy saplings and were soon romping past oaks and river birch with trunks the size of our own chests. I could feel my arms and face being cut by thin branches and had no idea what I was doing or why we were running or why I had made any of the decisions I had made in my life. So I concentrated only on the running itself. I counted my footfalls and enjoyed the deep breaths. I leapt over small and moonlit obstacles like roots and limbs and felt suddenly and without warning like I did when

352

I was a child and, in that feeling, I understood that it was a terrible thing that events had taken place in our lives to make it appear as if Jason and I or any of the kids on Piney Creek Road could ever be anything but children.

We splashed through slow-moving rivulets of water that made their way to a larger canal that Jason crossed by walking over a fallen tree. I stopped at the upturned roots of the tree, breathing heavy, and could see him only in silhouette, balancing himself with the box of Oatmeal Creme Pies in one hand. When he got to the other side, he turned around and looked at me. "Get your hand out of your pants and come on," he said. "It's not far."

I walked that fallen tree as if over a canyon and I could not see the bottom. I knew in my heart it wasn't deep, yet all the playful joy I had felt just moments ago was replaced by childish fear. The oak branches beneath the moon were now monster arms, a curved shadow before me a snake, the canal below an abyss. Although I understood that it was likely just mud and bracken and faded Coke cans and buried arrowheads a few feet below me, all like a wonderful novelty in the daylight, this was not daylight.

When I reached the other side of the

canal, Jason was gone. I heard him making owl noises up ahead, and I followed what looked like a trail. As the path narrowed and the vegetation thickened, my baggy jeans got stuck on a series of briars. I scratched up my forearms pulling them loose and fell into the clearing where Jason had made his home. He stood at the base of an oak tree and looked down at me. In one hand he held a white bedsheet. In the other, the large Rambo knife he had shown me in his room nearly three years before. It had a compass on the hilt, an empty handle to stash matches and fishing line, and both a sharp and serrated edge for cutting and sawing, perhaps gutting. He was grinning like a kid.

"Jesus," he said, and began cutting the sheet into strips. "What did you do, stop to jack off a couple of times?"

I got up and surveyed the area, which was lit dimly by a fading clamp light Jason had hooked to a car battery. The place looked like a hoarder's paradise, like a beach after a storm. I saw buckets, bottles, dirty towels, stacks of lumber, *Playboy* magazines, fishing poles, lawn equipment, chairs, and a bicycle. Then I saw more peculiar things like a shovel, a long-poled net to clean swimming pools, and a remote-control car, all made the more peculiar because they were mine. I also recognized Randy's tackle box, noticed a pair of shears with the name "Kern" on the handle, and saw a miniature trampoline that Artsy Julie used to jump on. The webbing of the trampoline was broken and most of the springs had been removed, and so Jason Landry, I understood, like the opossums and coons, had been visiting our trash while we slept. He had pilfered our open garages and carports, taken advantage of our presumed safety, and hauled away cartloads of our forgettables in the night. Yet I saw no blatant purpose to the items he'd chosen. A box of chlorine pellets, a rusty watering can, a bag of golf clubs. I walked around as if at a yard sale. And then, in the middle of this clearing, I saw Jason's shanty home in the branches.

"Not too bad, huh?" he said. "Is that how you pictured it?"

That this was the same tree Jason and I scouted those years ago uncorked a new sadness in me. The thousands of hours I had spent since that time falling in and out of things like love and mourning, Jason had likely spent by himself in these woods, bringing our childish vision to haphazard fruition. I walked around the base of the tree and studied it. Cradled between two of the strongest-looking branches, about ten feet off the ground, was a rickety shelter. It had plywood walls and a slanted wooden floor and was held together by nails, duct tape, and rope. It looked like it could fall at any moment. The roof was made of blue tarpaulin and sagged with enough stagnant rainwater to birth generations of mosquitoes. On each wall, crude circles had been cut through the plywood with hand tools and Jason had spray-painted phrases like "Fuck All!" and "No Survivors!" beneath them. Yet I didn't see a ladder leading up to it. I didn't even see an entrance.

"How do you get up there?" I asked.

Jason was now kneeling in the dirt, a small flashlight tucked beneath his arm, twisting the strips of bedsheet he had cut into what looked like small sections of rope with a knot on each end. He kept referring to a black book on the ground next to him, and in his diligence it was easy to imagine Jason earning a living one day, having a productive life in suburban America. But this would never happen.

"You've got to be skinny," he said. "And you've got to be able to climb. It's fat-ass-proof."

I walked beneath the fort and looked up. There was a space in the floor near the trunk, barely a foot wide. As thin as I was, I'd have to hold my breath to get through. And on the trunk itself, I could see where the bark had been scored, maybe knocked a couple times with a hatchet, and I fit one of my hands into the grooves. Jason opened up a box sitting next to him. It was full of brown glass bottles, the same kind Old Man Casemore used to bring to our Fourth of July parties, the kind that he would fill with home-brewed stuff like strawberry- and molasses-flavored beer, and it felt to me a strange breach of etiquette for Jason to steal from someone so old and benevolent. I suppose I was naïve in this way. I watched Jason carefully remove the bottles, one by one, and drop a piece of handmade rope into their mouths.

"They don't teach you how to do this in your bullshit high school, do they?" Jason said.

"How to do what?" I asked, but he didn't answer me.

I looked up at the fort.

"Mind if I go up there?" I asked.

"Sure," he said. "Just don't whack off all over the place."

I put my hands and feet in the trunk's hatching and made my way up to the fort. It wasn't easy, as this particular tree was not meant to be climbed. It didn't offer itself up in the way the knotty water oak by Lindy's driveway did and, because of this, I understood that Jason had chosen well. Plus, I was a different guy now than the kid who used to own these trees back in the days of moss, and the act of climbing a new tree felt as unnatural to me as anything I'd ever done. My shoes kept slipping out of the grooves. My hands hurt. A chain on my rock-and-roll jeans got stuck on a nub in the bark, and by the time I was able to grab hold of the opening in the floor and pull myself through it, I was breathing hard and sweating.

I sat in the fort with my feet dangling out of the opening and was immediately overcome by the heat of the place. It was so stifling and focused that it made me forget why I had come out there. I felt a quick desire to take off my shirt and go crazy in the old woods, to wipe my face with mud, to pour water all over my head. I began to have truly outlandish thoughts and felt nauseated and confused until I realized what was causing it all — the overwhelming smell of gasoline. I picked up a flashlight sitting by the entrance and looked around the dark and spare fort. I saw a pillow and yellowed blanket on the floor. In one of the corners, I saw stacks of instructional and pornographic magazines like *Popular Mechanics* and *Hustler.* Next to those, nearly half a dozen dismantled flashlights. And there, lining the far wall, a series of oil cartons and gasoline cans. The cans were gallon-sized, with ribbed spouts, striped red and yellow and made of metal in those days. I recognized them immediately, as I had seen every inhabitant of our block lugging them around at some point in my youth. The oil was primarily the two-stroke type, used for small engines, and the cardboard cartons they were sold in were already soiled and greasy near their mouths. I thought back to the last time I had heard a lawn mower in the neighborhood, the last time I'd heard a leaf blower. How could they run, I wondered, when all of the fuel of Piney Creek Road had been stolen? What did our neighborhood even look like anymore? How far had we let it go?

I noticed our own gas can along the wall as well. It was dented and scratched along its side from where I had accidentally dropped it, years ago, while bringing it out to my dad as he mowed the largest part of our property. The cap had popped off when it hit the ground and quickly spilled enough gas to soak and eventually kill a large swath of grass by the driveway. I was young, maybe eight years old, and upset with myself. I just stood around, watching the gas pour out. My dad saw me standing there and got off his riding mower to approach me. He put his hand on the back of my neck as we watched the last bit of it soak into the ground and he said, *Now, if we only had some salt, we could finish the whole yard off.* He was trying to be kind, but I was inconsolable. Later that night, after a few drinks from a Styrofoam cup, he came into my room and stood in the doorway as I flipped through some comics. *You're going to have a hard time in life if you let every little mistake bother you,* he said. *Life is good, son. Enjoy it.*

Okay, I said.

He was gone two years later. And it is hard for me not to wonder what he had already done at that point, when he told me how good life was. Was he already cheating on us? Was he with other women before Laura? Was he waiting until we all went to bed to make some clandestine phone call? If so, then did he mean that the good life, the life like he was living, was a life without virtue? Was that his advice? Or, as I like to think now, whenever we are together as men, was he just being honest? Was he possibly still in love with our family alone, but then life changed without his permission? I mean, was he saying that we should enjoy what we have because nobody, not even a person in love, knows what's coming? What was he telling me? What was I learning?

Down below, Jason asked if I could pass him the gas cans.

I'd almost forgotten where I was.

"Try not to breathe too much up there, man," he said. "Those fumes will mess you up. I thought I saw a fucking unicorn last night."

So I pulled my shirt up over my mouth and carefully dropped the cans through the hole in the floor to where Jason was standing. None of them were full, and as I pictured the shelf in our garage where my can should have been, I felt some strange guilt that it was empty. What else from my past could be missing? I wondered. What else were people just taking from me?

I watched Jason consolidate the gas into one master can.

"What are you doing with all this stuff?" I asked him.

"It's a science project," he said. "I want to keep up my grades so Mom and Dad will let me take Buffy to the prom."

He was joking, but neither of us laughed.

Jason had been missing from home for at least a week. I'd no idea how long he'd been missing from school, nor did I know how many schools he'd attended since he got kicked out of Perkins in the eighth grade. I knew so little about him at that time, so little about anyone, really. It stuns me, now, the limited information kids operate with. I watched as Jason began to mix the oil and gas in specific proportions outlined for him in his book and I began to feel an accomplice to something. "Jason," I said, "why did you bring me out here?"

"Two reasons," he said. "The *first* is in a blue envelope in the corner. Take a look."

I set down the flashlight and walked toward the corner of the small fort, where a blue envelope sat on a stack of magazines and spiral-bound notebooks. I picked it up, lifted the flap, and shook out a small key. And although there were hundreds of possibilities in that square mile, thousands of locks in our lives, I knew what that key was for as soon as I saw it. It was the key to Mr. Landry's private room, it had to be, and the immediate danger that it represented, the possibilities it created, twisted my stomach.

"I snatched it the night I split," Jason said. "My dad passed out with the door open. I almost smashed up the fucking place, I was so pissed. But what good would that have done? I just unlocked the window instead. Now we can open it from the outside so it doesn't matter how many combo locks he puts on that stupid door. I just wish I could have opened the shed."

"I don't understand," I said. "If you can get in that room through the window, then what do you need this key for?"

"I don't need it for shit," Jason said. "*You* do. That's the key to his safe."

I held the key between my thumb and index finger as if it was a lit match and I knew that Mr. Landry, if he hadn't already, would check the window of his private room soon. I knew the match would not have long to burn. Then, through one of the cut-out windows in Jason's fort, I saw something I never expected to see. Across the woods from us, maybe half a mile away, sat the Perkins School. I understood it was close, of course. I'd walked or biked to it thousands of times, but always on the sidewalks, always on the prescribed paths. And even though I'd ventured this deep into the woods before, I'd never achieved this particular vantage point. Yet there it was, glowing like a city in the darkness. The school buildings I knew so intimately were now rendered strange to me by their security lights and the grand old oaks of its quad were up-lit and beautiful. The football field and track were also lit, as if it was homecoming weekend, but the place was deserted. The sudden order of the manicured campus seemed a bizarre affront to the madness of the woods, and the school looked, from this angle, less like a school than a brochure for the school. It seemed an ad campaign for unattainable progress and it surprised me that Jason chose this view for his window.

More surprising, perhaps, was that I began to understand something important about humans and trees at that moment. I began to understand our shared history. To look at the world from a tree, as I had done so often in those years, is a fundamentally different way of seeing. It is contemplative and detached and the objects one studies from that height are rendered, at the same time, both majestic and small. A generally commonplace item, in other words, may stir admiration and mystery when viewed from that vantage point. Or, at worst, it may breed jealousy, desire, and contempt. It all depends on the viewer. And so, I have to wonder, what kind of viewer was I? What *was* that, exactly, up in the oak trees of Woodland Hills? An animal? Some sort of Peeping Tom? A sensitive boy racked with love and guilt?

Maybe.

My point is that climbing a tree to look at the world is primal. It is ancestral. So, as I imagine it now, the eyes in my head on that night were as dark and unreadable as an ape's. This may not have been the case, of course. I may have been only a nervous kid with a key in his hand. Still, it makes me wonder. Where is that missing link in our human history? Isn't it strange we can't find it? Australopithecus? Homo erectus? What was the exact moment we hopped down from the branches? When we said *Enough with all this looking* and became emotionally engaged with the world? When we became vulnerable? What dream were we so compelled to pursue? What was the prize? What was the hope? What was the goal?

"Hey," Jason said. "Come back down here. I need you to help me bury something."

31.

The soil of the Earth is made of horizons.

Beneath our feet, intricate layers of matter lead down to the core. The first layer is known as the O Horizon and is where most of your visible activity takes place. This is the domain of the earthworm and mole, of rotting leaves and flower root. It is called the O Horizon because it consists of primarily organic material, all of it still closely connected to the living or dead. Lean down and muss this stuff with your hand, kick it around with your feet, it is of little consequence. There is so much life traffic here that your tracks will be covered in no time. Below this is the A Horizon. This is the place where hardy trees and perennials tap and grow and go dormant and then wake again the next year, a place the weakest vine and weed roots never reach. It is settled and weathered and dark and rich and so long established that it will forever be a part of this ecosystem. Drop a geologist out of an airplane and, rather than orient themselves with the stars, they will dig for the A Horizon. It is so abundant with life-giving energies that even the falling rain, I'd imagine, is hoping to settle there. Below this is the B Horizon, where only trace elements of life still remain. The stuff of this place is ancient and cool and so entirely leached of desirable nutrients that it has collapsed upon itself and become too dense to scoop or sift by hand. It is instead thick like earthen clay and, once excavated, must be molded, formed, and often cooked in hot ovens for long periods of time to become something that we can once again recognize: a bowl, a plate, a human face.

Beneath this is solid bedrock, where no shovels go.

All to say that it is only by digging through the many horizons of my memory that I've come to understand how this particular night of my youth evolved into the one in which it all went down. It has taken me a while, in other words, to understand how a day that started so benevolently — with my genuine interest in the welfare of Lindy Simpson and Chris Garrett — could turn into a night in which I stood in the dark woods with Jason Landry, looking down at a corpse.

The fork-eared dog had been shot through the head in a manner I would later hear described as execution-style. As it lay on its side, the one eye visible to us was sheared of its lid and made it seem as if the dog were in perpetual amazement, perhaps witnessing some miracle ahead of us in the woods. Its dark tongue had bloated and fallen through the bottom of its jaw, which was gone, and the onset of rigor mortis had stiffened the legs to make it look as if it was stretching for a nap. It looked healthier, in a strange way, than the only other time I had seen it, which was when Jason fed and chased it away from his house those years ago.

Still, it broke my heart like life does.

"Jason," I said, "who did this?"

"Damn," he said. "You really don't get it, do you?"

I didn't.

Of all the permutations in my head on that occasion, none conjured the scene that I later learned to be true: that of my mother with a pair of gardening shears in her hand, a bucket full of clippings at her feet. And on a hot day in the yard while her son was at school for orientation, when she had perhaps paused to sip from a glass of lemonade on the wrought-iron table near the swimming pool, she heard the strange sound of a whimpering. Another sound, then, of a man's voice. And it was only a casual curiosity that led her to the fence of our yard, where she pushed aside the branches of the althea and azaleas that had grown so strong in that light. And once there, she saw through the chain-link fence the enormous body of her neighbor, Jacques Landry, dragging a dog by the scruff of its neck to the woods behind their properties. And wherein as soon as she recognized this dog as the fearful stray she'd stumbled across on occasion, one she'd felt a torn sympathy for, toggling between calling Animal Control or perhaps bringing it into her own home to share with her son and surviving daughter who could use some cheering up themselves, she saw her neighbor straddle the dog between his legs, pull a pistol from his belt, and shoot it in the head. And as she was still so stunned by what she had seen, still held motionless, the moment her neighbor with a bandaged hand made his way up the hill and glanced casually in her direction, meeting her eyes with his own, she was unable to keep yet another small part of her once hopeful nature from dying. And so she backed away from the fence and ran into her house, where the only remaining space left to retreat was inside of her mind. And this is where she found me, I suppose, in her memory, mentioning a dark room full of pictures in that large neighbor's house.

I didn't know any of this then. I only knew that my mom had been frightened that day and that Mr. Landry was frightening. I also knew that Jason Landry was old enough to be working in a convenience store, to be venturing out in life, and yet there he was pissing his blankets at night, sleeping alone in a childish fort. I knew that he had scars on his back shaped like dimes because I had seen them. I also knew there was a part of me that believed Jason himself could have killed the dog. And so, now that he had chosen me to confide in, to team up with, I also knew that our views of the world were so wildly disparate that the fond way I thought about Randy Stiller, my pal, my best friend in the good old days, was likely the way Jason Landry thought about me. Over all the other mounting evidence, it may have been *this* strange idea, that I was possibly the closest friend Jason Landry had, that convinced me of his father's guilt.

Jason handed me a shovel.

"Do you pray?" he asked me.

"No," I said. "Not in a long time."

"Fine," he said. "I'll do it." Jason stuck the blade of his shovel in the ground and squeezed the hilt like a microphone. "Dear Whatever," he said. "Please let my dog get lots of horny bitches in heaven. Or, if not that, let him come back to Earth infested with rabies and finish the job that he started when he was just trying to protect me from that asshole who is probably your biggest mistake. Or maybe just go back in time and switch life around so that my dad is the one that gets hunted for years and locked in a shed and then shot in the face by my dog. I'm good with any of these options. Okay, then. Fuck you very much. Amen."

"Amen," I said. We began to dig.

I like to think now that I was biting my tongue as we dug that hole, trying not to ask Jason for more details about his obviously horrible personal life. Or that I was trying to skillfully negotiate a way to offer some help without insulting him. I think the truth, though, is that I was already envisioning myself as some sort of local hero. The more we labored and sweat and slapped at the mosquitoes on our arms in the darkness, the more I imagined what Lindy might say if I crawled out of the Landrys' window with handfuls of evidence. I had no idea what that evidence could be, other than perhaps some more photos, but if I could find something to link Mr. Landry to the crime, something to put Lindy and her family at ease, something that would allow us all to move on and let me assuage my guilt without ever having to tell her about what I had done and seen while sitting in the branches of her water oak, then that would be nice. I imagined holding this evidence up like a trophy while my parents congratulated me. The Perkins School might even throw some sort of catered reception and invite Lindy back to the track team, give her a standing ovation. And by the time my fantasy had evolved into a vision of me traipsing across the stage to accept my Medal of Honor, Jason and I were covered in dirt.

"I think that's deep enough," he said, and he was right.

After we covered the hole back up, Jason encircled the grave with random junk as if to mark it: a rusty toaster, an elbow of PVC pipe, a birdcage, a broken speaker. It looked like the crown of some buried and monstrous king. He then gathered the bottles he'd filled with fuel, wrapped them loosely in a T-shirt, and put them in a backpack he slung over his shoulders.

"I guess that's it," he said. "Just make sure

you're out of the house in an hour. Don't start whacking off in there."

"Aren't you coming with me?" I asked.

"Fuck no," he said. He then looked past me toward the neighborhood, as if he could see straight through the woods and up the hill and into the living room of the home he'd fled from. "I'm never going back inside that house."

"Should we meet back here, then?" I asked him.

"Don't ever come back here," he told me. "I'm serious. Someone could follow you. This place is sacred ground now."

Jason tightened the straps on his shoulders and walked in the opposite direction of our neighborhood. I felt a quiet sadness that he was leaving, like we should shake hands or something. I suppose part of me knew I might not see him again.

"Jason," I asked him, "where are you going?"

"To the prom," he said. "You'll thank me later."

Then, after a few more steps, Jason stopped and tapped at his pockets like he was looking for something. He finally pulled out a lighter and flicked it twice in the darkness to make sure it worked. And I wonder, now, if I could go back in time and freeze that moment, how much would be lit up in those flint strikes? What else besides us was out there? Oaks? Owls? Mangroves? Gods? Could they tell any difference between me and Jason? Was there any difference? I don't know. Yet as I watched him disappear into the night, I felt pretty sure that something bad was about to happen.

And, possibly, something great.

So I ran. I broke back through the clearing and into the woods and felt no fear as I crossed the fallen tree over the canal. When I neared the edge of my property, instead of continuing toward the street, I took a sharp right and stayed hidden behind the tree line until I could see the lights from the back patio of the Landrys'. Their house, like all of ours, stood on a hill but was almost totally obscured by the metal storage shed Jason and I had leaned against the day I first saw that cur. I ducked behind an oak to catch my breath, and it struck me that I was likely hiding behind the same tree that fork-eared stray had hidden behind.

How long ago had that been? I wondered. It was before Lindy's rape, I knew. It was before my sister died. It was before I was in high school, before I ever did any drugs or drank alcohol or smoked cigarettes, and so we were truly just kids then. We sat in the grass and played with roly-polies and my life was so tremendous and simple that it hurt me to think about it. The more I considered the distance between these two moments, how much we had all changed since then, the angrier I became. I suddenly had no choice but to empathize with Jason Landry and, in many ways, this destroyed me. I knew, for instance, that what I had seen that day behind his shed was not an isolated event and when I began to do the math I realized that Jason had been caring for that dog for years — not weeks or months — by feeding it in secret, by petting it and then cussing it, and by doing everything he could imagine to protect it from his father, who would inevitably return home from work each day and try to kill it, who would stalk the woods for it, who would refresh bowls of antifreeze like others refilled their bird feeders, only because some part of his inexplicable nature was inexplicably offended by an undocumented animal on his property. Or, worse, that he was offended by it because his son loved it.

This horrible idea led me to think about the length of dog years, too, the old saying that dogs age at the rate of six or seven years to our one. And so where, I had to wonder, did our cur find shelter all those decades it lived alone in the woods? How often had it seen us play? How could it, while surrounded by well-to-do families, find no better situation than this one? How could it watch us eat and laugh and ignore it, day after day, and yet remain hopeful?

I suppose that it didn't.

So my anger expanded.

I was angry at Jason for letting it live like that and at Mr. Landry for being so cruel and at the dog for being so unfortunate and at myself for seeing it all those years before and not doing a single thing about it. And this brought to my attention that I had not done a single thing about any of the terrible events in my life. I had not dealt with my sister's death. I had not comforted my family. I had not dealt with my father's leaving us. I had not comforted Lindy. And, despite my inexhaustible attention toward her, I'd yet to even honestly deal with my own role in her sadness. Up until this point in my life, I understood, I had not been a person of much integrity and I wanted this to change.

So I moved up the hill toward the Landrys'. I jogged in a half squat like a movie soldier and had ludicrous thoughts of violence. Perhaps Mr. Landry would be waiting for me on the back porch, ready to beat me to death with his walking stick. Maybe he would pounce on me from the bushes, wrestle me to the ground, and shoot me through the back of the head. Or, perhaps he was already in his owl form and watching me, preparing his stinking nest for my bones. If this was the case, then so be it. I didn't care. I was out of my mind with adrenaline. I was rendered to nothing by guilt. My goals were simple. My ego was zero. It felt, very much, like my life was beginning.

I got to the top of the hill and hid behind the storage shed. I glanced inside the open door of it and saw dog feces all over the concrete, puddles of piss from where the cur must have been kept those last days, and the depth of my rage multiplied. It made sense to me now why Jason said he wished he could have unlocked the shed. It made sense how this particular assault on Jason's heart, of what I was sure had been one of many such assaults perpetrated by his father, had finally given him the courage to leave. Who could blame him.

I left the shed and entered the open garage. I moved slowly around the Landrys' cars, still on the opposite side of the house as the room I'd been called to loot. I wanted to make sure they were asleep before trying the window, and I needed a good look inside. I bent to all fours and crawled through the garage to the backyard, where my hands and knees got soaked from the grass. I didn't mind. I wanted it that way. I felt so much a part of the Louisiana landscape that I could sense the dew falling around me. It was a beautiful night and I know this because nearly everything that I remember so clearly — the corpse, the shed, the wet grass beneath my fingers — was lit only by the moon and I was a part of it, snaking up their yard to the back patio, where I could finally see through the big windows of their den, just as I would have been able to see through the big windows of mine. And sitting there, passed out in an armchair, was the enormous Mr. Landry.

He wore the same slacks and dress shirt I had seen him in earlier that day, and his hand remained bandaged. His shoes were off and his feet were splayed on an ottoman while his head rested on the fat of his own neck. Beside him on an end table sat a glowing lamp and an empty cocktail glass. Next to this sat a bottle of brown liquor that I did not recognize at that age. What was it? Scotch? Bourbon? Rye? I suppose it's no matter when a man takes it on by himself. And as I watched the terrible Mr. Landry sleep, I found it odd that a person who caused such pain could rest easily while his child and neighbor scurried about like night roaches.

And we were not the only ones up. Just as I was about to head to the front of their house, I saw Louise Landry walk through their den. I'd forgotten about her. She wore a thick blue robe that looked as simple as an oven mitt. I ducked out of sight, but she did not turn toward me. She was merely on some domestic trip from point A to point B and stopped only to stare at her husband for a while. She held a lit cigarette in her hand but did not bring it to her mouth in the time that I watched her. The way she stood there so still, with her unbraided hair spread scraggily across the back of her robe, made her look like a witch from a different era. It was eerie enough for me to wonder if she might disappear before my eyes or perhaps smother her sleeping husband with a pillow. But she did not. After a moment, she simply bent forward and dropped her cigarette into his empty cocktail glass. Then she walked around the corner into the hall.

I, too, changed position and kept to the shadows outside of the house until I got to their bedroom window. The blinds were down, but I was able to watch through a crack at the bottom as Louise Landry entered the far end of their shotgun-style hallway and opened the door to Jason's room which, in my house, would have been my room. She stood for a while in the same ghostly manner I'd seen in the den and finally closed the door. Then she walked toward me, through the long hall and into her bedroom, turning out the lights along the way.

Once she was inside her room, I watched her shut the door and remove her thick robe. Beneath it she wore an uncomfortable-looking nightgown that could have passed for a child's Easter dress. It had lace around the collar and a busy floral pattern and did nothing to suggest that there was a woman beneath it. She looked in the mirror and pressed her palms against her cheeks for what seemed to me like too long, and I wondered crazily if she might remove her entire face, if I was to bear witness to the real reason the Landrys behaved so differently. But she did not. She instead entered their bathroom and turned on the water that I could hear running through the outside meter I stood beside. When she returned, Louise Landry clicked off the overhead lights and was now illuminated only by a lamp on her bedside table. I then watched her walk to the foot of her bed, get down on her knees, and pray.

I couldn't believe it.

The image was so pure and unexpected that I felt sick to my stomach. I'd seen my mother do this so often in the time since Hannah's death that I could tell, without a doubt, Louise was praying for Jason. Despite their contentious relationship, despite her strange personality, the simple nature of her posture proved to me that she loved him. I had seen this type of worry before and I knew from whatever Jason was up to in the woods, and from whatever he had sent me to find in his father's private room, that things would only get worse for her. Perhaps I should have put a stop to it there.

Instead I hurried back across the patio to make sure Mr. Landry was still asleep and then ran halfway up their driveway before ducking into a hedge of azaleas that lined their house. I was sweating as I crouched in those bushes. I saw mosquitoes in their hundreds stir from the dead leaves I disturbed. They gnashed me in my progress. They covered me. I could feel them in my nose and ears and I had to hold my breath to press on. You must live in Louisiana to understand this. You must hide in our azaleas to tell this. And when I rounded the corner to the front of their house I shrugged the mosquitoes off my arms and neck and pulled the small key out of my jeans pocket. I listened intently for people and cars and heard nothing but the sound of frogs and my breathing and perhaps a distant siren. I went quick.

I scurried across the porch with my head down and when I reached the window to Mr. Landry's private room I saw that it was covered, on the inside, by blackout curtains. I put the key in my mouth and traced my hands along the slim metal ledge at the bottom of the window. I got a good grip and lifted the frame, and Jason was right. It was unlocked. I slid it open.

This is it, I thought. Finally, this is for Lindy. This is for my mom.

This is for the neighborhood.

Then I parted the curtains and crawled inside.

32.

It is important for me, whenever I relive this night at the Landrys', to first remind myself of other, better, memories. This is how I keep darkness from winning. This is how I stay healthy.

So, let me tell you:

My mother had a crush on Robert Stack.

This was after the divorce, after Hannah, after Lindy, after I had broken into the Landrys' house, and after Rachel had moved back out on her own, in a time when it was just me and my mom again on Piney Creek Road, in the fall of 1992, my senior year of high school. She had recently taken another part-time job to keep busy, this time at a beauty salon, working as a receptionist at the counter about four days a week and, on the days it was raining, or if we had decided to go out to dinner after one of my soccer practices, she would pick me up in her car that now smelled strongly of the rank acetone they used at the salon. I would throw my stuff in the backseat and sit down in the front and my mother would reach over and squeeze my arm to greet me. She would tell me how happy she was that I had started soccer again, how much better I was looking, how proud she was of me, and I'd say something like, *What's the big idea? You bucking for a promotion?*

Things were pretty good between us.

This was not the trouble.

The trouble was that my mother was still insatiably sad. She put on a brave face and filled as many days as she could manage with work but even this seemed only to remind her of what she had lost. The salon, for example, was frequented by women my mother had known in what she called her "previous life." These were ladies she'd played tennis with at the country club or gone to real estate conventions with along with their spouses and the constant re-appearance of these people in her "new life" seemed to throw my mother off-balance. While driving me home, for instance, she would say things like, *Do you remember Lucy Gifford? You played tennis with her son,* and I would say things like, *I don't know, Mom. That was a long time ago. Why?* Yet she rarely had an answer.

The obvious reason, I always imagined, was that she had seen Lucy Gifford at work that day and, whether or not Lucy Gifford looked ill or well, my mother had to wonder if Lucy Gifford knew about what my father was doing with the eighteen-year-old biology major who worked at the pro shop those years back, while he was still married. And who knows, my mom may have even been suspicious about Lucy Gifford herself. What was going on at those conventions when my father came back to the room later than she did? What did Lucy Gifford mean when she said she always enjoyed seeing us at the club? Once the trust is gone, you know, all of history changes. A person doesn't know what to believe. My mother was no different.

Worse still is that what surely followed these encounters was the way my mother backtracked in her mind to wonder about the Giffords' kids and how they'd come along, a boy near my age, she remembers, and a daughter near my sister's. And then there would be Hannah, always dead and waiting for her. There would be love and loss and regret and injustice and the inside knowledge that the way that life fleets can just crush you.

So despite her best efforts, my mother still

struggled to get through the days without exhaustion. This led her to give up dating, to stop being set up by friends, and to stop going to any social events that might require her to be emotionally engaging, although she was still a charming and beautiful woman. This also led her to become less energetic around the house. She began closing off doors to certain rooms and no longer dusting or vacuuming them as rigorously as she used to. She also spent less time cooking, which is a strange thing to do in Louisiana. This is not to suggest that she was lazy, because she wasn't, but if she came home from work excited about some new recipe the manicurists had passed along, it had nothing to do with the pleasure that meal might provide, but rather the fact that the whole thing took little time to prepare.

Meals that required forethought, like peeling or slow roasting or marinating, became rare. If they happened at all it was only on weekends or holidays and our weekly supper rotation came to consist of a predictable series of baked pork chops and sloppy joes and plain spaghetti, until even these dwindled down to skinless chicken breasts that my mother would buy in bulk and cook in the microwave. The results were pale and continent-shaped entrées that she would present to me with different names. Chicken a la Ranch Dressing. Chicken a la Ketchup. Maybe some peas on the side. I ate these meals without praise or complaint.

What does a boy say?

But on Wednesday nights my mom would order pizza that came to us in one large greasy box at seven forty-five p.m. The cash would be sitting on the planter by the front door, and I would hand it to a guy with long hair and a skull-and-crossbones earring in his left ear. He wore a Sony Discman attached to his belt, and I would often recognize the song blasting through the headphones around his neck. Each week he would take the money and flip through the bills and say, "Thanks, bro," and I would walk the pizza into the den, where my mother had set up trays. We'd lay our slices on paper plates and turn down the lights as my mom sat next to me on the couch to watch TV. Our entire house would then be transformed as the dark and eerie theme song for the show *Unsolved Mysteries* came on. The host, the actor Robert Stack, would then step out of a shadow on-screen and talk directly to us.

This hour was like a vacation.

At the height of its popularity, each episode of this show consisted of several retellings of "true" events both realistic and supernatural that even the most decorated detectives were unable to puzzle. The scenes would be dramatized by unknown actors and occasionally made use of special effects, all of which were narrated in voice-over by Stack.

If you don't know, Robert Stack's voice was a human miracle. His deep baritone had a strange influence on everything he said, and this, along with his good looks, sustained him through a long and varied Hollywood career at the back half of the twentieth century. It wasn't that his voice merely made things sound frightening or dangerous. It was that he made them sound important. The disappearance of a small-town girl from Utah, the abduction of a businessman from Des Moines, these sounded from Stack like a global crisis. So you couldn't help but listen when he explained the details of a case. You couldn't help but agree when he told you how necessary it was to come forward if you knew anything. And you couldn't help but legitimately wonder about the topics he pursued that no one else seemed willing to talk about, even when he began the show with impossible questions, such as, "Are we alone in the universe?"

This hour of the week became a true pleasure for both my mother and I, one of the few a teenager can share with a parent at that age, and our shadows sat like hills on the wall behind the couch as we watched. I remember it so well, and yet it is easy to underestimate moments like this when we're in them. It's easy to take life for granted. Everybody knows that.

But here's the thing.

It is also easy to dismiss the random ways in which these memories return to us, often in dreams or strange flashes, as merely the unpredictable shuffling of our human mind that is, in itself, an unsolvable mystery. How does it even work? Brain clouds? Electrical currents? Associative recall? Ask a doctor. They don't seem too sure. In fact, even some of our brightest psychologists and surgeons will tell you that the human memory, in its true intricacy, may never be parsed. But, I've come to think it's much simpler than that.

I believe the reasons we hang on to seemingly insignificant snippets of conversation, the smell of a particular pizza delivered by a particular guy, the shape of certain shadows on a particular wall, is that there may come a day when we are sitting in a hospital room visiting our mother as she lies on an uncomfortable bed, still recovering. And we are asking her questions and feeling nervous about what the doctor has said could be permanent damage caused by a blood clot the size of a pinpoint and we don't know if the way she is struggling to find the right words is a temporary exhaustion or the new reality and all we want to do is tell her we love her in a language no one has used before because we mean it in a way that no one has meant it before. And this will be a difficult time for us.

But then, in a break between the words, a commercial may come on the small television hung up in the corner of the room that we did not even know was playing. It may advertise some new drug, some insurance plan, and our mother will smile at the voice of the handsome actor standing in front of a green screen. She will then close her eyes and squeeze our hand, the one that she has been holding since we walked in, and say, "Oh, I used to have such a crush on him."

When she does this, our memory will be waiting.

As soon as we look at the actor, as soon as we recognize him, memory will gladly rebuild for us the flickering den, place again the taste of pizza on our tongues, and even fill the hospital room with the smell of acetone that clung to our mother's hair those decades ago. It will then perform other invisible miracles as well, allowing us to travel back in time to once again look at the woman sitting on the couch next to us watching TV, where she is now a much different person than the one we saw as a teenager. She is much more complicated, as with memory we are able to consider her life as a whole. We are able to consider both of our lives together. The sacrifices she made for us. The pain we went through. The trouble we caused her. The way she raised us. *Yes yes yes.* It is love that we feel here.

This is the purpose of memory.

But where memory fails is in touch.

We cannot physically go back to that dimly lit den and push aside the television trays to lie down and rest our head in that woman's lap. We cannot feel her fingers in our hair, her hand on our shoulder. We can try if we want to, sure. We can close our eyes. We can imagine as hard as we like. It doesn't matter. The touch is gone. Memory understands this.

So it enables the voice of Robert Stack or someone else like him to do for us what it needs to, which is remind us that every moment of our lives is plugged in. Every moment is crucial. And if we recognize this and embrace it, we will one day be able to look back and understand and feel and regret and reminisce and, if we are lucky, cherish. The way our sister tapped the top of a door frame. The way our father danced in the den. The way a grown man cried in the grass. The way Lindy, or at least some stolen version of her, once raced to a tree in the schoolyard. This is the best we can do.

And this is not so bad.

33.

Unfortunately, some things are so bad.

The inside of Jacques P. Landry's private room was fifteen by twelve feet and stank of cigar smoke. The carpet was thick and brown and felt dirty beneath my palms as I trespassed across it that night, scared thoughtless on my hands and knees. To my left was a table stacked with files and envelopes. On the wall above it, a dry-erase board scrawled with symbols I could not discern. Next to this stood three filing cabinets, the middle of which was topped with a television and other electronic devices, and the digital clocks of these machines provided one of my only two sources of light. The other came in a sliver from beneath the locked door and made the doorway look like the entrance to another dimension. It reminded me immediately of something in my past that I could not place. Then the hair on my arms stood up like an animal's.

I got the feeling I was not alone.

I stopped and listened for someone else in the room but heard only the soft whir of electronics. The place was so dark that I could barely make out even the largest objects and so I held my breath and scanned the wall to my right, making guesses as to what was there, and then my body went cold all over. In the far corner of the room I saw the outline of a head, what could be hair. It was hard not to scream. The shadow was so still, though, that I couldn't be sure. This made me doubt everything else in my vision, as well. Is that a lamp or a shotgun? A table or a cage?

I did not know the answers to these simple questions, and the shape I saw against the wall could have been a potted plant. It could have been the smiling face of Jacques Landry. Yet it remained freakishly still. So I sunk closer to the floor and invented simple rules for myself. If it moves, I fly out of the open window. If I hear breathing, I crawl backward and try not to wake it. Is that a chin or a handle? I wondered. A shoulder or a drawer? I pressed my belly to the ground to get a different vantage point and soon felt something cold beneath my forearm, a light square on the dark carpet. Once I noticed this one I saw others as well, spread across the room as if spilled or dealt out like cards. They were made of photographic paper, I could tell, the same size and shape as my picture of Lindy, and I carefully slid the nearest one toward me and turned it over. It was a close-up of male genitalia.

The image was so unexpected that I almost didn't recognize it. The picture looked posed and clinical, and yet this was not from a medical book. It was black and white and poorly lit, like pornography from a bygone era, and I immediately knew whose body it was. The thick mat of pubic hair, the sturdy thighs from which the organ stood erect all repulsed me. A trio of dark moles dotted the pelvis. The testicles hung like weights. It looked, to me, just like him.

When I glanced back up, I saw a person sitting in the corner. Her cheeks were thin and her neck long and I wondered wildly if some foster child had been tied to a chair and left for dead in this room. I worried too, even though it was irrational, that it could have been Lindy tied up in that chair because this is the nature of worry. Yet my fear of this was enough to motivate me to stand up and, once I moved toward her, I saw that this was not a person at all, but rather a life-sized female doll. She was stiff and naked and plastic, and the blank of her openmouthed gaze horrified me. I then saw another one, a male counterpart, crumpled to the floor beside her. He was facedown and undressed and the way his arms folded over his head made him look like a guilty penitent. I became clumsy with fear. I backed away and knocked an ashtray off an end table. I bumped against a video camera perched on a tripod. I tripped over cords that ran across the carpet to the far wall, and when I followed them to the filing cabinets I saw that they were plugged into the electronic devices stacked on top of the television. Once I got close enough, I could see that these devices were Betamax machines, outdated versions of the VCR. There were three of them, all plugged into one another, and I carefully ran my hands across their fronts. I flipped open their small viewing windows and, inside the middle machine, I saw a tape. I couldn't help myself.

I made sure the volume was off. I pressed play.

I expected the worst. Some part of me hoped for it. I knew that if I could find evidence of obvious atrocity then I could just grab this tape and go. This was my idea, I suppose, of being a hero. Instead, what materialized on the television was not immediately obvious. It was a series of pictures laid out like a grid and, in the eight or so squares that made a border around the screen, I saw the faces of foster children. The kids were thin and shirtless and stared blankly at something off camera like a Third World version of *The Brady Bunch*. I recognized the face of Tyler Bannister, the tattoo of a bird with one wing visible on his neck every time he looked away from the camera. The tattoos on his wrists visible when he covered his eyes. I also recognized Tin Tin and, in the other frames, saw kids from around eight to twelve years old that did not last long at the Landrys'. I did not see Jason at all. Every so often, one of these children would gaze into the camera and speak, but I could not hear what they were saying. For this, all these years later, I remain thankful.

In the middle of this grid — what the children were watching while being taped, I suppose — were two separate frames of black-and-white images from our neighborhood. One frame was comprised entirely of video footage and, in it, familiar cars pulled out of driveways, neighbors watered their lawns, we played football in the street. It was the ordinary stuff of our suburban lives in those days. The other frame shuffled through a collection of still photos, much like the close-ups scattered all over the floor. My mother at the mailbox. Bo Kern's harelip. A woman's vagina. Duke Kern's sculpted stomach. And then Lindy, one summer day before it all happened, I knew, with her hair fallen across her tanned shoulders. With her smile so innocent that I'd almost forgotten it.

Then everything changed.

I noticed a light on the walls, and its flicker was unmistakable. I ran over and peeked through the side of the curtains and it took me a long time to process what I saw. There was a police car on Piney Creek Road, parked two doors down at my house. The vehicle sat in our driveway, its lights spinning without sound, and in front of that, I saw my father's Mercedes. I watched two officers get out of their car as my father walked up our driveway to meet them and I'd no idea what to make of it. I remembered my mother calling him after Jacques Landry came to our door, telling us that he would stop by, but to show up in the middle of the night? How desperate must her voice have sounded? How long had he been at my house? Did I leave my window open? Were Mom and Rachel awake? Or was the reason he had shown up not because of that cur at all, not because of Jacques Landry, but rather because my mother had woken up to find me missing? Had she called him again? Had she also, this time, called the police? At what point did my decisions begin to hurt the people I loved?

I didn't have time to think.

Behind me, the Landrys' telephone rang. I nearly jumped through the window. The clang of the bell filled the house so aggressively that it was hard to recall the silence that preceded it. By the second ring, I heard Mr. Landry moving around in the den. It sounded like someone was rousing a bear. I heard a glass break, a piece of furniture fall over. I then heard him calling out for Louise to answer the phone and I knew I had to get out of there. I took another quick glance around the room for the safe, for the entire reason I came, and I spotted it, the size of a dormitory refrigerator, sitting beneath the desk.

Before I could get to it, three more patrol cars came screaming down Piney Creek Road. They had their sirens on, their lights flashing, and I turned to watch through the side of the curtains as they stopped in front of the Landrys', maybe thirty yards from where I hid. I shut the curtains and heard the heavy sound of Jacques Landry running down the hallway toward me. I couldn't move. This was it. I was sure of it. He was going to open the door and find me and he was going to kill me. If a person could shoot an innocent dog, why not shoot a meddlesome boy? I found no logical reason. So I put my back to the wall and stared at the door and in this almost ecstatic fear realized what the sliver of light beneath it reminded me of.

It reminded me of Christmas Eve, every year but that last one.

It reminded me of the way my sisters would return home from college for this holiday or, back when we all lived together, simply play along with the idea of Santa Claus because I was their brother and I was younger than them and I had rushed through supper to take my bath and put on my pajamas so that I could sleep where I always slept on Christmas Eve, which was on the pullout trundle of my sister Hannah's bed. She and Rachel would turn in early that night, as well, to share the bed above me as they did only that one time per year where they would tease me by wondering aloud if we had forgotten to put out food for the reindeer, cookies for the big guy. And even after they eventually told me the truth, which they claimed it their big-sisterly duty to do, we continued to sleep in Hannah's room on Christmas Eve for what we said was our mother's sake, and I would have sold my soul, at that moment, to do it again.

But the reason I was reminded of this was that in those youngest years, when I still believed in nearly everything a child is supposed to believe in, I would stare at the sliver of light beneath Hannah's door long after she and Rachel had fallen asleep and want desperately to be the one boy on Earth who saw Santa's feet and could testify to it, as he stopped outside of our room to give my sisters and I a quiet blessing. Yet when I finally did see a pair of feet stop at a door exactly like Hannah's, in a room the exact shape of Hannah's, it did little but confirm to me that Hannah was dead and my childhood was over and that blessings are as easily taken away as they are given.

So I dove beneath his desk to hide. I had no real plan. When Mr. Landry rattled the doorknob I closed my eyes and clenched my body and prayed like a coward for help from the same God I'd so often dismissed. And yet he did not open the door. He instead began securing the locks outside of it and the rattling noise of this endeavor traveled up the door frame like it was being zipped. In the street, the police cut off their sirens. I heard their footsteps on the sidewalk outside. Inside the house, I could hear Mr. Landry and Louise bickering with each other as they both moved toward the front door. When they opened it, Mr. Landry said, "What is the meaning of this?"

A policeman said, "Are you the parents of Jason Landry?"

I knew we were going down after this.

So I did what Jason suggested I do and opened the safe beneath the desk. If I was going to be arrested for breaking and entering, I at least wanted my hands full of evidence. Who knows what I expected to find. Lindy's underwear? A signed confession? The entire enterprise suddenly seemed ridiculous. Still, I twisted the key and opened the safe and there was not much inside of it: six Betamax tapes with the word "Master" written on the labels, a few documents that looked official and scientific but were incomprehensible, and a medical case full of glass vials. In a cardboard box next to this sat a pile of syringes still in their plastic. I carefully removed the case and pulled a vial from its package. I did not recognize the name of this drug but recalled the pained face Tyler Bannister had made those years back upon the mention of this room and understood that no matter what Jacques Landry was up to with those children, it was abominable. I've never gone back to research this. I've never had the stomach. Call me what you will. Yet on that night I took this vial and grabbed as many photos from the floor as I could. I thought about grabbing the tapes, the camera, the spent cigars that were as round as dimes, and then I heard my father's voice.

He was outside, calling Jacques Landry's name.

I went to the window and nudged the curtain to see my father barreling down the street. Behind him, two police officers walked with my mother and sister, both of whom were in their robes. "Jacques!" my father yelled. "Where the hell is my son?" Mr. Landry stood talking to two policemen. He seemed totally unaware of my father's presence until my dad broke through their huddle to confront him. He grabbed Mr. Landry by the shirt, and for one split second, before the voices all rose beyond comprehension, before the police pulled my father off Mr. Landry as easily as lint from a suit coat, it looked like my father was honorable. It looked like he was valorous.

And hereabout came a change in me.

Although it was dark outside and the

lighting was bad, just a few rotating sirens, two streetlights lit and a third still broken, it looked like my father was invincible. If you could have frozen that moment in time, like we so often do in our photos, you would have seen my father about to reach into the throat of Jacques Landry and pull out his bullying heart. You would also see genuine fear in Mr. Landry's broad face. More important, though, and what I am trying to tell you is that within this quick exchange I understood that it is inside all of us men to be both menacing and cowardly. It is in all of us to have virtue and value and yet it is also in our power to fall into irrelevant novelty or, even worse, elicit indifference from the people we've loved. This is the challenge, I suppose, of fatherhood. And so I knew that, despite my father's errors, he loved me. He loved us. I also knew that big and important parts of him were sorry because I knew that he was willing to fight. What more could I ask for? I will never apologize for loving him back.

But it was my mother's face that brought me out of the window.

She stood to the side of the growing crowd as confusion, in general, began to bloom. She watched my father argue with Mr. Landry, but I could tell by her expression that she was not listening to them. My mother, instead, was in some internal place, looking around at her life. I wondered what she was thinking then, in the same way I so often wonder that now. Was she considering her time with my father? Was she wondering how it had come to this? What is the exact path from old wedding photos to a night of horror outside of your dream house? What are the odds of one child dead and another one missing? The truth is, of course, there are no odds for this, and that is when I realized what my mother must have been doing. She must have been preparing herself. That's why, when everyone else was yelling and getting emotional, my mother stood quietly off to the side, as if doing math in her head.

And me, I wanted to solve her problem.

I lifted the curtain and stepped out of the Landrys' house.

For a second, I thought I was going to walk right through the yard, unnoticed, and into my mother's arms. But this did not happen. Instead, I heard a policeman yell for me to stop. So I did. I imagine that he drew his gun and approached me, but I really don't know. The only thing I saw was my mother's face. She had not even looked up. I put my hands in the air and called to her.

"I'm right here, Mom," I said. "I'm fine."

The officer demanded that I drop my weapon, and I immediately realized how I must have appeared. I was sweaty and covered with mud. I had fistfuls of contraband. My mother finally looked up, and I still today cannot decipher the expression that broke over her face. I am not sure, in other words, if the lighting cast me in such shadow that she was trying to understand how her son's voice came from this criminal surrounded by cops or if my voice on that night, so full of fear, sounded foreign to her coming from a shape she so obviously knew. If I had to guess, I'd think that my mother, in doing her private calculations, had likely advanced so far into the unfortunate algorithms of her future sadness that she had simply forgotten the possibility that I might be okay and that she would not have to suffer yet another loss. So the confusion on her face was not about my life, really, but about hers, and the idea that it might go on.

I looked at the policemen.

"I don't have a weapon," I said. "I have evidence in the rape of Lindy Simpson."

I suppose there are five things to know

about the next ten minutes on Piney Creek Road.

One: Jacques Landry had to be restrained when he learned I had been in his house. Two: my father had to be restrained when he saw that cop shove my face in the lawn. Three: the police thought I was Jason Landry. Four: unbeknownst to us, the actual Jason Landry was approaching the house from the woods. And, five: Lindy was standing in the street, watching all of this.

This was not good.

Lindy's parents were out there, too, as was nearly the whole neighborhood. This type of entertainment was not typical on Piney Creek Road and so everyone wanted answers. Lindy's father, for example, began frantically swooping up the photos I'd dropped on the ground. Lindy's mom, on the other hand, put her arms around Lindy as if attending to a person in shock. I heard my father threaten a lawsuit, Mr. Landry demand my arrest. The police, of course, were totally unprepared for the totality of what they'd stumbled upon in Woodland Hills, and when the officer finally pushed me into the backseat of the patrol car, I began to understand why.

Past our houses, way off in the distance, I could see an orange light.

407

The Perkins School was on fire.

And although I later found out that Jason had spray-painted his name all over the school chapel and thrown his father's business cards around the manicured quad before he set the place ablaze, I could not yet empathize with his desperate need for attention in the way that I do now. I could instead only watch this colored sky become a backdrop as Lindy walked toward the police car I was sitting in. It was obvious she had been crying, and I thought, for a second, that she might be grateful for what I had done. I smiled at her as she put her hands on the glass of the half-open window.

She yelled at me.

"What the fuck is your problem?" she said.

I had no idea how to answer.

"Are you trying to ruin my life?" she said. "Is that your goal?"

"No," I said. "What are you talking about? I was trying to help you. I thought if maybe you knew."

Lindy did not want to hear it. She turned in a circle. She was beside herself.

"If I knew what?" she said. "If I knew what his face looked like? How would that help me, you sick fuck?"

"You don't understand," I told her. "Mr. Landry has all these pictures of you. He has

408

all these twisted pictures of everybody. He has all these drugs. I think he might have done it."

She looked over at Jacques Landry, who was now surrounded by police, by Lindy's father, by Old Man Casemore, by every male out there. "That fat ass?" she said. "He didn't do it, you idiot. The guy was skinny. He was bony. He felt like a goddamned skeleton on my back."

"He did?" I said.

The last couple years of my life appeared pretty naïve to me then.

I thought, for instance, that explanations healed scars, when they didn't, and that the way I wanted life to be was more important than the way life was, which it wasn't. In fact, I think I honestly believed in those years that if I could get Lindy to again be who she was before her rape, rather than admitting to the fact that she had been raped and was now different because of it, then maybe I could get the entire world to go back to how it was when we were little, when my father was around, and when my sister was alive.

"I didn't know that," I told Lindy. "I didn't know that he was skinny."

Lindy cut her eyes so sharply in my direction that I understood, despite my years of trying, that I didn't know a thing about her. Our talks about Dahmer. Our idle gossip. Our misguided phone sex. They had nothing to do with her real life. That had nothing to do with her heart.

She again leaned toward the open window.

"Does it make you feel better to know that he was skinny?" Lindy asked me. "Is that why you talk to me all the time? You want to know some more details? You act like you're my friend, but that's total bullshit. You just feel bad because you told everybody and now you want to make it better, but you can't. That's why you act so interested in me. So you can be a little detective and solve the case and feel better about fucking up my life."

I noticed people looking over at us. I saw Lindy's mom coming our way.

"Lindy," I said, "that's not true."

Lindy slammed her fists on the roof of the police car. "Yes, it is," she said. She stood on her toes as if wired with energy. She was so angry that she couldn't even look at me. "Let's get it over with, shall we?" she said. "What else do you want to know? Do you want to know that I get sick when I see a man's sweat sock? Like in the gym or in the road or anywhere else. Some idiot loses a sock and I fucking puke because I taste it

410

all over again. Do you like that? What else? Do you want to know that I remember hitting the ground and smelling ink and I have no idea why? That's why I got a fucking C in Ms. Price's class last semester, by the way, because she counts off for not using a goddamned pen but every time I smell one I am right back on that sidewalk and it is happening again right now and not in the past but right now and I want to fucking kill myself."

Lindy beat her hand against the window.

"What else do you want to know?" she said. "Let's get it all out so you can feel better. You want to know what he said to me before I blacked out? That's a good one. Everybody acts like I don't remember, but I do. I felt his body and heard his voice and I still don't know whose it fucking was, no matter how many times you or a cop or my fucking dad might ask me, but I do know what he said. Do you want to know? I bet you do, you sick shit."

At this point, Mrs. Peggy put her hand on Lindy's shoulder.

"Lindy," she said. "You're upset, honey. Let's go home."

"Leave me alone," Lindy told her. "I'm talking to my friend here. He wants to know all about me."

"Sweetheart," Mrs. Peggy said. "He was only trying to help."

"I'm so sorry," I said. "I really was trying to help."

Lindy broke away from her mother and turned toward me. We looked into each other's eyes, both sober and clear, for the first time in years. And, as she stood there staring at me, I knew that I had hurt her. I truly felt it, for perhaps the first time.

"Do you want to know?" she said.

"I'm so sorry," I told her.

Lindy put her mouth to the crack of the window.

"I'll tell you what he said," she whispered.

Lindy then lowered her voice to a grunt, to a growl, and it sounded like neither a boy nor a man but some feral animal given power to speak.

"You think you're so pretty," she said, and then Lindy walked away.

I let my head fall against the window and watched the scene before me dissolve through tears that had built up for a long time before this. It was Lindy, yes, and her shredded heart and my self-deception and my parents bearing witness to the person I'd become. And it was also, of course, my own bearing witness.

But I did not get much time to dwell.

Soon Louise Landry tapped on the glass. She was still wearing her thick and knitted nightgown. "Why did you break into our house?" she asked me. "Did Jason ask you to do this? Did he help you?"

I wiped my cheek on my shoulder. I nodded my head.

"I should have gotten us out of here a long time ago," she said.

I looked up at her, and, in her remorse, Louise Landry appeared a thousand years old.

"Do you know where he is now?" she asked me. "Please. He needs help. He needs real help. I never planned for things to turn out this way. I hope you know that."

I knew that she was telling the truth.

In my experience, nothing ever turned out as planned.

Except, perhaps, for Jason Landry on this one night, for whom everything had turned out perfectly. After all, what more could he have wanted? The Perkins School was on fire. His father was being investigated. His mother was pleading for forgiveness. And, meanwhile, Jason himself had walked unseen from the dark woods up the hill to face the back windows of his abusive suburban home. He still had a couple of bottles left in his backpack. He had his lighter. He had his aim. Nobody even knew he was there.

Yet we all heard the glass shatter.

We all heard the woof of his fire, the sound of his laughter.

It was only a matter of time.

34.

I did not see Lindy Simpson again until 2007, nearly sixteen years after that night, outside of an LSU football game. We were both settling into our thirties at that point, only memories to each other now, and we had our own separate lives. To tell you anything more romantic would be dishonest. Not that I didn't try to stay in touch. After the insanity of that debacle on Piney Creek Road was sorted out (the fires extinguished, Jason caught and arrested, Mr. Landry permanently stripped of his medical license and arrested, my name cleared of all charges at the request of Louise Landry), I made several attempts to call and apologize to Lindy. I wanted desperately to see her, to tell her that I knew there were many ways in which she was right about me, and that I was sorry, but she was gone. Whenever her father answered the telephone, he always sounded grateful that I had called, but then told me that she and her mother had still not returned from Shreveport, where they were visiting an aunt. I am not sure if he knew, then, that they would never come back.

I found this out a few weeks later when I learned that Lindy, like scores of other kids, had transferred out of the Perkins School after the fire. Since the damage to the main school building was so extensive, and our semester pushed back and abbreviated, other places had opened their doors to us, extended their generosity, and a number of parents accepted. Randy Stiller, for instance, spent his last two years at Parkview Baptist, where he became a football star. (On the day after I was arrested, by the way, Randy came over to my house. He'd stayed that previous night at a friend's whom I didn't even know and therefore missed all the action. Yet when he entered my room to see if I was okay, we hugged and laughed as if we were best friends again and to this day there is not anything I wouldn't do for him.) But not everybody transferred out of Perkins.

Artsy Julie and I, for example, we stayed. This was a good thing.

We spent that next year walking to school together, where we would shuffle through plywood corridors to find our new lockers made of plastic milk crates with our pictures taped to them. We made up funny nicknames for the men who walked around in asbestos-proof space suits behind the orange caution tape and we practiced our Spanish with the carpenters who showed up by the truckload. We sat through half-empty classes in double-wide trailers, where it was impossible to hear the teacher over the sound of the hammers and saws being used to create a much bigger, much better Perkins School for the future. But we didn't care. For once, we enjoyed the present. We ate lunch out of brown paper sacks in the gymnasium and I found out the soccer team was low on athletes. She heard the pep squad was low on dancers. So, we both said what the hell and joined up and therefore became successful and popular deals in this alternate and burned-down universe. We never forgot how good that felt.

The year 2007, as we later grew to know it, also felt good, and when I ran across Lindy Simpson it was almost midnight on the Parade Grounds of the LSU campus. The date was October 6, and LSU had just defeated the hated Florida Gators in a dramatic and improbable fashion that included five successful fourth-down conversions. That type of thing, if you don't

417

know, just does not happen. This win would vault us into first place in the national rankings and so fans of all ages walked around the campus as if hallucinating. Occasions like this surpass the Rapture where I'm from and I would not be surprised if every living person I knew was in attendance.

But even in a crowd that size, after all those years without her, Lindy was easy to see.

She was dancing in the bed of a pickup truck, at the edge of a large group of people our age. Around her, beer and champagne shot off like fireworks. In the middle of the Parade Grounds, a band had set up a stage and played funk music at full blast and the only lyrics were celebratory chants so earnest that you couldn't believe the game could have ever turned out differently. Lindy's hair on that night was red and stylish, and she wore a purple shirt and fitted blue jeans. She was, as she had always been, gorgeous, and I was thrilled at the sight of her. When she spun around in her dance and saw me standing there, she doubled over and put her hands on her mouth. She jumped out of the truck and ran toward me.

I suppose I should have been terrified at what she might say to me, but I could see in her face, already, that time had been good to us.

"Oh my God," she said, and hugged me around the neck in the same drunken way she had those years before. Her breath, too, was as sweet and smoky as I remembered it, but she was not out of control. She looked happy and fit, and I hugged her back with both arms.

"Can you believe it?" she yelled. "Can you believe that we won?"

"I know," I said. "It's crazy. It's wonderful."

It was so loud and chaotic around us that it was difficult to hear and so we just stood there smiling until Lindy pulled me over behind a screen of trees to talk. "It's good to see you," she said. "Jesus, it's been so long. Do you still live here?"

"I do," I said.

"That's great," she said. "What are you doing these days? I mean, like, for a living."

It was a strange thing but, on that occasion, I felt none of the anxiety around her that I did as a boy. I felt no need to impress her. I had no agenda. Instead I felt as simple and clear as the evening itself because Lindy and I were, perhaps for the first time in our lives, exactly what we looked like: just two people among many, glad to see each other.

"I'm a botanist," I told her. "I study plants and trees and stuff."

Lindy seemed to find this hilarious. "A botanist?" she asked. She looked around. She pointed up. "Okay," she said. "Prove it. What kind of trees are these?"

"Those are crepe myrtles," I said. *"Lagerstroemia indica."*

"What is that, Latin?" she asked, and I nodded. "My God," she said. "Do you remember taking Latin with Ms. Abbott? What a windbag. All I remember is *veni vidi vici. Veni vidi vici.* I think we spent an entire year just saying *veni vidi vici* and watching shit like *Ben-Hur.*"

I smiled. She was right.

It was good to see her.

"What about you?" I asked. "What are you doing these days?"

"I'm a stylist," she said, and dramatically primped her hair. "You know, I study hair and stuff."

"Wow," I said. "That's great."

"Well," she said. "It lets me play with scissors."

And before I could even recall the soft white scars that I am sure still line her inner thighs, Lindy clapped her hands. She grabbed my wrist.

"You've got to meet my husband!" she

said, and pulled me a few steps toward the crowd. "He's a sad little puppy right now. Maybe you can cheer him up. Stay right here." Lindy then turned away from me and sort of half walked and half danced to a guy standing in a small group of people wearing Florida Gator jackets. I'd seen the ring on her finger the moment I first spotted her and so I was curious to meet the man she'd married. I watched her sneak up and slap one of the guys on the butt and give him a long and generous kiss on the cheek and it filled me with pleasure to see this. Then she whispered in his ear and led him over to me.

"This is Sean," she said. "He is, like, the *biggest* Florida fan."

We shook hands. "Sorry, man," I said.

"It's okay," he said. "Who gives up five fourth-down conversions in one game?"

"Nobody," I said. "I know."

"What a nightmare," he said.

"Wait!" Lindy said, and put her hands on my shoulders. "You have *got* to tell Sean about that time Old Man Casemore drove his boat around the neighborhood handing out Cokes and jambalaya and stuff after the street flooded. And tell him about how we used to make those huge beds of moss. He never believes any of the stuff I tell him

421

about growing up."

"It's all true," I said.

Sean laughed. He was clean cut and handsome. He looked like a pretty good guy.

"It sounds like some kind of wonderland to hear her talk about it," he said. "I'm from Gainesville, man. All I remember is being really bored as a kid. We lived in Florida but we weren't on the beach. We didn't have Disney World. It was just hot. I don't know, when she talks about Baton Rouge, it all sounds made up."

"It gets a bad rap sometimes," I said. "But it's a pretty good place."

"It is," Lindy said, and looked at me. "I mean, it was weird, you know, and it took me a while before I started missing it. But now I think about the good times a lot. Do you keep in touch with anybody else from the neighborhood? What about Randy? The Kern boys? Artsy Julie?"

I smiled a little.

"What?" she asked. "Do you have gossip?"

"Well," I said, and held up my left hand. "I keep in touch with Artsy Julie pretty well."

Lindy went nuts. It was like she had won the lottery.

She jumped up and down and hugged me. She nearly knocked me over. "That's incredible," she said. "My God, it was so obvious even then. You two are *perfect.* I'm so glad you finally saw that." She clapped her hands again. She punched her husband on the shoulder. "You don't understand," she told him. "That's like some storybook shit right there. You don't even know."

I smiled. I was happy and embarrassed and we were all a little drunk. Plus the football game, the atmosphere, the Louisiana night, it had all been so good. "Yeah," I said. "It turned out really great."

Then, as if on cue, Julie and her father, who we always go to football games with, came walking toward us across the parking lot. They'd been talking to some family friends who'd wanted to feel Julie's belly and make their predictions. I found out later that they'd also given Julie a list of names, written on a purple napkin, that we should call the child if it was a boy. The names were LSU-related things like *Tiger* and *Geaux Boy* and *Charlie Mac.* One person, I saw, had simply written down the date, that night of our victory on October 6, 2007, and then scribbled *No, I'm serious. Name him that.*

When Lindy saw Julie waddling our way, a good seven months pregnant by then, she grabbed my arm. "She looks so beautiful," she said, and then whispered in my ear,

"Don't you dare fuck this up."

I smiled as Lindy ran over to give Julie a hug and I could hear her complimenting Julie's dress, telling her how she always knew we'd get together. Julie looked at me, sober and amused by this turn of events, and said, "Pish-posh. I practically had to beat him over the head with an anvil."

As the two of them caught up, and Julie's father wandered over to listen to the band, Lindy's husband, Sean, handed me a beer. I had no idea where he got it from. They appear by magic in this place. "So," he said, "tell me this. Is it true that there was this crazy giant psychiatrist guy on your block who took weird porno pictures of all the kids?"

"Yep," I said. "Pretty much."

"Okay," he said. "And is it true that he experimented on all these foster kids with drugs and whatnot? And that his own son basically blew up his house trying to kill him?"

"Yeah," I said. "It was his adopted son, but still. He'd made all these Molotov cocktails. The whole place burned to the ground. He burned down our school, too."

"Jesus," Sean said. "And what about the guy who tried to gather all this evidence to protect the girls in the neighborhood? Lindy said he got caught in the crossfire. She said it was kind of tragic."

I looked at Sean. Out of all the men in the world Lindy could have ended up with, this guy seemed all right to me. I suppose this is because I knew that behind his easy smile was a man in love with a woman who had struggled in life and that he was aware of this. I knew, in other words, that Lindy had scars on her thighs that she could not hide and that, by their marriage, this man, at the very least, had made himself vulnerable enough to share them with her. I also saw that below his heavy Florida jacket Sean wore nice khaki pants that were pressed. And, below this, he wore a pair of dress shoes, not the kind you typically put on to go to a football game, and not the kind you would ever pair with sweat socks. So, we were okay from the start. He had no idea who I was, I understood, but we were okay.

"Is that what Lindy told you?" I asked him. "She said some guy was trying to protect her?"

"She's got a million stories," he said. "But what I don't get is that she tells me these things like it was the most exciting stuff that ever happened, like it was a good time. No offense, but that sounds horrible to me. Floods and fires and psychopath neighbors?

It sounds like a freak show."

"Yeah," I said. "I understand what you mean. It's hard to explain."

Then the two of us stood there and watched our wives laugh and talk. We watched Lindy reach down and rub Julie's belly, and I think we both knew we were pretty lucky in life.

I raised my can of beer, and Sean toasted it without a word. We took a long gulp.

"Who even goes for it on fourth down five times in one game?" he asked me.

"Nobody," I said. "I know."

And later that night, while Julie and I lay in bed and I put my hands on her belly to feel our unborn child do its little knee-and-elbow dance, I began to experience a guilt so tremendous that I knew I would eventually tell you this story, or that I would at least tell someone. It just seemed so strange to me, all of a sudden, that I could still have secrets in the world like the ones I had in regard to the rape of Lindy Simpson.

After all, with Julie, I felt I had no secrets. Anything she had asked me, I told her. Even after we had parted for college and dated other people and then reunited for graduate school (she's a literature professor now, by the way, a smart cookie), I'd told her the truth about all of my feelings. But then, after I saw Lindy again, the legitimate joy I'd experienced at learning she was happy and healthy slowly faded into self-loathing. It was like I was back in high school, shaving the sides of my head, trying so hard to impress her. This made me think of my uncle Barry, and what he'd said to me about love always being the same. It began to make a certain sense to me. I felt antsy and nerve-wracked. I felt full of a tremendous vulnerability. And although there didn't seem to be any similarities between Lindy and Julie, I understood that they were connected by the pain I felt when I was keeping secrets from them. Or, to put it another way, that they were connected by the tremendous potential for love I imagined if they knew the whole truth about me.

So, "Jewels," I said, "I need to tell you something."

Julie rolled over on her side to face me. At seven months, this took some doing, but she didn't seem to mind. She held a pillow between her legs and wore an oversized T-shirt with a cartoon Tyrannosaurus rex on the front of it. The dinosaur was lying facedown, its mouth and feet on the ground, while its short arms flailed around uselessly. The caption read "I hate doing push-ups!"

She smiled.

"Are you going to tell me that you used to be madly in love with Lindy Simpson?" she said. "Because I already knew that."

"No," I said. "That's not what I was going to say."

"It was nice to see her, wasn't it?" Julie said. "She looks good, don't you think?"

"She does look good," I said. "I mean, you know what I mean. She looks happy."

Julie smirked. "What else could you mean, young squire?"

She gave me a playful little pinch under the sheets, and I pulled the covers up to my shoulders. I closed my eyes.

"Do you remember what happened to her?" I asked.

"Of course," Julie said. "She was like Little Red Riding Hood in my house. She was my cautionary tale. It was how my parents told me to be careful, you know, even in our neighborhood."

The idea of this bothered me.

"But Lindy was careful, wasn't she?" I said. "And our neighborhood was safe, wasn't it?"

"Who knows," Julie said. "I'm sure my parents just used her as an example because she was the only one they knew about. Who knows how many others there were."

"Other what?" I asked. "You mean vic-

428

tims? In our neighborhood?"

"Sure," Julie said. "In our neighborhood, or anywhere. Who knows how many more there are out there. That's just not the type of thing women go around talking about."

I thought about this. It seemed to me a horrible version of the world I love.

"I would die if that ever happened to you," I told her.

"Who's to say it hasn't?" she said.

I sat up in bed and looked at Julie. My heart started pounding. I felt frantic.

"You would tell me," I said. "Wouldn't you?"

"I guess I would if I wanted to," she said. "But that would really be up to me."

Then, after a while, she touched my arm.

"Relax, Lancelot," she said. "We're just talking."

I lay down again and looked at the ceiling. I had this painful lump in my throat and was so afraid, already, of becoming a parent.

"If you were Lindy," I said, "do you think you'd want to know who did that to you? Whether you found out now or back then, do you think that would change things for you? Would it make it better, if you had someone to blame?"

"I think a lot of women know who did it,"

Julie said. "I think they might rather not. Still, it's not like either one is a good option."

I kept staring at the ceiling as Julie watched me. She saw that I was close to crying. I know she did.

"They never arrested anybody, did they?" she asked me.

"No," I said. "But they should have."

She took a moment. I could feel her still watching me.

"You're the one who told everybody at school, aren't you," she said.

"I was," I said. "I am."

I then turned to look Julie in the eye and beneath the covers she took my hand and placed it again on her belly. "Hey," she said. "Before you tell me that thing you were going to tell me, will you do me a favor? Will you think about whether or not it will help us? Will it help the baby? I mean, even in the long term. I know how you are. Even if you're thinking about big-picture stuff like honesty and trust, will you also think about how good things seem for Lindy now? And think about how good they are for us? And think about whether or not what you say will help that goodness continue?"

I didn't understand what she was getting at.

"Are you suggesting that the point of the truth is to help people?" I asked her. "Isn't it more complicated than that?"

"Just think about it, okay?" Julie said.

So, I did think about it.

I'm still thinking about it now.

But on that night, Julie rolled back over to her other side, where it was more comfortable for her to sleep in those days. It wasn't personal that she turned her back to me. I understood that. I reached out and adjusted the crease in her shirt. I straightened the covers on her legs.

"Hey," Julie said. "Can I tell *you* something?"

"Yes," I said. "Anything."

"It doesn't bother me that you used to be in love with Lindy, or that you got arrested trying to save her like some comic-book hero."

I smiled at this.

"Why not?" I said. "Shouldn't you be insane with jealousy?"

"No," she said, "because you are in love with me now and we are going to have a kid and you will be our real-life hero."

"Ouch," I said. "No pressure."

Then, after a minute, I said, "You're right about that, though. I am in love with you."

"Plus," Julie said, "I've got like forty

pounds on her now. I've got a ninja in my belly. If Lindy tried anything, it could get ugly."

I lay there and smiled for a good long time.

And then a couple of years went by and our child was healthy and bright and everything I believed I knew about love and humanity deepened in ways I could have never predicted. Still, I understand that we are just getting started, Julie and I. Our daughter is three years old now, and every leap she makes, even the simple sound of her singing in her room when she thinks that no one is listening, it fills me with an irreplaceable joy. It does this to Julie, as well, and so we are happily crushed, like so many others, by parenthood.

But just the other day, as my daughter and I were playing around outside, drawing chalk figures on the driveway, washing the car, and picking a few stray weeds from the flower beds, a small group of neighborhood kids came by. They range from around my daughter's age up to maybe nine years old or so. They are polite and energetic and we see them in the neighborhood often. We wave at them when we pass by. I recognize each of their parents. I hope that Baton Rouge will always be this way. Still, this was the first time they had come to our house in a group to ask if my daughter could join them a few houses down, where they were doing things like riding their bikes in a circle, building an igloo out of milk jugs, and eating popsicles.

I looked down to ask my daughter what she thought of this idea and the look in her eyes was so hopeful that all I said was, "Okay." She ran to the patio to grab her tricycle, a pink getup with a basket on the back, and she was gone. The older kids were kicking off on their skateboards and rip-sticks, the younger kids still with their training wheels, and in that scene I saw what felt to me like the entirety of my life. The plump kid on the Big Wheel, that was Randy Stiller. The older kid on the skateboard was Duke Kern. The girl on the bike, pedaling hard to get to the front of the pack, was Lindy. I did not know who my daughter was yet, or if she would ever be like any of us. I only knew that, whoever she might be, I would love her.

And then a number of things made sense to me — the research I'd found myself doing lately, the old photo albums I'd been looking through, the way I kept steering the conversations with my mother and sister toward Lindy and Hannah and the old days, and even the conversations with my father and Laura, who are now married. These past few years, ever since we had our first child, our daughter, I understood, I've only been trying to say this one thing.

35.

I was up in the tree that night.

It was June and it was hot and I was young and turned completely inside out by what I thought at that time was love. And on that night I had finished supper and helped my mom with the dishes and without even the slightest bit of hesitation I lied and told her that I wasn't in the mood for television. I said that I was instead going to my room to play video games, maybe fall asleep a bit early. And these were the days when every-one I knew was alive, remember. My father was gone, yes, but Lindy and Hannah were untouched. We were all young. So, I knew that my mom would do what she always did in the young summer evenings of 1989 and sit at the dining room table to call Rachel in her dorm room in Lafayette, call Hannah at her apartment on the other side of Baton Rouge. If she got hold of them, they would chat pleasantly for a few minutes and tell each other they loved each other and my mom would then walk the phone back to the wall to hang it up. She might then have called her father or perhaps a friend to reconfirm a lunch date, but not much more, though I am sure she wanted, at times, to call my dad. I am sure she wanted, at other times, to knock on my door and say, *Hey, you, come visit with me. It's barely eight o'clock.* But she did not. She instead walked through the house turning off the lights and picking up little odds and ends like socks and discarded food wrappers until she got to her room, where she began the long process of undressing and taking off her makeup before she would lie in bed and fall asleep reading a self-help book about how to parent through a divorce.

Meanwhile, in my room, I watched the clock.

The thing was, I knew the routine of the Simpson girl.

So when I heard my mother's door shut at eight o'clock, I waited fifteen more minutes and then opened my window to sprint across our darkening street. Lindy would return from the track at eight-thirty, and this gave me enough time to run from one yard to the next while making sure all of the neighbors were inside. I had done this a few times since I learned how to spy on her from the water oak and the results had been tremendous. I saw her, once, talking on the phone and painting her toenails. On another occasion, I watched her fold some laundry and put it away and I honestly never imagined there would come a time when I regretted this.

But that night, as I made like a cat across the street, I couldn't help but look a bit farther down the block to where that broken streetlight looked so peculiar to me. It was still new to us at that time, maybe a couple weeks old, and as I sprinted toward the tree, I saw someone beneath it. I did not *think* I saw someone. I *did* see someone. It was a man, I thought, or perhaps a boy, and the truth is that it was impossible for me to tell because I was running. In other words, I did not get a good look because I did not stop to get a good look.

What I did see was a shadow working hurriedly, moving back and forth from the pole to the azalea bushes, and I thought it was perhaps Old Man Casemore, or maybe some utility worker who'd come to fix the light. I did not care as long I was not seen.

I cannot go back and change this. I cannot go back and fix this.

All I can do is confess that a few minutes

later, when I was up in that tree, I heard something happen on Piney Creek Road. The sound of it was quick and muted and has no other reference for me than that single event. So I have no way to describe it to you, no way to make you hear it. Yet I can tell you this. It was a sound that gave me a feeling. I immediately felt that something was not right and I knew that, whatever it was, it was happening around the corner. I also knew that Lindy, at that time of night, would likely be around the corner. I thought to climb down and go see. That's what kills me. I thought to check on her. Yet I was so afraid of being caught that I decided not to.

So, I never really saw what happened. And I did not commit the act myself.

That's the truth.

What I did see, however, was Lindy, a few minutes later, walking her bike up the sidewalk. Her face was as blank as the day of the *Challenger,* the day I fell in love with her, and I noticed that her shoe was missing. The scraping sound of her uneven walk up the driveway is as clear to me now as it was then. It is as clear as the way I saw her bathroom light turn on, the way I stayed in the tree against my better judgment and listened to the shower go, and the way I watched through my binoculars as she walked into her bedroom still wrapped in a towel, still wearing the exact same blank expression, and curled into a ball on top of her bed. It is also as clear to me as our street was empty, by the time I finally went back home.

So, I am guilty in the most specific sense.

I had an opportunity to help someone and I chose not to. For a large part of my life, I've felt that this decision defined me and I've worn my guilt like a locket.

What am I trying to say?

After my mother's stroke, a minor one that occurred in 2006, a year or so before my daughter was born, she told me that she kept a box in her closet. She was still in the hospital, doing fine but a little shaken and confused, and asked me to go retrieve it for her. When I brought it back to the hospital she unlocked it with a simple combination and opened it up. She pulled out a manila envelope.

"This is my will," she said. "This is the boring part. The rest of this stuff, I figured we could take a look at."

I imagine there is little need for me to describe the bittersweet exhaustion of that afternoon. My mother had a smattering of old photos, strange personal favorites she had collected that were pretty much evenly distributed between Hannah, Rachel, and I. She also had some mementos that didn't mean much to me, but that I enjoyed hearing about. She had a dried corsage from her wedding to my father. She had a blue piece of silk that she told me was from her mother's wedding to her father, both of whom had passed by then. She had letters that had been especially meaningful to her, one from my dad's remorseful parents who had drifted away from us after my father's adultery, another from Finally Douglas after Hannah had died. She had a photograph clipped from the newspaper that showed Rachel playing the wife in a kindergarten version of *'Twas the Night Before Christmas,* and she had a poem that I had written to her for a Mother's Day present when I was in the second grade that I had no recollection of. She also had a yellow Duncan yo-yo that my uncle Barry had asked her to give me.

"I'm sorry I never gave this to you," she said. "Things were just so difficult back then. Barry was so confused and I could tell how much you looked up to him. I don't know. I was afraid of everything."

"I know, Mom," I said. "I was, too."

Other people came to visit throughout the

afternoon, like Rachel and her family, and although the crying jags passed through the room like weather fronts, the majority of the day, interrupted by nurses' visits, was cheerful with memory. When visiting hours were over and we were packing up to leave, my mother pulled out a small notebook from the bottom of the box and asked me if I would like to take it home.

It was Hannah's journal.

"You were so young when that happened," my mom said. "I figured you might not appreciate this until later. And then, you know, time went by and I didn't know what to do."

I looked over at Rachel. I knew she and Hannah were closer than we had ever been.

"You can take it," Rachel said. "Trust me. I've read it a hundred times."

I got home that night to a series of messages on our machine from Julie, who had been at an academic conference in Chicago when my mother had her stroke the day before. I'd told her to stay and deliver her paper, and she had called me to say that she managed a way to deliver it early and get a flight that would have her home the next morning. She asked me to call her in her hotel room and I did.

After this I sat at the kitchen counter of our rental home, on a bar stool I rarely sat on, and opened Hannah's journal. I'd never been so nervous. I imagine now it is because I was old enough to realize that I never really knew my sister and perhaps, at this moment, I was about to.

To my surprise, the journal spanned the entirety of her writing life. The entries were sporadic and often undated and consisted of everything from poems to stories to songs to random observations about the happenings of our family from times both before and after I became a part of it. The tough parts that dealt with her disappointment with my father, her string of bad and even dangerous-sounding relationships with guys her age, these were difficult to read. Some of the pages were even glued together or blacked out in Sharpie so that no one could read them and I imagine that Hannah did this herself, for whatever private reasons she had, and that we all do this with our pasts. Still, the well-earned skepticism about men that I could see coming through, about their intentions, it reminded me of things Lindy might have said on the phone those years back. And yet the lighthearted stuff from when she was a kid, the tales of princesses and dragons she'd cooked up, it all seemed steeped with a certain unorthodox wisdom that reminded me of Julie. It was powerful stuff, all of it, and I couldn't get enough.

But two specific entries were of particular note.

One was dated from the early summer 1989, the summer of Lindy's rape, when Hannah must have been home visiting or stopping by for a swim. The setting seemed to be a window at our house, facing Piney Creek Road, where she was composing a love song about Finally Douglas, called "This Lucky Heart." On the margins of the page, Hannah had scribbled details from our neighborhood as she saw them outside. Perhaps they were for future songs. Perhaps they were just practice. I am sure, however, that she had no idea of what they might mean to me all those years later.

Some of the lines read awkwardly, like:

A missing Mercedes / can't hide the pain
Oak trees drop / what will be theirs again.

Maybe this is where I'd gotten my bad taste in poetry.

But then, near the bottom of this page, I saw this line:

A skinny boy slinks / tattoos blue as night.
His head as bald as the street / he throws
    rocks at the light.

And there it was.

Tyler Bannister. It had to have been him. He was the only kid with tattoos and a shaved head that Piney Creek Road had ever known. He must have returned to the neighborhood after leaving the Landrys' and knocked out the light. He must have planned the whole thing. I felt sick to my stomach as I recalled the day that Tyler, Jason, and I stood in front of Lindy's house talking about the water oak, the way we pretended to be fiddling with a remote-control car as Lindy's father pulled up and smiled and asked his daughter, yet again, to remind him of what time she was to return from the track. It would be eight-thirty, Daddy, she told him, the same as every day, and in this way the whole awful thing became obvious to me.

The fact that Tyler Bannister had moved out months before — that he no longer lived with the Landrys at the time of the crime — meant nothing, because the simple truth is that there was a stretch of time in his life in which Woodland Hills was his home, and a home, no matter how wonderful or menacing, is a thing you don't forget. Ask anybody.

So, my mystery was solved.

Yet I didn't feel any better.

I had my reasons.

For starters, how had we not stumbled upon this connection before? Although Hannah lived across town at that point, although she was busy with her own life, hadn't my mom or Rachel or perhaps even the police spoken to her about Lindy's rape? Hadn't everyone given their best effort, discussing simple clues like a busted streetlight or the reappearance of suspicious boys? I'd always thought so. This made me wonder if there was perhaps another, darker, reason that we'd missed this. It made me wonder if maybe my mother or Rachel, knowing what they did about Hannah's history with men that was just now unfolding for me, felt it better not to mention to her what had happened to the Simpson girl in our very own neighborhood. It made me wonder if perhaps this was the reason my mother took that police officer's card off the refrigerator and slipped it into the drawer that day, if maybe she didn't want her daughters seeing a thing like this, being reminded of realities like this, every time they wanted a little something to eat.

This type of care, I understood, would not be dissimilar to the way people had been so wary to mention Hannah around my mother after she had died. I then began to wonder

445

what Julie meant, exactly, when she said that rape is not a thing that women go around talking about, and this made me wonder what other dreadful knowledge is passed silently among the hearts of women and I suddenly had a hard time understanding men, in general, and the damage we can do, and how it is even possible that I am one of them.

So, from the time I read that journal until now, a period of a few years, I've buried what I'd learned about the rape of Lindy Simpson. I didn't tell anyone about it. Yet I went so far as to look Tyler Bannister up and, unsurprisingly, found out that he was already in prison on various other charges, including sexual battery. This didn't make things easier on my conscience and so I began to take strange and nostalgic trips back to the old neighborhood, wondering if I should track Lindy down and tell her what I'd uncovered. I suppose this is why I felt so awful after I ran into her that night at the football game.

It was the first time I had seen her since I knew, or at least believed I knew, who had changed her life so dramatically, and since I'd come to grips with my own cowardice on that night of her rape, and yet I didn't even think to apologize. So, in an awful way,

I felt again like I was in on the crime.

Maybe I was.

That's why I am so lucky to have Julie around now, and to have had my mother and Rachel around for so long, to make me realize that life is not always about me and the unloading of my conscience. The story of Lindy's rape, for instance.

It is about Lindy. And that is all.

However, what is about me, and the reason I am talking to you, is the other entry in Hannah's journal.

It was from a time when Hannah was around eleven years old and, I've gathered, on a school field trip, a thing we all had to do in our youth. This seemed to be one of those wilderness camps they sent us to, where the rustic setting is meant to remind you of how fortunate you are in life and how beautiful nature can be. And so Hannah had been sent out to sit by herself in the woods and construct a list of things she was thankful for. Her handwriting was cursive and big and, near the top of her list, beside a collection of butterfly doodles, she had thanked God for her "new baby brother," which she described as a miracle.

It hit me so hard when I saw this.

Don't you understand?

My sister had written my name before I

ever knew her. She had believed in my goodness in the same way that I now believe in my daughter's innate goodness and in your innate goodness, and when I read that it was like I could hear Hannah again. It was like I could see her. And it was like I was whole again. I felt no guilt. I had no regrets. It was as if I'd been forgiven.

After I read those words, my own future suddenly seemed as sunlit to me as it had to Hannah all those years ago, and I guess I would like, very much, to share this feeling. Because no one can change what has happened to Lindy or to Hannah or to anybody. Our histories are just that. But what's most amazing about the connection I felt with my sister is that it was made possible only by the love she showed to me before I could ever possibly return it.

And so, *you*.

The doctors tell us you will be a boy.

And they say that you are healthy.

Your mother and sister are ecstatic about this, as am I, but with my excitement comes the fear that I will not be able to raise you from this boy to the man that I know you can be: a better man than I have been, surely, but one like I am trying to become. And so I have spoken honestly to you about my youth and my mistakes, and also of the incredible fortune that has come my way through the kindness of our family, for one simple reason. I want us to get off on the right foot. I want the two of us, together in this world, to be good men.

And when I tell you that I love you I want, so badly, for you to understand what I mean.

ACKNOWLEDGMENTS

The first person I'd like to thank is you — anyone who took time to read this — for your generosity and spirit. Thank you for reading every single book you've ever read by any author from anywhere. It's important. My family would also like to express their enormous thanks to Renee Zuckerbrot and Amy Einhorn, who floated into our lives like young fairy godmothers. I could not dream up a better team. Thanks also to Ivan Held and Elizabeth Stein and everyone else at G. P. Putnam's Sons and the Penguin Group. You are all incredible.

I am also in the debt of my friends who, for some reason, agreed to read the early pages of this book and yet still let me carry on with it for another seven years. These good people are Matt Brock, Sean Ennis, and Alex Taylor. Special thanks also go to the Sewanee Writers' Conference, especially Steve Yarbrough and Diane Johnson, who gave me the exact push I needed when I needed it, as well as the Faulkner Society, in particular Rosemary James and Jeff Kleinman, who also gave me a huge boost. Thanks also to my students and colleagues in the Creative Writing Workshop at the UNO, at the Yokshop in Oxford, and to my former teachers at the University of Mississippi and the University of Tennessee, for what seems like a never-ending parade of goodwill. And finally a big thanks to the Chimes Tap Room in Baton Rouge and the Parkview Tavern in New Orleans, where much of this book was figured out.

The deepest thanks, of course, go to my mother and father and my sisters. Where would I be without you? That is a question that actually has an answer. Also, to the extended Walsh, Prater, Anselmo, Jones, Berdon, Madere, Patterson, and Taylor families. Thank you for taking me in.

Lastly but never leastly, to my good luck charms: Sarah and Magnolia and Sherwood. Thank you for laughing at how I type instead of what I type. You've no idea how happy you make me.

ABOUT THE AUTHOR

Milton O'Neal Walsh, Jr., is a writer from Baton Rouge, Louisiana. His stories and essays have appeared in the *New York Times, Oxford American, American Short Fiction, Epoch,* and *Best New American Voices,* among others. His first book, the story collection *The Prospect of Magic,* was the winner of the Tartt's Fiction Prize and a finalist for the Eric Hoffer Award for fiction. He is a graduate of the MFA program at the University of Mississippi and is currently the director of the Creative Writing Workshop at the University of New Orleans, where he lives and works, happily, with his wife and family.

The employees of Thorndike Press hope you have enjoyed this Large Print book. All our Thorndike, Wheeler, and Kennebec Large Print titles are designed for easy reading, and all our books are made to last. Other Thorndike Press Large Print books are available at your library, through selected bookstores, or directly from us.

For information about titles, please call:
  (800) 223-1244

or visit our Web site at:
  http://gale.cengage.com/thorndike

To share your comments, please write:
Publisher
Thorndike Press
10 Water St., Suite 310
Waterville, ME 04901

LARGE TYPE
Walsh, M. O.
My sunshine away